BENC

Judith leaned obediently forward over the padded edge and felt a finger trace one of the fading lines left by Marjory's cane.

'I see you are into discipline, Judith.' Nancy kept her voice low. It seemed she intended it to be unheard beyond their small space. 'With buttocks like these you must be much in demand. It is plain they would permit the most rigorous treatment.' Hands lifted and separated the cheeks, squeezing hard, and Judith's loins responded at once. The speaker sighed and released her grip. 'If I had my way with you for just one evening you would be left unable ever to forget. But I should not be saying this. We have a job to do. Come, up on the table . . .'

By the same author:

DRAWN TO DISCIPLINE
RITUAL STRIPES

BENCH-MARKS

Tara Black

This book is a work of fiction.
In real life, make sure you practise safe, sane and consensual sex.

First published in 2003 by
Nexus
Thames Wharf Studios
Rainville Road
London W6 9HA

www.nexus-books.co.uk

Typeset by TW Typesetting, Plymouth, Devon

Printed and bound by
Clays Ltd, St Ives PLC

ISBN 0 352 33797 4

Contents

PART 1

1

Past and Present

Judith shifted in her chair and instantly regretted it. The weals freshly scored into her behind made sitting down an act that required care, and once it had been accomplished any change in position was best avoided. While it might seem surprising that the young woman seated in an office with the designation ASSISTANT DIRECTOR should be carrying marks as extreme as any inflicted on offending boys at the old approved schools, the incumbent herself bore the discomfort of them with a degree of equanimity. The two years spent at the Nemesis Archive had seen her bent tight over a tall desk on a number of occasions to receive a dose of her superior's favourite length of rattan. It was, after all, in the nature of the post she held. And, as she acknowledged only to a select few, being formally beaten – by the right person, of course – induced in her an erotic charge to which she had become addicted. The pain was invariably severe, but in its wake, and especially with a sympathetic touch, there could be the most intense pleasure. Judith had come to think since her appointment that such a sexual disposition was an essential qualification for the task of assembling the critical database on female masochism that was the institution's founding purpose and she took her recent promotion to be a welcome confirmation of that belief.

What had caused the wince-making move in her seat was a letter she had just opened. On silky cerise-coloured paper that was headed 'CatWork, 1325 East Simpson Street, Seattle', it began 'Dear Judith Wilson' and what followed was brief but arresting:

> You do not know me, but you know Cate, and I think that you guys were once close. So I am telling you she went away and she took with her my great-aunt's secret writing, but I made a copy. If you will contact me – please, SOON – I can explain. You are the archivist, Judith, and I am hoping that a story of discipline in old Europe will have interest for you.

It was signed Zadia Marlova and there was a home phone number underneath the name. But Judith was no longer taking in what she read for her mind was spinning back to the two nights she had spent with Cate during their escapade in the north. It had been in the summer of the year before but it was as though the sharp scent of the American's arousal in the bedroom of that country hotel was back in her nostrils. The passion between them had been fierce if short-lived and loins prickling at the memory Judith felt a keen sense of lack in her present existence.

Then the door opened and secretary Grace appeared with a white porcelain jar and a questioning look. Judith nodded with a half smile and eased herself out of the chair: no words were required as she moved to the chaise longue and knelt upright on it. Eyes drawn to the fine brown hair wound demurely into a bun, she savoured the contrast between the chaste demeanour and what the young girl was about to do, though not without a tinge of regret. While her physical need was to be assuaged, and willingly, it would be done without any of the ardour of which she had just been reminded.

Judith began by unbuttoning the waistband of the tailored trousers, after which she lowered the zip and folded them neatly down. When the tiny black briefs had joined them, she went forward on to her elbows and pressed the dark crop of her head into the surface of the couch, causing her blouse to ride up under her small breasts and expose her bottom fully to Grace's nimble hands. As soon as *their* job had been done, she would contact the exotically named Zadia as requested (she was intrigued by the manuscript referred to and Cate's alleged disappearance), but the present business was urgent. The hot throb of her caned buttocks had fired the genitals and as the soothing cream was applied Judith luxuriated in a rising tide of sensation. At last the massaging fingers delved into the wetness between the mistreated globes and the newly appointed executive abandoned herself noisily to the breaking waves of her climax, safe in the knowledge that she and the versatile secretary of the Archive were quite alone within the thick walls of the old building.

As it turned out, Ms Marlova proved difficult to get hold of. Judith tried ringing at intervals throughout that afternoon, the evening and the following morning, then gave up for two whole days before she tried again. This time she was determined to be systematic by phoning on the hour every hour for a whole twenty-four-hour period if necessary. At last, yawning at her desk at 3 a.m. she heard the receiver picked up at the other end.

'Hallo, yes? Oh. Oh please, you must wait while I turn off the water. Don't go away, I come back.' After all this time and effort she had caught the elusive woman about to enjoy a soak in the tub. Despite a small flash of irritation, Judith found it hard to suppress a smile and when a rather breathless voice returned to the phone she said simply, 'I'm calling from the Nemesis Archive in England.'

'Judith! At last. I have been drumming – two dates out of the blue, and exactly when I was wanting your call. I am very sorry not to be here before. And now I am sweaty and run a bath and so keep you waiting again.'

'That's OK. No problem.' Disarmed by the candid speech Judith left unsaid the acid remarks about answering machines she had rehearsed. Maybe the lady was hard up and if regular contact was going to be needed the Archive could fund one for her. In fact she could authorise that herself from her newly elevated position. But that idea was, to say the least, jumping the gun, and Judith reined her thoughts in to the immediate job. 'Right, Zadia. Now that I've got you here, tell me all about this secret document. And what Cate is up to *this time?*'

On reflection it was perhaps not a good idea asking to be told *all* about anything on a transatlantic call, especially by one whose native tongue was plainly not English. Judith thought the accent to be German (though the surname sounded Slavonic) but that in itself was no real obstacle. Not in comparison to the way the speaker's basic grasp of the language weakened in direct proportion to her enthusiasm and when she got really excited her syntax threatened to unravel altogether. So it took a long time to piece together a coherent story but what she heard was compelling enough for Judith to persist until she had the bones of one. If the expense of the call was queried on the Director's return then so be it: at worst it would provide another excuse for Miss James to exercise her disciplinary prerogative on the seat of Judith's trousers. She had of course done just that five days ago leaving marks still plainly visible, but now she was 'on retreat' in Brittany for the rest of the summer. So the Assistant Director could afford to shrug off the distant prospect of further correction and concentrate on Zadia's tale.

What had happened – as far as Judith understood it – was that great-aunt Marlova had left something behind that had only lately come to light. Not that her death was recent: born in 1905 she had not survived beyond 73 years of age, so was gone over twenty years before. But a cousin was entrusted at that time with a chest of papers and books that had lain untouched until in her own terminal illness she had had it sent on to the the last she knew of in the family line. On examination it was a more appealing legacy than the expected collection of old photographs, or even the bundle of faded letters testifying to an adulterous affair – more appealing, at least, to a young woman with Judith's special interest. For, according to the grandniece's account, it consisted of several chapters of autobiography that covered the period of her ancestor's residence in the St Thomas Academy For Young Ladies in 1920s Bohemia. She had begun at seventeen as a pupil and been taken on as a personal assistant to the Acting Headmistress for two further years, the 'assistance' required being mostly with the administration of corporal punishment to the senior girls with the aid of what was called 'The Bench'. That, it appeared, was a kind of punishment frame complete with restraining straps, mention of whose name was enough to cause a chill of apprehension to spread amongst the students. Unfortunately no more details were forthcoming since Zadia's attempts to convey its precise horrors lapsed into excited incoherence.

However, it was all quite enough to whet the appetite and knowing that her old adversary turned brief lover had decamped with the manuscript was a further piquant morsel. What on earth did Cate plan to do with it? Judith decided that she must take this further. Understandably, after the theft, Zadia was reluctant to send another copy of her prize anywhere, so there was only one thing for it: she would have to go where the text was. When in addition she learned that it had been translated from the original German with the help of Zadia's stepsister's excellent English, that clinched the matter. She would be able to go over the thing in detail with the two women and return with a valuable addition to the Archive's materials; in fact, just the kind of thing her job description required her to collect. In spite of the expense involved, the outcome – with a decent break of luck – should have the Director patting her on the back rather than laying the cane across her bottom.

By the time she had taken down the address, forestalled Zadia's attempts to give directions ('I'll take a cab, OK?'), made her promise to stay in for the next forty-eight hours and – finally – put down the phone it was fully light. Judith stretched luxuriously and swivelled her chair, taking in the midsummer dawn light that suffused with a rosy glow the weathered stone of the quadrangle and the rich texture of slate roofing overlooked from her top-floor perch. She was in the part of the old university library known in its day as the stacks. The exterior displayed three levels and a half-basement of high-Georgian proportions, but for the purposes of maximising accessible book storage the interior had been remodelled into six floors supported by a metal frame without making any outward change. Beside where she sat at the computer terminal the original sash window extended well below her floor into the next and so provided a dizzying line of sight almost vertically down to the grass far below.

While the new office was a place to pose and imagine the impression she could make on an important client, Judith did all her real work at the cubbyhole she now sat in. And, she felt, for good reason. Following immersion in the lovingly related details of a girl's public whipping, that she could look up and out into the light and apparent order (however bogus she knew it to be) of this small university town in the middle of

England was a kind of restorative that helped her hang on to what little sanity she possessed. This was now the beginning of her third year of employment among the dark perversity of the Nemesis collections and she thought back to her previous life as a first-year hoping to make it into Honours English.

There had been quite a stir caused in academic circles when the mysterious Oceanus Corporation, based in Chicago, made an offer for the building that was to falling empty on the library's move to the growing campus on the edge of town. Or rather, a mere half of the building that comprised the stacks together with an access stairwell, although the price mooted was enough to buy the whole thing twice over. While no one on the Senate was exactly happy about having in their midst an archive dedicated to sadomasochism whose director was rumoured to be a practising dominatrix, the sum paid would allow several university properties to be completely refurbished. Once this fact dawned on the governing body the remaining opposition melted quietly away. It was one of the pleasing ironies of the situation that the once most vociferous critics – the academic psychologists – were now housed in a lavishly equipped set of laboratories in the remainder of the vacated library. The fact that Oceanus had also contracted to maintain the complete structure indefinitely served as an added incentive to curtail further expressions of hostility to their neighbours.

Judith pulled herself up. Reminiscing was all very well, but there was stuff to do even if it wasn't yet 5 a.m. She reactivated her screen, and in two minutes had located a direct flight to Seattle leaving in the mid-evening. There would be plenty of time to make the connection if she was on the train to town after lunch, so she logged in to Oceanus with her revised code number, took a deep breath and entered the airline and flight number. Then, after an anxious moment, there it was: Booking Confirmed for Ms J Wilson, Nemesis Archive; Check-in 19.35 hrs. Well, no one could say she wasn't taking advantage of her new privileges: just as long as the outcome was going to justify it . . . Judith leaned back and swung her chair round, suddenly drained by lack of sleep. It was time to go home, pack a bag and then get her head down. But not for too long because before she made the train she just *had* to drop in on a friend and announce what was on.

'So you make this call at three in the morning and by five you're booked on a fucking flight?' The bar manager of the Phoenix was wide-eyed and the sight made Judith chuckle. It was rare to see Marsha's cool slip, even by a fraction of an inch, and true to form it was back in place almost at once.

'Oh, honey,' she drawled, rolling her eyes, 'can't you see I'm jealous: it's my old stamping ground. Won't you take me with you? I'll tell you what. How about the, ahem –' she cleared her throat ostentatiously '– *senior* member of staff I'm talking to hires a gofer for her important expedition?'

They both laughed then the American woman pushed over an opened bottle of Pils. 'Drink this, girl, and while you do you can spill the beans. That means like *right now*.' Out of term the place was busy only at weekends, and on that Thursday lunchtime they had it to themselves. Marsha settled back behind the bar and cocked her head expectantly. She had the slight spare build that made it difficult to guess her age though Judith knew that it was more than ten years since she too had been a student at the university. Active in feminist circles in the town, and with disciplinary inclinations herself, she had provided essential support during Judith's first faltering steps at the Archive. Marsha's role as principal confidante had been less in demand lately, so it was time for Judith to restore it by trying to piece together out

10

loud what she knew. It seemed that she had been contacted through CatWork – an s/m agency that Miss James herself had visited the year before – just because Zadia could get the use of the computer and some headed paper there. And the reason she could do that was because the agency's prime mover was also the singer in the band she played with.

'Jynx,' announced the American, 'and Marissa is a stunning vocalist.'

It was Judith's turn to gape. 'Marsha, you're having me on,' she said sternly.

'Their name's Jynx, and I caught one of their gigs last summer. Aha! You didn't know I was back in the place I used to call home for a couple of weeks, did you? You were too busy fighting with a woman called Cate somewhere up north to notice.'

'OK, OK. Don't remind me. So if you've seen the German lady, tell me what she looks like.'

'Well, she's fair-skinned and totally beautiful and she shaves her head. Even though she was sitting down at the back you could see how big she was. Don't go falling out with her, Jude, because judging by the way she whacked those drums . . .'

It was often difficult to know how seriously to take Marsha, and when in doubt Judith had learned to keep a poker face. So she demanded another beer and then carried on with her account until she could think of nothing more.

'Sounds like juicy stuff, girl: Severe Schoolgirl Punishments of the 1920s. Good title for a vid, eh? Organise a cast – you'd look great in uniform for a start – and get the cameras running in your basement over there.'

Judith swallowed some lager, not sure what the speaker was driving at.

'Look, honey,' Marsha said, laying a hand on Judith's arm, 'I don't want to put a damper on things, but how do you know it isn't all just at that level. I don't mean

11

that our skinhead is a fraud, but someone else down the line may well be. And while the whole thing would be fun as a fantasy, it would be a whole lot more than that if it's for real.'

Judith considered this, the germ of an idea forming. 'Well, I need to read the thing first and see what I think. But there's got to be ways of checking some of the details.' She thought suddenly of Harry at the British Library who might be willing to do some European digging on her behalf, but she had kept her dalliance there from the lesbian separatists of her acquaintance. All that is save the Nemesis Director, who had somehow divined what was going on, and her disapproval was tempered by the professional usefulness of the liaison. Feeling awkward, Judith emptied the bottle and looked pointedly at her watch. 'Shit. If I don't head off, I might not get on this expenses-paid flight. So thanks for the drinks and I'll give you a full report when I get back.'

So saying, she grabbed her bag and headed out the back door with Marsha's 'Good luck!' sounding in her ears. But she took with her too the distinctly quizzical look in those steady grey eyes. Damn. Judith hated having secrets from her American friend, not least because she usually got caught out. But honesty *was* the best policy, and as she hurried into the entrance of the station she vowed to make a clean breast of her sins on returning. Well, that one anyway. It would make a start.

2

Stepsisters

The flight seemed to go on for ever, yet by time-zone trickery the clock in the arrivals lounge was claiming it to be just two hours since take-off. Enthusiasm waning fast, Judith humped her stuff into the ladies' toilets, splashed water on her face and dried herself with a paper towel. What the fuck was she doing there? She interrogated the image that stared back at her from above the washbasin but it held no answer; though what she saw was – if anything – reassuring. Last year's radical crewcut had been allowed to grow into a short dark crop, and while the eyes showed strain the doggedly straight nose was softened by the warm full lips below it. That wasn't the face of someone who would embark on a foolhardy mission on a mere whim, was it?

There was a full-length mirror on the wall and Judith turned to inspect her clothes. In what seemed to have become the regulation black – and she was far from ashamed to acknowledge there the influence of the formidable Miss James – they had survived the journey in surprisingly good shape. The thin cotton top hung loosely over her small breasts and was short enough not to hide the way the trousers moulded themselves closely to hips and thighs. Swivelling to get a better view, she studied the full curves of the bum. Its ripeness was wholly appropriate to the owner's special tastes, she always thought, and the sight cheered her up at once.

'It is nearly good enough to eat, I think, yes?'

Judith gave a start and felt the hot flush rise from her neck. At her back stood a tall woman with a shaved head, startlingly clad in tiny hotpants and matching crop top that displayed acres of glowing flesh.

'Oh God, how embarrassing! You must be Zadia.' She had emailed her travel details to CatWork before she left in case they could get a message through. Obviously they had, and not only was the lady there in person, she had caught Judith in the act of ogling her own arse. She stuck out her hand in an effort to retrieve the situation.

'I'm Judith, as, er, I'm sure you've guessed. Hi. You didn't need to come, I was just going to get a cab.'

'I am sorry, the cab will be necessary yet. I go to play again until late. It is not convenient but we must take what offers we get. You understand, yes?' Judith nodded assent: she was not going to start by disagreeing with this powerful beauty.

Zadia fished in the pouch strapped at her waist and pressed a key into Judith's hand. 'I must go to my lift. You have the address: make it your home. Eat and drink, I leave plenty. And do not wait up, the small bed is for you. We talk tomorrow, yes? Again I say sorry not to be there.' She made for the exit and Judith's eyes followed the movement of the muscular buttocks sheathed in their scarlet lycra, then at the door the striking figure turned with a serious expression. 'Judith, do not be ashamed of what I see when I find you. It is right to admire one's good shape, I think.'

With that she was gone, leaving her listener blushing afresh. But she was pleased, and despite the voice in Judith's head that said it was all very well for the fair Amazon to talk, she went out to the taxi rank with a lighter heart.

* * *

The apartment was above a flower shop, reached from an outside stair, and its shabbiness was somehow comforting. Judith located the single bed and dumped her bag, then wandered into the kitchen. The sight of a fridge that would have swallowed the small one in her own flat three times over made her suddenly aware that she was ravenous. True to the lady's word, inside was a feast of cold meats and cheese together with several bottles of Chardonnay and half a dozen cans of lager. On the table was a fresh crusty loaf and it overcame the last reservations she had about making the most of a stranger's hospitality.

The food was soon set out, and Judith found plates and cutlery in an old-fashioned dresser, together with the essential corkscrew. She ate with concentration for some minutes, glad she had passed on most of the stuff on the plane. When a second glass of wine had followed the first she sat back and yawned as a wave of tiredness washed over her. It was barely after ten and if she could hang on for a couple of hours she might sleep through to the morning. She had spotted a coffee maker on the counter by the sink and on a quick inspection it appeared to be manageable and there was a grinder right beside it. All that she needed now was to lay her hands on some beans.

Twice round the kitchen into all the likely places brought her no nearer to her goal so she stood on a chair to look in a container on the top of a fitted cupboard. Unlikely maybe (though Zadia could probably reach up there unaided) but she had to check all possibilities. When she picked it up a small bundle behind toppled to the floor and at the same time she saw out of the corner of her eye the handle of a door round at the side of the counter. It had to be, didn't it, sitting right below the machine. What was in her hand was empty, so she put it back and climbed down to retrieve what she had dislodged. They were photographs that had spread out over the linoleum in an untidy heap and Judith knelt down to retrieve them only to be brought up with a jolt. There, on top of the pile, was Cate, grinning wolfishly at the camera with a leather strap dangling from her fingers. *And she was quite naked.*

Judith left the fallen items exactly where they lay and confirmed her guess about the whereabouts of the coffee. Mechanically she set about pouring in water and grinding beans and only when the appropriate glugging and hissing was underway did she rescue the pictures. But then she placed them carefully face down and waited until the jug would supply her with a full cup to take to the table. Once she was seated she sipped at the hot liquid for a few moments then made herself turn over the pile in front of her. There she was – a blonde bombshell if ever there was one – and the first sight of her had taken Judith's breath away. In the back of her mind she had known how deeply the fling with Cate had affected her but that's where she had kept it, and for what was now almost a year. There had been no contact after the American was back in the States – after all, she'd had a new girlfriend while Judith was occupied with the novelty of her man at the British Library. But that was then, whereas now ...

She sat up and riffled through the images. Most were snaps taken of the band in action and Judith put them to one side. That left two in addition to the solo portrait she had first stumbled on and in both of them there was another woman as well. The first showed only a rear view of her, though a striking one at that. She was down on all fours presenting a well-streaked posterior while Cate sat astride her back, hands pulling apart the purple cheeks to give a full genital display. But the second left no doubt about the disciplined woman's identity, for while her behind was again the focus she looked back over her shoulder into the camera. It was plainly Zadia, transported with screwed-up eyes and mouth a round O,

16

while the blonde head was busy with face buried between the handsome striped cheeks. Judith recoiled and reached for the rest of the wine with a trembling hand. Oh fuck, oh fuck. She emptied the glass in one and banged it down on the table, then took the second bottle from the fridge and angrily wrenched at the cork. After she had glugged out more into her tumbler she stared morosely at it for a couple of seconds and swallowed it down.

Her brief lover had once so enthused about doing to her just what she was shown doing in the glossy photograph, and she felt grossly betrayed. Her much-praised bum was, it seemed, just one among many for Cate to get down and dirty with. At the edge hovered the thought that she was in the grip of an absurd overreaction fuelled by fatigue and booze; that a three-day fling a year ago, however passionate, gave her no right to indulge in a fit of jealous rage. But emotion, once unleashed, was not easily restrained by anything as mundane as a sense of perspective, especially when there was plenty more to drink. So for a good half hour the faults of the blonde American were rehearsed in detail and the occasion of her come-uppance at the Archive relished once again. But of course the story had an ending in entwined bodies, and in an hour there was weeping not in anger but at what had been lost.

'There'll be tears before bedtime,' muttered Judith drunkenly to herself. 'Well, we've had them, so it's gotta be time to crash. Right?' She pulled herself together enough to clear the table and gather up the pictures. Getting her clothes off was nearly too much but somehow she persisted, and at last naked under the sheet sank her head into the pillow in the welcoming darkness.

There was the bang of a door and Judith came wide awake in the strange bed. Her mouth was dry and her head was muzzy. Oh God, she was in Seattle. And the night before she'd done her best to drink her host's fridge dry. Shit. The mental tirade came flooding back and she winced with shame. You've got to get over her, girl. That's past history and there's work to do here. The voice in her head was firm and Judith sat up to consult her watch. Nearly ten. She pulled on a baggy T-shirt and peered out into the passage. There were raised voices coming from the left but the door was closed so she decided to let them get on with it while she took a shower. It sounded as if they would be occupied for a while.

When she emerged from the bathroom Zadia appeared in the doorway. 'Judith! You slept, yes? Good. I need your help now, please.'

It could be just her manner of speaking or it could be an order. Either way Judith wasn't going to argue. She followed the imposing lady into the kitchen where there was a slighter figure with bleached-blonde hair dressed in a halter top, flared mini and knee boots. Leaning on the counter on one elbow, hand on hip, she looked every inch the bratty American teen.

'This is my stepsister, Petra. She provoked me all the night, so now we are home she will be punished. It is – how do you say – much overdue.'

'But you can't. I'm not a schoolgirl any more, Zee, for God's sake. I'm almost twenty. So you just *can't*.' It was pure nasal whine that would make anyone want to slap her, and at the thought Judith realised with a quickening pulse where this was heading.

'Bad girls get spanked,' announced Zadia decisively, 'and I choose the time when I have my assistant to help with discipline. Now you say you are the adult, Petra, so will you be dignified in front of Judith, or do you fight me?' She towered fiercely over the blonde who looked small and helpless.

Judith put her hands up and took a step back, stammering. 'I, er, I dunno . . . It's not, er, my business, really, is it?' Things were moving a bit too fast.

But all at once the girl pulled herself up almost with a shrug. 'OK, OK, *Mama*. I'll take what's coming to me. I'm going to get it anyway, so you may as well join in, Jay, yeah?' The look she flashed was almost salacious and Judith saw that what was between these two was as much ritual as real dispute. And she was being invited to take part.

Two high stools were placed together in the middle of the floor while Petra was dispatched to fetch 'the instruments', which turned out to be a paddle and a bundle of leather thongs bound into a handle. But before they were put to use it appeared there was more to be said and the skinhead looked stern.

'Each time I look round from my drums I see you in the corner, Petra. With that boy, kissing and cuddling.' She reached forward with a sudden movement and flipped up the hem of the girl's skirt to reveal an uncovered triangle of pubic hair. 'Ha! See what I find. No panties.'

'Oh, I only had one pair with me and, and . . .'

'And that guy is petting you, so you were wetting them, and then you went out the back and they came off and –'

'No!' Petra looked for a moment really cross. 'No, Zee, I didn't, I wouldn't. You *know* that.'

'Right. I am the fool, I believe you. But what you do is bad enough, yes? So you get down. Now!' The young blonde took the skirt right off and draped herself obediently across the padded tops. 'Judith, you will stand astride, please, to keep her in the place.'

A little flustered by the – to say the least – personal talk about the state of Petra's knickers, Judith took a moment to work out that she was required to straddle the prone form with its head between her thighs and then hold her wrists up into the small of her back. With her own already moist genitals pressing into the young woman's neck, this was getting downright intimate. Add

19

in the fact she had a close-up view of the bare cheeks enticingly spread for punishment, and it could all go to a girl's head. Especially one who had been expecting to investigate only a manuscript.

Zadia took up the leather oval and swung it hard to left and then right. Each time there was a terrific *smack!* and the buttock bounced along with a sharp intake of breath from the victim. Again and again it landed and as the chastiser found her stride the rhythm became steady and purposeful. It was plain that in Zadia's hands a spanking was no trivial juvenile affair. Judith could feel the impact of each blow through her grip on the body and marvelled that the flesh-tone of the target area had deepened into crimson without eliciting from Petra anything more than a few gasps.

Eventually, there was a pause and Zadia laid down the paddle, but the event was far from over. Without a word she stripped off her top and her faded denims and reached for the many-tailed whip. Standing erect in a black thong with jutting breasts, she was an Amazon indeed and Judith gawped. Then the instrument came down and drew the first cry of the morning. Now the body squirmed and writhed with every lash and after a dozen or so there was a loud wail from the immobilised head.

'Ah-ah-ah! Fuck, that hurts. Oh, Zee, I can't take any more. Plee-ee-ease.'

It would have melted the hardest heart, Judith thought, eyes dwelling on the purple streaks that covered the exposed posterior. But Zadia was implacable.

'Twelve more, Petra, you earned twelve more I think, yes?'

The only answer was a choking noise and the strokes were duly delivered, with the wielder rising on to her toes to add that bit of extra force to her already powerful arm. It was all Judith could do to restrain the body that bucked and howled, but at last it was done, and after a pause filled with heavy breathing Zadia signalled she should stand back.

Petra lay moaning gently with no attempt to rise from her position and attend to her blistered arse. Had it been Judith she knew what she would be doing: hopping about the room clutching the assaulted parts then diving for a towel to make a cold compress. It seemed, however, that the young stepsister was made of sterner (not to say more dignified) stuff, but then it appeared there was another reason for her behaviour that might have weighed with Judith herself. Alongside the weapons there sat a bottle of oil she hadn't noticed and the strict chastiser pulled out the cork and knelt down. She poured a little into a cupped hand and ran it over the bruised flesh in a soft, circular motion. Before long, the moaning began to take on a different character and Zadia's thumbs began to press into the dark cleft between the abused hemispheres.

Oh God. Judith pulled herself back with an effort. What *was* she doing? It was one thing being part of a punishment scene by invitation, but she wasn't needed here. This was turning into sex pure and simple and it was between the two of them. She was definitely surplus to requirements and began to move out of the room, feeling excluded and very much alone. A last glance cast her down even further for it showed Zadia taking up the position Cate had occupied in the upsetting photograph. In her aroused condition Judith could imagine only too well how Petra would feel with that eager tongue working in her wet cunt. Damn it, she could *remember* what it had been like with Cate.

She closed the door and leaned weakly against the wall. Five minutes ago her arousal was such that a mere touch to the clitoris would have made her explode on the instant; now she was choked up with desire turned sour. How could she even wank while the two of them

21

made love in the same flat. Shit, shit, shit. There was only one thing for it. Angrily she hauled jeans up over her still oozing crotch and laced on boots. They were bang in the centre of the gay/lesbian corridor of the city and she was going out and she was going to get a beer. And with any luck some horny broad – that's what they had here, wasn't it? – would catch the smell of her and drag her home for a spanking and a good fuck.

3

Unfinished Business

'Why don't you come and keep me company for a while, sister? I'll buy.' Judith was peering at the notice 'Dykes 'n' Sluts Only' on the door under the foot-high flashing letters of THE CANDY BAR and looked round doubtfully at the stranger. She was a burly woman in leathers with short grizzled hair who was locking up the bike she had just parked at the end of a side-alley.

'I don't know. I'm – I'm new here.'

'English, yeah? Well then, I guess you need someone to show you the ropes. And don't worry honey, I won't bite. Not unless you ask real nice.'

After the hard light of the city street, the gloom of the interior was comforting. Judith picked her way to a corner table while as promised the lady ordered a couple of draughts at the counter. She brought them over, sat down and shucked off her jacket, revealing a singlet top and a pair of tattooed shoulders. After an exchange of toasts they drank in silence for several seconds.

'I needed that,' said Judith as she put down the already half-empty glass.

'Correct me if I'm wrong –' the biker was toying with a beer mat '– but you don't seem the type who'd come to our fair city to trawl the gay bars on her own.'

Unsure what to say, Judith looked at her new companion, but she had her eyes fixed on the table.

'What I mean is, I'd reckon you came here to do a job but something's happened. Something not easy to deal with and it's sent you out for a beer or six in the hope of an answer, or maybe just to get away from it. Am I close?'

It was disconcertingly near the mark and Judith stared. This time the leatherwoman met her gaze and turned down the corners of her mouth.

'Me and my long nose. You don't want the third degree from an old dyke and why should you? Have one more and give me a bit more of your tasty young presence then I'll let you go. And you get to choose the topic from here on.'

When she came back Judith had made up her mind. It would be good to talk and who better to listen than an anonymous woman as observant as this one. So it all came out including a few tears: the job she did, the story of Cate, the night before's photograph and finally being out in the cold the morning after.

'Well, it's enough to drive anyone to drink. That's my opinion. So you'll have to have another.'

But this time Judith jumped up and insisted on standing her round. When she came back the greying lady offered her hand. 'Pat. That's all you need to know.'

'Call me Jude. God, I feel better, though why you should want to hear my juvenile ramblings . . .'

There was an amused chuckle from across the table. 'Honey, you really got no idea, do you? And when I think of some of the preening young femmes I meet these days. Jude, that mouth of yours alone makes my knees tremble, but when we add in the ass . . . I know it's not on show today, girl, but to the practised eye of one sadistically angled, a rear end like yours don't disguise easy.'

Judith's face burned, but the compliments were difficult to resist and she managed an awkward 'Thanks'.

'Since you ain't walked out on me yet, sister, I'm going to say one more thing. I got the afternoon free, and I also got the biggest collection of implements to tickle a young dyke's fancy in the whole of the north-west. And of course it don't take much to get to a whole lot more than tickling once the pants come off...'

Judith felt a stab in her loins as sharp as a pain. To put herself in the hands of this woman, to be petted and smacked, caressed and even whipped, entirely according to whim seemed in that instant to be utterly thrilling. Then she drew back from the vertiginous edge and saw that Pat was watching her.

'You got better things to do,' the older woman said gently, 'and I shouldn't be trying to hook you for myself.' Judith shook her head, feeling a door was shutting that she wanted open, but the older woman was firm. 'Girl, there's unfinished business out there you were telling me about. Go sort it, yeah? But first come this way with me.' Judith followed her to the bar where she handed over a bunch of notes.

'Cal, this is Jude. Take a good look, will you, and if she shows again make her at home. OK?' At the exit she said: 'If you do come back, odds are it won't be because you're chasing me. But this *would* be the place to ask.' With that she turned back into the saloon and the door swung shut behind her.

'It is very wrong to make love and ignore a guest. Worse when she is in at the start. And then you are gone...' When Judith let herself back into the flat an unhappy Zadia had been waiting for her.

'It's OK. Don't worry about it.'

'You see, one day Petra will go off with a man, I know it.' The German was frowning with the effort to communicate her meaning. 'While she is here, we sleep together like proper sisters mostly. We are in the same bed but with no sex, you understand? Then after two

25

weeks or three it is like you see today. We do the s/m scene and we fuck like *bad* sisters.' A foxy grin broke through the apologetic manner and it melted what was left of Judith's anger.

'I think I get the picture, Zadia. You don't need to say any more.'

'But I should put it right. You will correct me – that is the word in England, yes? – you will correct me with the cat I use on Petra?'

Judith slowly shook her head. 'Thanks for the offer, but I don't. Well, that's not true, I do sometimes, but only . . .' She tailed off: it was all too complicated to explain. Then she had a brainwave. 'Right, Zadia. If you want to make it up to me, then it needs to be the other way round. That's what gets me going.'

The shaved Amazon stared, then Judith saw comprehension dawn. 'I understand, I think. You don't beat me, instead I give you the spanking. Not hard like Petra – just the hand.' She held up a palm more substantial than most of the paddles Judith had seen but she resisted the temptation to smile. Things were working out.

'It seems wrong way round,' said Zadia, 'but I promise to give much pleasure.' She stood up, decisively. 'Very good. Then you will go and take all clothes off. It is best nude, yes?'

When Judith came back a flat-topped chest had been moved out from the wall and Zadia sat at one end, stripped to the thong worn for Petra's discipline. She signalled Judith to come to her then turned her round. 'It is a most lovely thing, your behind,' she said solemnly, hands resting one on each hip while Judith was glad that her other, blushing cheeks faced away. 'There is enough meat here for serious corporal punishment, yes? And these marks –' there was a fingernail tracing a line across her bottom and then another '– are old but they do not fade yet. I am guessing that it is the cane of your Director that made them.'

Judith had more or less stopped trying to give an account of herself to those who choked on the fact that an independent-minded young woman – a career woman, even, in the wake of her promotion – would submit to such treatment. A bit of erotic spanking was a thing many people could entertain to spice up their tired vanilla sex, but the application of an instrument that raised welts and left bruises that lasted for weeks, well, that was simply *sick*. However, she was that day in better company for Zadia rose magnificently to the occasion. With no apparent need for explanation, she said, finding a rare moment of succinct clarity, 'It is such exquisite pain. And then there is afterwards . . .' Got it in one, lady, thought Judith, and she lowered her nakedness across the bare thighs and waited for the firm hand to begin its work.

When it did there were six hard slaps the shock of which made her squeal. Then she felt the lightest of fingertips running up and down her inner thighs and a little flurry of sharp smacks to the back of them. Judith gave herself up to a riot of sensation as the most sensual stroking was interspersed with stinging blows that took her breath away. Before long she was lubricating uncontrollably and there were fingers spreading the juices up over the hot cheeks.

'Oh, we have such a bad girl here! We spank and spank and she gets so wet. Ah, bad girl, my bad girl . . .' It was a hoarse murmur that seemed right inside Judith's head as she writhed and squirmed in a state of arousal so intense that pleasure and pain were the same thing. And then the slaps were landing with full force and the restraining grip tightened around her. On and on they rained down until the spanked girl burned from waist to knees; on and on until at last the fire flamed inside and she convulsed shrieking, held in the strong arms of the vigorous chastiser.

* * *

'Keep still now, please, or I cannot be gentle with the oil.' Zadia sounded impatient and Judith tried to obey but even the smallest touch to the crimsoned rump made her flinch. Its condition had taken her conception of a sore behind to a new level and she would not have believed that a mere hand spanking could have achieved such a thing. Of course, the cane could do worse, but a typical application would leave its trauma in localised bands; here she was afflicted with two swollen globes that felt as if they had been rigorously tenderised in every single pore.

'OK, I do not persist. It must soak in by itself. Maybe I get carried away a little when I smack.'

'You can say *that* again, sister.' Judith's attempt at levity missed its mark for the German looked dismayed. Then she saw the grin and shook her shaved head.

'You cannot be so bad if you joke. Now, get up on the bed and kneel. Also spread your legs. Like so.' Judith obeyed orders, then as she was being propped up and positioned Zadia spoke in a softer tone. 'You saw the photographs, yes? Of Cate?'

Shit, she hadn't put them back and they'd been noticed.

'It was long ago, you understand. Back before you ever meet her. But you will let me do this for you now, I hope.' She pushed Judith right forward and down and at first the stretching of the skin made her cry out. But then the pain eased and she felt a mouth pressed to the splayed cunt she was presenting like a bitch in heat. Hands held firmly to her hips while a long tongue probed into her liquefying depths and as its tip found her clitoris the keenness of the sensation cut like a blade. But when the climax came it did not wrench her like the first; instead she rode a great wave of feeling until she could bear it no longer then fell in gentle slow motion, utterly drained, back into the downy softness of her nest of pillows.

'Now that's what I call a spanked bottom.' The quiet voice spoke into the post-orgasmic bedroom and Judith jerked up and swivelled round. In the doorway stood Petra, immaculate in a plain white blouse and pinstriped trousers and the contrast with the naked bodies that reeked of sex was absolute. For God's sake, how long had she been there? Zadia was already on her feet and had taken a step forward. 'Petra. What you must think. I only make up to Judith for the morning, and then –'

'Zee, spare me, please. Don't even *try* to talk yourself out of this one. I kiss a boy on the mouth a couple of times in public and get well leathered for it. And then I come home and find you with your head halfway up Judith's ass. Now that's what I call being intimate: *damn* fucking intimate. It has to be long past time that Mama got a taste of her own medicine and I reckon it's gonna take the proper heavy strap to do this one justice. So why don't you just *go fetch it*.' The last three words were snapped out at a raised pitch and Judith saw the conflicting emotions in Zadia's face. Then she bowed her head a little and left the room.

At once Petra gave a snort of glee and made a thumbs-up sign. 'I don't often get the chance to do this, Jay, so back me up, eh? Look, I'm real sorry about earlier, OK? And I promise you later I'll show that I can give head just as good as big sister. Deal?' When the lady in question returned she stiffened up and demanded the instrument, which she started to whack menacingly against the palm of her hand. 'Right, retribution time. We'll have you over the high-backed kitchen chair – you're going to need all the support you can get.'

The formality of the façade was nigh-perfect and Zadia looked at a loss. But she made no objection to what was proposed and Judith guessed that the fear she had expressed of losing Petra was keeping her compliant.

'Well, what are you waiting for? Get in there and take up your position. And I can guarantee this is *not* going

to hurt me more than it hurts you. In fact, it's not going
to hurt *me* one little bit.'

During the night Judith awoke to find a naked figure
sliding into the bed beside her. In the darkness lips teased
at a nipple while a hand slipped between her thighs but
she reached out and clicked on the light. Petra stuck out
her tongue. 'Spoilsport! You mad at me for making Zee
pay? She's gone off on the tourbus quite happy: after
you'd left I made her come like a steam engine.'

She giggled and the young face was appealing in the
candle-bulb that glowed softly on the table. Judith lay
back and opened her legs a little to let the fingers further
in. How could she be cross with this gorgeous creature
who'd come at her word to make love to her? What the
stepsisters did with each other wasn't her business; it
was just that she feared the older one's awkward
honesty made her too vulnerable. This one had the
confidence and cunning to bounce back from most
things whereas she feared that the outwardly powerful
Zadia could end up badly hurt.

Then Petra was sliding down her body, planting kisses
all the way to the pubic bush, where she looked up with
a impish smile. 'You gonna turn over then, so I can
inspect the famous butt? Well, you'd think it was to hear
Zee talk about the thing!'

Judith's blushes fuelled the girl's merriment so she hid
her face by doing as asked while her visitor plumped up
pillows and placed them under her belly. 'The swelling
isn't too bad now,' she pronounced, 'but you're gonna
be bruised as fuck.' The phrase rolled off her tongue
with a relish that made Judith wince. Oh God, she was
going to be carrying revealing marks for days to come
by the sound of it. She grimaced round at Petra who
chuckled some more. 'Yeah, my sister did the biz all
right. But don't worry about it, Jay. You'll just have to
stick to partners in the know for the next month or two.'

Month? *Month?* Then it dawned that the pretty blonde was winding her up something rotten so she fell on her, pinned her down and applied a few smart slaps to the neat little bum. 'Ow! Ow! You can't do that, Jay. I got mine earlier, remember.'

The pout went straight to Judith's loins and she pulled the girl up by the hips and nuzzled into the dark cleft between the cheeks. But Petra twisted out of her grasp and pushed her down. 'Kneel!' she ordered, mock-stern. 'Madam gets served first. Of course, if after that she wanted to reward her dutiful servant . . .'

It was five in the morning before the lovers' games subsided into sleep and then at six Judith opened her eyes to find Petra gone. There were noises from the bathroom so she lay back and drowsed in a happy satiety until she was woken by the appearance of the perfectly groomed and tailored PA heading off for her weekend assignment in California. Here she was once again nude in the sweaty aftermath of sex, fixed by the cool gaze of glossy perfection; and it gave Judith quite a buzz that such a creature as now looked on had a mere hour before been rutting with her in all the ripe secretions.

'This is it,' she said, placing a substantial folder carefully beside the bed. 'You'll have the place to yourself until Monday to take it apart and put it back together again. So I'll leave it with you. But not too much sniping at the English style because that's *me*! OK?' The cheeky grin brought back the feel of her naked body and Judith reached out. But Petra backed off. 'Uh uh. You can't touch *this* dame, lady, not in her paint. And it could be you've had all you're gonna have, cos Zee'll be around when I get back. See ya!'

The spasm of lust that pulsed through her took Judith by surprise and she shook her head ruefully. There she was worrying about Zadia and now it was her getting entangled with the skittish siren of a teenager. Then the bleached curls appeared once more round the door.

'Pay no attention, I love you really, Jay. Don't tell me, I need a good spanking. Well, maybe you'll get your chance yet, eh?' This time the front door banged shut and Judith sank back into the pillows. More sleep was a must before the manuscript could be tackled, but first things first. An exploring hand found the renewed wetness she was expecting – she was becoming a real slut, no doubt about it – so Judith drew up her knees and began, ever so gently, to stroke the slippery button . . .

4

Lesson

It is eleven o'clock in the morning when Mrs K interrupts our Classics period to announce that I must report to Dr Schermann forthwith. It is the feared summons and I rack my brains: what have I done? A ripple runs through the class and I hear the shocked whisper of a girl by me to her neighbour: 'It'll be the bench – she's for *the bench*!' It dawns on me that I am in danger of finding out exactly how the infamous device is put to use and the thought makes me shudder. In the corridor it is explained that I am to be punished for insolence to Miss Werther, who is our English teacher. I do remember being somewhat familiar with her and now I think of it she may have been a little offended, but I do not understand why the Headmaster is to take action. When he does, what action it is reputed to be! I have heard terrible stories and already my knees are trembling.

At the door of the study I realise that I must use the toilet before I face this ordeal, or else the ultimate indignity may occur. The First Mistress (that is her title as deputy to the Head, but everybody refers to her as Mrs K) frowns but she knocks and puts her head into the room with a few words of apology. Then she accompanies me to the cubicles (does she

33

think I will run away if left alone?) which are very smart with their new plumbing, but I am so nervous that I cannot go. I say I am sorry for the delay and Mrs K comes in beside me and takes my hand. I am embarrassed, of course, to have her there as if I were a little child on its chamber pot, but she is quite unperturbed and says that however terrible it is going be in the study, in half an hour's time it will be a thing in the past. She gives forth on the theme of how the fear of a thing can be far worse than the thing itself and before I know it my bladder is giving forth too. Once the mistress hears the flow she leaves me to finish and restore my clothes with their fussy buttons and frills. *Very* old-fashioned they are, having passed out of use everywhere since the war – everywhere, that is, except in St Thomas Academy.

Judith pushed her chair back and got to her feet. The textual 'flow' had proved contagious so she padded through, dropped her knickers and squatted on the lavatory seat. Having come wide awake before ten she was moved to deposit her bed linen in the washing machine and take a long hot bath. Then, pink and glowing, she located clean sheets in the hall cupboard, remade the bed and found a new T-shirt and white cotton pants for herself. It was as though she needed to put behind her – for a day or two at least – the highly charged sexual triangle she had landed in and bring a fresh mind to bear on the memoir that was the reason for her visit.

She returned from the bathroom and stood in the humid air that drifted through the screen window. The kitchen looked out across a jumble of backyards and the traffic noise from the street was muted, though it served as a reminder that she was far from her usual place of study. Back at the table she looked again at the pile of materials in front of her. Amongst it was a sheaf of circumstantial detail on the author Jana (at a glance it made her look real, though of course these things could be faked) but Judith had decided to plunge straight in at the first page of the typescript proper and trust to her feel for authenticity. So, now that her bladder had been emptied along with the narrator's, she had better press on and learn of her disciplinary fate.

In the study I stand in front of the desk with the Mistress at my side. While the Headmaster is old and shortly to retire, he is tall and straight and holds the cane at the ready in his hands. I have kept him waiting and am afraid it will be the worse for me. He asks me what I intend to do with my future and I say that if I succeed in my examinations I shall be seeking a private position as a tutor. This gives him the excuse to deliver a lecture on the importance of manners for a young lady with my aims whose pomposity drives me in the end to protest – oh so foolishly, if I had known the consequence of it – that mine was only a small lapse. Surely, I go on, Miss Werther did not report me for such a minor matter.

'No,' says Mrs K, 'she is far too forgiving. It was I who overheard you and when Dr Schermann learned of it he decided that you need a lesson.'

There is no doubt that the two are of a single mind for he nods solemnly and says, 'You did well to come to me, ma'am, for I fear the case is worse than I thought. I was considering the application of six strokes for the single offence, but it seems that our young lady is reluctant to own the gravity of her misbehaviour. That piece of impertinence, Miss Marlova, earns you a further six plus one for good measure: what is generally known, I believe, as a butcher's dozen.'

'Indeed it is, sir.' They smile at each other as I try to grasp the enormity of my sentence. To be lashed thirteen times with that thing quivering in his grasp: how can I possibly bear it?

With a dry mouth and trembling limbs I am led over to the object that is the focus of so much nervous gossip and which occupies a prominent position in one half of the rectangular room. That view of the dreaded 'bench' will stay with me for ever, I know, for in the few seconds I wait before it my fevered brain registers every one of its features with a hallucinatory clarity. It is a stout wooden frame around the size of an upright armchair but without the back so that it stands at the height of a dining table. The top is wider than it was deep and curved down in the middle, while the four upright timbers are fixed into long lintels at the base that are no doubt intended to make the apparatus difficult to topple.

Then Mrs K instructs me to lift my skirt and petticoat and lower my drawers and when this is done she pushes me forward so my belly presses into the slatted hollow. (Thus my objective examination comes alas to an end: for the rest I shall be all-too-directly involved.) After my clothing is tucked up out of the way, a leather belt is secured tightly across the small of my back, followed by two straps that fix my legs just above the knee. Two more buckle the wrists high in a way that keep the elbows up by my sides and the fastenings are done. There is thus little support for the upper body which can droop down or rear right up, as I shall no doubt soon demonstrate. But one thing is quite clear: however much a victim may writhe and struggle, the bared hind parts will be held in prime position to receive every last stroke of the thrashing prescribed her.

Now I wait while Mrs K occupies herself with small adjustments to my folded-down underclothes and my anticipation is screwed up to a dreadful pitch. It is not really the nakedness which upsets me, for it is a common enough feature of home punishments (and my friends report this too), so it seems natural that the school patriarch should by extension have such disciplinary access. I do not feel *shame*, only fear: fear of what the rattan instrument will do to my uncovered behind. To put it bluntly, it is Mrs K alone – one of my own sex – who can have any view of my private parts as she stoops at my back. From his lofty height, all the Headmaster will see are the curves on which to paint his stripes of suffering.

I am almost glad when the rod touches me to signal the start and, as with a loud *whup!* my hips are thrust against the wood, it seems for a fraction of a second not quite as bad as I thought. But that is just the impact; then the pain strikes and my head is wrenched up. I should be screaming but the shock is so great that I cannot make a sound. Two more blows follow in short order and I find my voice in a desperate howl. If any girl is passing it will confirm her worst fears of what goes on in this room. Another two make me think I must faint with the agony of the cane's bite into my left side, and indeed two more leave me slumped forward with a mist before my eyes and a buzzing in my ears. Gradually I become aware of a pause and a consultation; there is a touch to where the hurt is worst and I cry out.

'Hush, Jana.' It is Mrs K's voice, then the Head speaks.

'Very well, ma'am. We do not want to break the skin. She will feel the remainder all the more on a fresh target.' Twisting my head I see that the Mistress has taken up the cane in her right hand and is standing on the opposite side. Now the other flank is to be as cruelly used as the first and I feel a sob rising in my throat. But it goes no further for then she strikes and once again I am shrieking.

* * *

37

It is to the Literature lesson that I am returned after an interval allowed for me to wash my face and regain a degree of control. While Mrs K speaks quietly in her ear the listening Miss Werther looks pale and troubled. For my part I stand stiffly before her desk with the throbbing smart of my posterior in the forefront of my consciousness. The silence in the class is total and I feel the pressure of eyes that would strip away my coverings if they could and feast on the horror of the welted flesh beneath. When I am told I may use the tall desk to the side for the rest of the day's classes it breaks the spell and there is a hum of excited murmuring that spreads amongst the girls until they are called to order.

At the end of the period they are dismissed for lunch but Miss Werther keeps me back and turns the key in the door. 'You must understand, Jana, that I had nothing to do with your punishment.'

She is agitated but I repeat what Mrs K said in the study and I can see it relieves her. Then, after an awkward pause, she blurts out: 'You'll think *me* impertinent now, Jana, but will you show me how you have been treated? In case I make a report I shall need to see for myself.' Now her colour is high and I guess that this 'report' is not the whole story (could she just be as curious as my class-mates undoubtedly are to inspect the results of a real beating?), but I do not mind: she is, as a trainee teacher, scarcely older than I am. So I lift my skirt and petticoat and bend forward while she finds the buttons of my drawers and opens the flap.

'Oh! My poor girl, these marks are as thick as my finger. And you are blistered too!' Her touch is light and the pain is by now dulled so I keep silent. 'This is a terrible place,' she sighs, 'I shall be glad to leave at the end of the year. Don't think me merely squeamish, dear Jana, for where I come from in Saxony girls are raised by corporal punishment too.

And I had my share at school in England – but never such a thing as this!'

My clothing restored, I am feeling much restored in myself under all the sympathetic attention, though I anticipate it will be some time before my bottom is recovered enough to let me sit in comfort. I am ready to go now but it shows in her face that the young teacher has not quite finished, and again she looks embarrassed. 'Perhaps I shouldn't say this – and please don't gossip to the other students – but I believe that Mrs K has – how shall I put it? – a defect of character. The Headmaster is simply of the old school, as they say, and believes it his duty to punish strictly. But she – well, she takes pleasure in it, I think the wrong kind of pleasure, if you understand me. You know, Jana, she has several times suggested that my skirts are too tight and she often stares at my, my – well, where you've just been chastised. I need to have a good report from her as First Mistress when I leave and she has hinted that she might have to deal with my 'laxity' before she could write one. What else can that mean except that I will have to submit to her cane in order to –'

The door handle rattles and there is a sharp knocking that brings the conversation to an end. In confusion, Miss Werther jumps to turn the key and let the janitor in, and I escape to have my belated lunch. Now she has said it I am sure she is right about Mrs K, though it is not something I have thought of before. But the idea of Miss Werther's own hindquarters being in danger seems fanciful to say the least and I put it out of my mind. At the present the important question for me is where I shall be able to stand to eat my lunch.

Mmmm, this was shaping up. First a rather classy bit of 'traditional' rattan-wielding with the promise of more, and, if she were not mistaken, the definite hint of lesbian doings to come from Mrs K and the English teacher. But was it a document from 1920s Bohemia as billed, or was it a disciplinary romance in a period setting? Much too early to say, Judith decided, but one plus point had to be the singular – and rather chilling – bench. Another was the way Miss W lacked the word she needed to pigeon-hole the First Mistress: it was indeed unlikely that a provincial trainee in the 1920s would have known anything of sexology. The tense of the narrative, on the other hand – *historic present* was the name she recalled from her student days – was that how it had been written or had it been Petra's idea to make it more vivid? Well, maybe she could find out.

While it was a neat bundle of properly printed pages that she had started to read, the rest of the papers in the box file took some time to sort through. There was the sheaf of notes about the ostensible writer which had yet to be put into a readable form and another wad of material that seemed to have the makings of a family tree, as yet far from complete. Then Judith came upon a printed page she had not noticed before whose paragraphs contained exactly what she was seeking.

I could justify setting down this story to supplement the work of Dr Ellis on the sexual perversions or to provide a testing-ground for some of Dr Freud's speculations about sado-masochism. I was not, of course, familiar with any of that work when the events took place: how could I have been as a girl of seventeen and one who was even naïve for her age at that time? So what I have tried to do is recapture my state of mind – in all its ignorance – and drawing as I was on the impressions of my diary pages, I found the task easier if I imagined it all to be happening in front of me as I wrote.

But however well this material may serve as a case-study, I have to own that it is principally an attempt to lay some ghosts. Over a period of little more than eighteen months I grew up forcibly, and in a hothouse of sex and pain. Now, two years on and abandoned by my lover, I am trying to trace what happened to me in the hope that understanding the past may sow the seeds of change. Perhaps this will occur in the future; but I have to report that at the time of writing this I remain, alas, every inch the sexual pervert that has come into existence by the end of my short narrative.

The difference in tone was palpable: suddenly Judith was convinced that what she had here was exactly what it pretended to be. And the bluntness of the final sentence was like a shock of cold water in the face. Immersion in the materials of her work made her now and then forget how the world at large viewed such things, and Jana's unhappiness was a salutory reminder of it. She stood up from the table, went to her travel bag and laid out a pair of black satin hotpants and lace-up 'governess' boots she had bought as an outfit and never had the courage to wear on home turf. They had been packed in case she got invited to a gig (without much idea of how odd they might look in latter-day punk circles in Seattle) but now Judith knew exactly where they were likely to go down a treat. First, there had to be a couple of hours' solid work on the background notes to the case of the reluctant deviant; but after that she was going to take up the standing invitation she'd been granted and seek out some of her own kind among the fellow perverts of this new town.

5

Dedicated

At the foot of the outside stair Judith's nerve almost failed. There was a block and a half to cover and in her get-up she was certain to be propositioned several times over before she made it to the bar. Moving slowly in the Saturday sunshine the pedestrian traffic was depressingly straight in dress and manner: where were all the exotic flowers of gaydom marking out this territory as their own? Then the door of the shop was thrust open and an arm appeared flourishing a huge bouquet of hyacinths and gladioli. The bearer of the blooms was very tall and very black and clad in a white PVC miniskirt with bra-top. Judith felt herself scanned up and down with an easy curiosity.

'Honey, you look divine. Are you walking my way this fine afternoon?' In rapid succession her judgements were woman, then drag queen, then transsexual and then woman again. But who was worrying? The direction indicated by the tilt of the head was her intended one and it seemed rescue had come. So when s/he hooked an arm into her own Judith turned and fell happily into step alongside as they set off down the street. Now that she was linked with a real affront to convention, the eyes of the passers-by as they separated to let them through no longer held any threat; instead, if anything they seemed to contain envy rather than hostility.

At the door of The Candy Bar the pair parted company. 'Well, girl, do *you* think they would let me in?' The eyebrows were arched theatrically. 'Now, of course, *after* the op . . .' What more was there to say? Unsure whether to shake the offered hand or put her lips to it, Judith settled for a squeeze and then watched the departing form cutting a swathe through the city walkers with a smile. Inside, however, her new-found confidence took a knock when the woman charged with looking after her was nowhere to be seen. She hadn't caught the name or enough of her appearance to offer a description and the way the skinny redhead who was serving had her lips set in a thin line wasn't inviting. But the prospect of retracing her steps alone made going on the lesser evil, so Judith went up to the bar. Not knowing what to ask for she pointed at a conspicuous tap she had seen being used the last time and put down a five-dollar bill. Then she took her glass away to the far end of the counter and sat on a high stool from where she could keep an eye on the room.

It was long and dimly lit except for the pool table where two women in biker gear were playing in silent concentration. Across from them sat a lady in a business suit with a broadsheet newspaper spread out in front of her, and nearer the entrance a group with shopping bags and cocktail glasses were talking in low voices that broke now and then into ripples of laughter. Hardly a scene that lived up to the establishment's name, yet it wasn't six o'clock and for all she knew there could be a riot going on come ten. Judith swallowed the last inch of her beer and decided to have another. Then if the worst came to the worst she could phone for a cab back to Zadia's place and get on with what she should be doing in the first place.

'Well, I was wondering when you were going to turn round. It's Jude, right? You should have said who you were because they were all primed. And on the orders of the dame in the leathers that no one, but no one, argues with. I guess Lolly don't look too friendly but that's just an act to keep the kids in line.' A pair of slate-blue eyes under a short fringe topped the smile as she took and refilled the glass. 'This is on the house. Name's Cal, by the way, in case you didn't get it yesterday.' Judith was speechless at the change of bartender that had taken place silently behind her and took a good swallow.

'Cheers, Cal. I, er, thought I'd come back.'

'Attagirl. I'm pleased you did. Now, you just wait there while I haul one of my sweeties in to cover the bar and we can sit down and put our heads together before the customers start tearing the place apart. OK?'

The proprietor of the premises cut a youthful figure although close-up the crow's-feet put her nearer forty than thirty. She wore a red check shirt and Judith noticed the worn denims turned up over scuffed boots were of a heavy gauge despite the summer heat. Slightly short of her own five feet six, the compact body had a coiled strength about it that made the difference seem the other way round. Most of all there was an air of experience that had Judith opening up and telling her story for the second time in two days. After she'd brought over another round of beers, Cal sat down and took a swig.

'You made quite an impression on our Pat, y'know, and I guess I see why. She's left town for a week so you're gonna be outa here before she gets back. Could be that's for the best.' She spoke in a laid-back drawl, yet the words were obviously chosen with care. 'See, Jude, a girl needs to be *dedicated* to do a number with her. I don't mean she forces anything on you that you don't want, just that she has a way of getting you in deeper and deeper, and then before you know it you're wallowing in heavy shit you'd normally run a mile from.'

Judith nodded, but she was feeling out of her depth. While she had read around the kind of literature kick-started by the Samois group in the eighties, much of it was polemic that didn't spell out the details of precisely what was involved in 'heavy shit'. And when Cal got to the next question, Judith realised she'd been afraid of it all along.

'That Archive of yours sounds neat, and I could fancy staging a basement number there myself. But what about when you wanna push out the boat – y'know, like take a few risks. Where d'you guys go to do that stuff?'

'Well, um, er –' Better face it, they didn't. Or rather *she* didn't. Oh fuck. Judith saw the sum total of her experience flash before her: maybe a dozen canings from Miss James and a good few spankings that were more erotic than punitive. There had been one thrashing in Brittany that still made her sweat to think of, but that was two years ago. No boats came into the picture at all: it was a case of being stuck firmly on the shore. She felt like an imposter and looked down in confusion.

'Hey, girl. I don't mean to put you on the spot. I got a few years on you, Jude, and it's a fool who thinks that this game is any kind of contest.' Cal stood up and looked at Judith, hands on hips. 'I got an idea. How many beers you had – it's only the three, yeah? OK, no problem there, so why don't you come through the back of the bar with me right now.'

It was a smallish room with a desk cluttered with papers and a couple of easy chairs. Cal asked Lolly to give them a few minutes then closed the door behind her and bolted the one on the opposite wall. When she spoke it was with a slow deliberation. 'Now you can say I've got a fucking nerve and if you feel like smacking my face and walking out no one's gonna stop you. What I want to do is pull down those pants of yours and take a proper look at what fills them out so nice.'

At a loss Judith stared, caught somewhere between the urge to smirk at the popularity of her behind and frown at an overdramatic pass. 'I promise you there's a good reason for this, Jude. So how's about it?' The eyes that met hers were earnest, so Judith capitulated with a little shrug and bent forward over the upright chair. Then, the shorts round her knees, she submitted to the requested inspection from the boss woman hunkered down at her back.

'One thing I gotta say for Pat – the lady has taste. But don't let it go to your head, girl.' As she spoke, Cal lifted first one cheek then the other and gently kneaded the flesh. 'While I can't deny I'm enjoying my work at the minute, there is a serious point to it. And what we find here is very good. First there's been a quite thorough spanking in the past couple of days, yeah? And definitely by hand.'

'That's right, but how –'

'You can tell by the way the fingers leave lines that you don't get with a paddle or a strap. But then, underneath that are the remains of a pretty tough caning, maybe a dozen strokes, say last Monday?'

'All right, Sherlock. Now come clean and admit that was a guess. And can I pull my pants up, please?' Her tension had dissipated into light-headed giggles and Judith was relieved to see Cal wearing an indulgent smile.

'Two questions and I've done with the examination. Now we know nobody *enjoys* that English discipline of yours (it's the whole idea, right?) but does it always make you wet? And if your ass feels like it's been cut to ribbons after, does the pussy drool even more?'

Judith nodded, trying to control her rising colour at the explicit images being evoked.

'And do you come like crazy if you get a *proper* spanking? I mean where you get good hard slaps, not the fanny-patting a lot of kids stop at these days.'

'Yes, I do. If it's done right.' She may as well speak clearly and try to downplay the fact of her burning face.

'Well, Jude, I have to tell you there's only one possible diagnosis. You are a *natural*. But like with any talent, it needs work to flower into something real wild. And what the doctor prescribes to begin with is a few simple exercises. We could start off right here and right now if you wanted. So what do you say?'

Standing naked in her black ankle-boots Judith watched the large orange bulb being filled with growing apprehension. What *had* she done? But only one answer had been possible to Cal's question if she were not forever to reproach herself for a missed opportunity. There was no arguing with the woman's point: it was high time to build on her deep-seated inclinations. The wilder journeys taken were almost without exception in her head – courtesy of some of the materials in the secure section of the Nemesis collection – and there had been a distinct lack of real-life exploration, certainly in the last twelve months. However, it had come as a bit of a shock that by saying yes she had signed herself up for an immediate session in the specially equipped club open only to bona fide 'dykes and sluts' who frequented The Candy Bar.

Exactly what was to happen had not been explained: the point would be lost if she were prepared for what was to come. But first, there was to be the 'irrigation' – mandatory, insisted Cal – and Judith bent reluctantly over while the white-coated assistant inserted the greased nozzle into her. The swoosh of warm water inside was not itself unpleasant, but there was something quite disconcerting about the explosive discharge of her bowels into the lavatory bowl that followed. After three goes she was pronounced clean and submitted to the silk band that was placed over her eyes and the cuffs that held her wrists in front. Both were to remain there until she was returned to the examination room. One definite piece of information had been imparted and Judith clung on to it as she was led out into the passage: there was a safe word. If it all got too much and she said *home* then it would come to a stop.

A door was opened ahead of her and she was guided down a set of wooden steps. There was a draught of air in her face which had the faint mustiness of a windowless basement and she felt a thick carpet under her feet. Then her thighs pressed against some sort of padded bar and her top half was bent over it. While arms held her ankles, something hooked between the wrists and with the sound of a ratchet mechanism she was jerked, gasping, forward and down. Then each leg was pulled up and strapped tight at the knee and something cold and smooth was pressed for a moment to her gaping genitals. Judith squirmed and choked but she was held fast: never before had she been so obscenely on display. There was the sound of a door closing and then nothing. She strained her ears but could detect no sound that might indicate the presence of another person in the room.

Minutes passed without perceptible change. Once the initial distress of her extreme openness had passed she found the position to be not in itself uncomfortable. The hips and belly were well cushioned and the leather bonds quite soft against the skin, so after a while Judith relaxed gradually into her restraints. There was a background hum caused no doubt by air conditioning and its drone began to make her feel drowsy. At first barely detectable, it seemed to have acquired a rhythmic pulse which was expanding and deepening to fill her entire consciousness ... Then she snapped back wide awake for lightly, but unmistakably, a slippery finger had just circled her anus. It was followed by a squirt of grease that hung unpleasantly between the buttocks until it was worked into the outer ring of muscle.

Judith willed herself to relax: since she'd been sluiced out it didn't take a genius to deduce something would be going in. And indeed there was. After the third dollup of lubricant had gone as far inside as a finger would take it she felt a solid object nosing into the tight opening. Under steady pressure the sphincter expanded and kept expanding as the thing pushed relentlessly deeper. Oh God, it was big – *too* fucking big. She cried out and then the head of the plug pulled inside and the strain eased. Her muscle closed round the narrower neck of the device and she felt its end held against the furrow between her buttocks. Denied visual feedback, in her imagination the inserted dildo grew until it seemed that all of her insides had been shifted to create the gigantic space it must be occupying. She lay frozen, panicked at the thought of a sudden movement causing internal rupture and let out a shaming whimper of violation.

But before self-pity could take more of a hold there was a new development to occupy her mind. Something hard was laid down the inner line of her arse-cheek almost touching the cunt and it felt very much like a slender cane. Oh Jesus, not there. Please not there. With a sharp crack the instrument cut three times to the left, then three times to the right. It was not hard as canings went but the hot sting was like a knife into her centre, and Judith clenched her fists with the anguish of it. In the pause she hung panting over the trestle and fought for self-control. She could – would – take that once more if she had to. In the event she endured the sequence repeated and repeated again without crying for 'home', though it was a close-run thing. Then she realised that the interval was growing longer without any fresh strokes or any sound above the steady attendant hum and Judith allowed herself a few tears of relief.

However, it soon became obvious that she was not out of the woods yet. As the smart of the lines faded an itch grew in the genitals right beside them and the small writhing movements her bonds allowed just made it worse. Moreover, they caused the once-frightening object buried in her colon to shift with an erotic frisson all of its own. After five minutes of this Judith was at screaming pitch: she wanted, more than anything else in the world, to be vigorously fucked and thoroughly buggered at one and the same time and her mind filled with images of the huge phallic objects with bulbous heads that would be needed to accomplish this operation. Reluctant before to vocalise for fear of capitulating, now she moaned and hissed in the mounting lust she had no means of slaking. For some years after Judith would cringe at the memory of it; at the time she bit her tongue in shocked embarrassment as two pairs of firm hands out of nowhere took hold of arms and legs and released her from the bondage.

In the small office at the back of the bar Cal was lounging in the swivel chair tapping a pencil against her teeth. 'I hear you did not bad – for a beginner. But there is something more. If, of course, you're up for it.' Judith was standing against the wall as naked as she had been in the basement, though the blindfold was gone and her hands were now free.

'Absolutely.' She must try to redeem that disgraceful exhibition but the arousal was still leaking from between her legs. It was not a good start and she shifted uncomfortably. The proprietor was watching her with a half smile.

'It's OK, girl. I'm gonna fix that tickling down there that won't give you any peace. And I reckon you're gonna taste something real special. But there's just one thing: it gets done here and now or not at all.' Judith looked at the speaker as the implication sank in. It was bad enough standing here starkers with the top half of the connecting door open but if Cal was going to bring her off . . .

'That's it, Jude.' There was a grin, but it seemed to have acquired a predatory edge. 'You gotta keep the noise down this time if you don't want to draw an audience. It's getting busy through there by the sound of it and these ladies ain't shy. If they get wind there's a girlie in here having her honeypot licked clean you'll be hauled out to do a floor show in front of the whole bar.'

'If you were mine, I'd get you waxed, babe. And then I'd be able to study every sweet pink fold you got in this pussy while I drove you crazy all night long.'

It sent shivers up Judith's spine to think of being a dyke's, well, *femme* it had to be though she couldn't be doing with the soft-porn lingerie the word implied. No, she would hate it of course, Jude the independent agent beholden to no one, but yet . . . but yet . . . And then the probing tongue moved around the root of her clitoris and she had to bite back the first cry.

Later a voice floated through demanding, 'Where the fuck is Cal? I ain't seen her all night,' then it was swallowed back into the general hubbub from the saloon. Judith felt the sweat running in rivulets between shoulder blades and breasts and her thighs ached with the strain of keeping her legs wide. But the long-delayed climax was starting to break and Cal's hands were clasping the cheeks of her behind, fingers kneading the cane marks and pressing into the anal plug. The impossible riot of sensation demanded that she cry and yell and shriek, but somehow, tearing at Cal's shoulders and thumping her back against the wall she held it in as the tide swept her up until, in the end, her knees buckled and she slid to the floor.

When the dildo came out in the examination room it proved to be a thing of rather ordinary proportions though she felt oddly deprived without it. Once showered and dressed she made her way down the passage, but Cal was nowhere to be seen. Lolly pressed a tall glass of iced liquid on her in the office with a broad wink. 'That sounded good, hon. Wish it'd been me. Now you sit and drink this and I'll call you a cab in a half hour.'

While Judith was ready to protest that she was up to a few at the bar, before the glass was half empty she felt used up and woozy and was glad to leave when the ride came. Back at the apartment she made an attempt to sit at the table with the typescript but her head was full of her own doings. Well, the next day was Sunday and there would be no adventures. There was serious reading to do.

In bed she found her cunt moist, but for once forbore to masturbate. The feel of Cal's mouth was fresh in her mind and she wanted to keep it there a while longer and savour it. Was this what one of her 'sweeties' felt like, even just once in a while? To be a dyke's plaything – to be delivered for cruel punishment games and afterwards sucked and nibbled into delirious pleasure – was that a possible life? The answer had to be no, but the business of submission was distressingly complicated. Or did she mean complex? Probably both. Judith sighed and turned over. It was time to sleep.

Later, as her thoughts wandered on the edge of consciousness it came to her there was one thing – it would be like a *token*, that was all – this waxing to remove the hairs, it couldn't hurt *that* much now, surely . . .

6

First Mistress

My story moves on a full four months into the middle of the autumn term. Until the summer I managed to keep out of trouble – at least I made no further acquaintance with the fearful bench – and I obtained the grading in my examinations to enable me to tutor if I could find a placing. But then I was most surprised to be offered a position at the Academy itself. Now that Dr Schermann has officially retired, Mrs K is *de facto* Head but she must retain her old title and report to the Board on a regular basis because they will not give a *woman* formal governance of a *girls'* school. However, no doubt in recompense for the absurdity of the ruling, they have approved funding for the new post of Assistant to the First Mistress. So far I have been used solely to substitute for a teacher unable to take her class, and indeed the knowledge of our curriculum for which I was ostensibly chosen obviously stands me in good stead to do just that. However, Mrs K has alluded to future work of a more 'personal' nature and while I have little idea what she intends, I suspect that it will not be my academic side that is put to use.

This morning I have been in charge of Miss Werther's classes since 8.30 a.m. I am glad at the opportunity to practise my English though of course sorry it is occasioned by her leaving of us tomorrow. While she will have things to attend to I am surprised that it has reached eleven o' clock without her making an appearance. I decide to find her, only to come upon the First Mistress in the corridor who enquires where I am going. I tell her my business and explain, with some nervousness, that I have left a senior girl in charge for the short time I shall be absent. She waves aside any worry that I may have gone beyond my authority in leaving my class and as she does so I notice there is a cane under her arm. Her colour is high and for a long moment she stares as if trying to read something from my face. Then she speaks rather in a rush: it is as though she has passed a point of no return and must keep going. 'Yes, by all means, Jana. Go to Miss Werther. You will find her in her room. And take the time you need: I shall attend personally to your girls.'

I cross the yard into the resident staff quarters and knock on the door I am seeking but there is no answer. With my ear to the wood I am sure there is movement inside so I tap again quite sharply. A muffled voice asks, 'Who is it?' and I say, 'Magda, it's me – Jana.' Since the time I paid dearly for my overfamiliarity we have become in fact familiar, which is considered acceptable now that I am a colleague, albeit a lowly one. But there is no answer coming to my statement, and it dawns on me that what I can hear are sounds of distress. So I open the door without waiting for an invitation and then stop in my tracks, unable at first to comprehend what I see. My friend is stretched out across the bed in her bloomers with pillows under her that raise the hips. At the sight of me she cries out, 'Oh Jana, how it hurts!' and breaks into a fit of sobbing. Suddenly I perceive that when I spoke to her Mrs K had come directly from this room where she must have used the instrument she was still carrying. Now I recall the threat I was told of last term and feel a little ashamed of my scepticism.

'Oh, poor Magda,' I say, 'please let me look. It will help if I bathe you.' She makes no objection as I draw down the silk undergarment to uncover the damage that has been done. I am familiar with what greets my eyes, having once seen my own posterior in a similar state with the aid of a mirror. I set to bathing the livid stripes with a face cloth and cold water from the washbasin and during the process I am given an account of the ultimatum delivered by the First Mistress that very morning: either Miss Werther submit to the correction of her behaviour in the approved manner, or the letter of recommendation she needed would criticise her lack of proper formal distance from the students.

'I was too soft and she would show me proper discipline. That is what she said. Jana, I had no choice. I have a position waiting for me if I get a good report. At least I managed to persuade her not to bare me completely, but I had to take twelve strokes and the pain was so bad I rolled on to the floor. Oh, I know the bench is terrible, but there you *cannot* move. As it was I earned an extra six for not keeping in place, with the results you can see.' She turns a woebegone face to me with tears starting afresh, so I make soothing noises and talk of how tomorrow she will be beyond Mrs K's reach for ever. At this Magda quietens and lies still while I finish off my ministrations to her chastised bottom. I have to own I am becoming quite absorbed in the task, for the downy skin around the horrid weals is deliciously pale except where it darkens mysteriously into the secret cleft. The cheeks are rather full with doubled lines where they join the thighs and suddenly I want to slip my fingers in and stroke her there. Of course I restrain myself but the urge makes *me* feel peculiar in the place I want to touch on *her*. I suppose this is how I am meant to react to young men (I have no experience of that) but she is a woman. Does that mean I am abnormal?

It is a troubling question that stays with me through the afternoon, but as the evening wears on and I am attempting some preparation for the morning's classes my mind turns more toward regret that I did not follow my impulse. I reason that as of today Miss Werther the trainee is no longer employed at the Academy and will be leaving first thing in the morning, so if I make a disastrous error I shall not have to live with the consequences of it. Once this thought has entered my head I know I cannot rest and as soon as the passage lights are extinguished at 10 p.m. I steal out and up the stairs. At her door I dare not knock for fear of attracting attention so I open it a crack and call her name softly.

'Jana, is that you?' she says back and I am inside at once. Suitcases stand packed by the desk and Magda herself is lying on the bed in her nightgown with a book open in front of her. I explain I have brought a herbal lotion for her bruises and apologise for the lateness of the hour. Then I blurt out that I was afraid she would think me too forward and it has taken me all evening to work up my courage. She smiles and shakes her head at my silliness and I am relieved but also nervously excited. We arrange the pillows as before and she goes over them with her gown up around her waist to allow for my inspection.

Her condition is much improved from the morning for already most of the swelling has gone though the worst of the purple marks have now turned almost black. I concentrate first on these, then broaden out the area I am anointing to the dimpled flanks. The long skirts Magda wears have a snugness of fit to the thighs which has earned her the disapproval of some older mistresses (and may, it seems, have been instrumental in prompting Mrs K's course of action). To follow her down a corridor was to have one's eye drawn to those undulating curves, the very ones to which I am now – and I cannot quite believe it – giving my close attention in all their unclothed glory.

Magda is moving with the rhythm of my gentle massage, saying, 'Oh, that is lovely, Jana. I am *so* much recovered. You have become such a good friend to me and I shall miss you greatly.' She promises to write with her address when she is settled so that I can visit her. Emboldened by these declarations I trace the line of one low stripe and go the extra inch so that my hand is amongst wisps of brown curls. My heart is in my mouth, but far from objecting Magda pushes against me and my fingers are into hot wetness between her legs.

'Oh! Oh! Oh!' she cries and jerks her hips several times. Then she starts up, clasps me in her arms and kisses me on the mouth, breathing, 'Jana, Jana . . .' But this sudden development is too much for me and I pull away, muttering, 'Sorry, sorry,' and I am out of the door before she can stop me. Back in my room I sit on the bed waiting for the thudding in my chest to subside. It is a long time before sleep comes, and in the morning I am told that the trainee mistress left by taxi some time before breakfast to catch the early train.

'Jana, I expect that you think the worse of me for my treatment of Miss Werther. I remember that you were drawn to her some time ago when it was not appropriate, which made it necessary for me to intervene as I did.' From the way the First Mistress is regarding me I *know* she has a picture in her mind of me bared and strapped down for punishment and I look away blushing.

'Since your appointment, of course, there has been no objection to it and I understand the two of you to have formed a relationship.' One eyebrow is slightly raised on the last word and again I shy away from her gaze. Can she know anything of that final encounter on Friday night? It occurs to me that Mrs K did all but send me to Magda in the wake of her caning: could it be that she envisaged our becoming closer as a result?

'I don't expect you to understand this yet, Jana, but there are some young women for whom discipline is vital. Miss Werther is one such, I believe, though she may well deny the fact without further experiences to teach her otherwise.' We are standing in the corridor which has become busy with the mid-morning break, so I am ushered into the office and seated by Mrs K's desk.

'Tell me, Jana,' she says, 'do you bear me any resentment for the caning *you* received last term? Be frank with me, please.'

I say I don't believe so, and it is true. There is something *impersonal* in her devotion to corporal punishment that makes it difficult to harbour a grudge. I know that Magda thought the enthusiasm unhealthy: that she took too much pleasure in it. Perhaps so, but I have to admit that the subject has been much in *my* mind in the last few days.

'I'm glad to hear that.' The First Mistress has taken up a cane that hangs from the desktop and is toying with it while she speaks. 'Now go back in your mind to the occasion and tell me how you felt afterwards.'

I stare – is the answer not rather obvious? – and she sees that I am at a loss. 'I realise an instrument like this –' she flicks the thing so that it quivers in the air '– causes considerable pain at the time of its use. It is, after all, what it is intended to do. But when that began to fade – and within minutes the worst is usually over – did you not feel a sense of release, perhaps?'

Still I do not understand. At the time she speaks of I was shocked and back in class with all eyes on me, wishing that the floor would open and swallow me up. So I shake my head: there was nothing positive about the experience that I can recall. However, it does occur to me that much later I was the centre of attention in the dormitory among the small number of boarding girls at the school, so I tell of how I was inspected by moonlight once the duty mistress had left and felt the pride of one who has survived an ordeal.

Mrs K clicks her tongue but it is clear that this misdemeanour from the past is of little concern. However, my reply is plainly not the one she is seeking and she persists in her questioning. 'Well then, Jana, let me ask you something else. If you do not wish to answer me, I shall not hold it against you. When you went to Miss Werther on Friday, did you find anything about her reactions that you were not expecting?'

I say no, she was very distressed. I am feeling under pressure to produce something so I divulge that I bathed her and then left her still upset. Mrs K does not appear the least surprised by my revelation and she goes on. 'But how about later, Jana? Did you perhaps visit Miss Werther – your friend Magda – again before she left us?' This is said in a soft, persuasive tone I have never heard before and it makes my words come tumbling out. I tell of my restlessness and the lotion, the massage and how she, she . . . But I cannot say it and hang my head, ending instead with the lame statement that she was much recovered. There is a silence while I stare at the floor then Mrs K stands up, back to her old brisk self.

'That is fine. I do not mean to pry into your personal affairs. But what I have heard inclines me to think it may be time to widen the scope of your duties. You have the afternoon free, is that not so?' I nod, relieved the interrogation has come to a stop.

'Then I wish you to assist me, if you will, in a little disciplinary matter. We shall meet here at 3 p.m. sharp.'

By the time the knock comes at the door I have been treated to a rather full explanation of the experimental policy the First Mistress has recently adopted. Her idea seems to be to supplement the exclusive use of the cane characteristic of the Headmaster's régime with milder punishments like spanking and strapping, but to apply them at the earliest signs of bad behaviour in order to nip it in the bud. Today's culprit was thus punished last week for poor homework which has regrettably been repeated. After the offender has been berated for the lapse, Mrs K announces her decision to try the effects of a second dose and indicates with her hand the stout table against the wall with a cushion on its top.

'Since there has been a *slight* improvement our Miss Bergmann will be spared the bench. *This* time. I hope you are grateful for my leniency, Monika.' The girl looks anything but grateful, but she moves over without demur, lifts her blue tunic dress and lies forward on her elbows. Along with the new uniform, Mrs K has at last brought the underwear into the modern age, so we are greeted by the sight of a pair of, it has to be said, rather well-filled white cotton knickers.

'However, we have not yet cured the problem,' the First Mistress continues, 'so the fine young belle of the Saturday ball becomes on the Monday a schoolgirl offering her bottom for a sound spanking.' My job is to curb the girl's habit of leaping up which proved troublesome on the previous occasion so I take up position and press down firmly on her back. She swivels her neck and I see she is flushed and looks close to tears.

Mrs K swings her arm with an easy rhythm that is no doubt designed to be sustainable for a lengthy delivery and the slaps fall to left and right in a regular pattern. The movement of the hind cheeks under the stretched fabric is quite enticing and as I watch I experience again the feeling that made me return to Magda's room. After a while I am instructed to lower the pants and the handspanking continues. Already the skin is a deep pink and each smack is met with an 'Ow!' from the victim although she makes no serious attempt to break away. Perhaps it is because I have such a firm grip, I think.

However, such a conclusion is premature for when the short but thick strap makes its first contact Monika yelps and twists violently, thrusting me aside in the process. Mrs K directs me to take the girl's arms round behind her and hold the wrists tight up between the shoulder blades. She has become annoyed by the fuss and decrees a further two dozen strokes, each of which the culprit must count in the form 'One, thank you, Mistress' and so on to the end. Now we hear a definite sob, but the head goes down and there is no further struggle. The thwack of the leather across the bouncing buttocks directly below my eyes is enthralling, and towards the end of the tally I can almost feel the heat radiating from the crimson posterior. I should like nothing more in the whole world than to soothe the burning flesh with my caresses and I feel weak with the strength of the desire that must be denied.

Then it is over. The girl's clothing is restored, tears are dried and her face is washed at a basin in the corner. Once the penalty has been paid the First Mistress is all smiles.

'Now, Monika, we do *not* want to see you here next week. Isn't that right, Miss Marlova? So make more time for your studies at the weekend, please. You may go home early if you wish, and don't worry about any further consequences. I see no reason why your father need be informed of what has happened today.' The assurance provokes a smile from the student too, if a rather watery one, and I see how pretty she is as she gives a little curtsy and retreats out of the door.

Mrs K turns to me and says, 'Thank you for your help, Jana. I'm sure I shall call upon your services again. But you do look a little heated. Why not take the last period off. I'll arrange for Miss Jansch to cover for you.' She seems to be studying me but her expression gives nothing away, so I mutter my thanks and flee.

In my room I stand in front of the mirror and remove my pleated skirt. I have such a feeling inside my private parts – it is almost a *pain* – that I can no longer hold back from the thing I have never done though I know girls who have. That it is regarded by proper people as shameful is suddenly of no account and I pull down my own knickers just as I did Monika's pair. I think of her swelling cheeks as I put my hand to the opening between my legs. With a shock I find it brimming with slippery juice and I cannot stop my hand touching deeper. The spasms begin at once and continue until I sink exhausted on to the bed and curl into a tight ball, my mind reeling. Of course, *that* is what happened to Magda before she kissed me . . . And it can – it will – happen to me again. Oh, I had no idea of such a thing, such *sensations* . . .

7

Self-Help

After supper I decide to set down these momentous events, and since I believe they originate in my first experience of corporal punishment I must make an effort – disagreeable though it be – to recall every detail of my encounter with the Headmaster's bench. Soon I am drawn into reliving the past and when there is a sharp rap at my door it makes me jump. I am a little shocked to find that it is the First Mistress who is already in my mind through what I am writing. I stand guiltily in front of the table but she shows no interest in the papers on it.

'I am here because I have been thinking about the way Monika's punishment seemed to affect you rather deeply, and it occurred to me that such things may be more foreign to you than I had considered.' I am able to confirm what she suspects and explain my position as an only child who had come late and was much indulged by an ageing father (my mother having died young).

'Even at school I escaped any form of physical punishment,' I go on, 'until I came here and – and –' I break off for the incident is painfully fresh in my thoughts.

'I know it must have been a shock to you, Jana, especially in the light of what I now learn of your upbringing. I generally expect that a girl on the receiving end of the cane will have at the very least met with a good dose of the strap at some point in her career. But perhaps that is not a safe assumption to make.' Mrs K looks a little discomfited and I am moved to reassure her until I remember what we are talking about: an occasion when she consigned me to a thrashing that had no real justification and then helped to administer it.

'Whether that was truly merited or not,' she continues and I blush that my thoughts seem so transparent, 'it was pure punishment, intended to sear itself into the brain. And you have made me very aware that it has done exactly as planned.' The sardonic edge has returned to her manner and I feel more at ease as she develops her theme. 'However, discipline can take other forms that do not call for the rigours of a punishment frame. For instance, between a woman of experience and one, like yourself, who may be in some respects naïve but is willing to learn . . .' She lets the sentence hang and sits down on the edge of my bed. I have an inkling where this is heading and I get a rush of excitement rather than the fear which would be much more appropriate in view of my past treatment. So when the First Mistress says that before I play a regular part in the spanking of errant seniors she would like me to take a sample of what they will undergo, I am ready to put myself in her hands.

On instruction I strip from the waist down promptly, if with heart a-flutter, and lie over the lap of her prickly tweed skirt.

She does not hit at all hard at first, and when there is an increase in force, the sting of each smack stimulates more than it actually hurts. I cannot describe the feeling of being held across the firm thighs of this handsome woman with my vulnerable flesh entirely at her disposal. I want it to go on for ever and am almost bereft when she stops and I have to get up. She cups my bottom in her hand and kisses me on the forehead.

'One day, dear Jana, you may graduate to the cane,' she says, staring into my eyes, 'but do not fear, I shall never again force it on you as I once did.' Then I get another kiss and she is gone.

My hind parts are hot and heavy, and I examine their pink curves in the mirror, wondering at the strange turn my life is taking. This time one touch is enough for the seizure to shake my body but when it has passed I want more. I spread a towel on my bed to avoid staining the sheet with what wells up from inside me and stretch out on it. Has Mrs K divined that I have learned how to help myself to such pleasure? Is that why she came tonight to –

Judith broke off her reading and pushed the manuscript aside. Talk about things welling up ... In a second she was squatting on the lavatory seat with the wet-crotched pants on the floor beside her, two fingers hooked into the sensitive folds. To judge from her own reactions, this was more than worthy of a place in the Nemesis Archive. Miss James had expressed the desire to launch a series of monographs and this could be just the thing to set the ball rolling. She should make the German lady an offer. But first things first. As with Jana, this wasn't going to take much. Not much at all. Judith hunched forward with eyes closed, breath quickening while her mind dwelt on the spanked and masturbating girl of some eighty years before. Then she heard a sound from the passage and started up in horror grabbing at the discarded knickers. There in open doorway of the bathroom was a grinning Petra.

'Don't you *dare* stop, Jay. I am totally stressed and a nice sex show is *exactly* what I need.' She pushed Judith back down gently into position and there was a teasing waft of perfume.

'Shit. This is becoming a habit.'

'My party piece.' Petra giggled. 'It's amazing what you can discover at this place if you creep in when you're not expected. Now that's how *I* sit when it's urgent, so you just carry on while I hold you, OK?' With her head against the girl's blouse Judith began to relax, and as a hand reached inside her T-shirt to stroke a breast she turned her attention back to the interrupted task. There was something very erotic about doing this private thing in front of another woman and the climax came fast and loud.

Afterwards Petra said, 'I bet I know what set you off. It was where she gets the first spanking and has to wank twice, yeah? Well, if it got you horny reading it, what do you think it was like to write?' She giggled again and stepped back. 'Hey, I have an idea. Here am I all dressed up like Mrs K and there you are minus underpants like Jana: let's re-enact the first bit. Come on through to the bedroom.'

Judith needed little persuasion to go over the suited knee and her level of arousal leapt when Petra fondled her bottom, separating the cheeks. 'Well, what have we here – new marks, if I'm not mistaken. Where *did* you get these? I want the full story later, madam. First, though, there is a job to be done and I reckon it might need me to smack a tad harder than the lady did in the story. But you'll wear that won't you, Jay?'

A while later she lay sprawled on her bed, satiated in the wake of a second orgasm while Petra demanded to be told all about the club and the initiation, if that's what you could call it. Judith wasn't sure of that, but she was sure that she had to pay them another visit, even more so as the tale had her audience hanging on every word.

'Sounds really cool. I've never met an up-front old-style dyke, it's a no-no to advertise the fact in corporation land.'

'Oh, Petra, they wouldn't let you in. It's a drag know but they're dead strict on ID.' In fact Judith was rather relieved: she could just see Cal bypassing her in favour of this juicy teenager. Especially if she wore – as she did at that moment – a sulky pout that positively invited the application of a firm hand to its owner's bottom. One thing led to another and the best part of an hour had passed before Judith surfaced from between the young girl's legs, awash with the taste of her desire.

'A year and a half to wait. It's a fucking slow business this growing up.' Petra's mind had clearly returned to the same topic. 'So, Jay, I'll have to make do with a hand-me-down. You just must go there again for the material to give me another episode. Or before you know it you'll have jetted off to England and left us all to it.'

Judith sat up: the idea was not exactly an appealing one. All too soon she would indeed be leaving this wild place she'd landed in to return to the routine of life among her files and folders. She would have to phone Grace first thing in the morning and then arrange a flight for the day after. Even if nothing had come up she couldn't expect a secretary to run the show for long in the absence of both her seniors.

'OK, Petra, I'll fit it in somehow, don't worry. You'll get another instalment of the doings in The Candy Bar.' It was like being held to the promise of a bedtime story by this young woman with the smart job who flipped alarmingly between personas. One moment there was a child hungry for information and the next a sexual sophisticate bragging she gave the best head in town. At present she was curled up on the bed stroking Judith's pubic mound as if it were the fur of a cat, and the action brought to mind Cal's talk of how she liked her women bare. Supposing she – Judith – went for it: the whole works. Much more than a mere memento of this time it

67

a quite literal embodiment of the new direction ‌p was making seem imperative. She cleared her ‌t in order to put the thought into words. Maybe the enticing bundle of contradictions beside her would know where to go to get such a thing done.

'Sure. I have a card somewhere from a good place. Rhoda in the office took the plunge after wavering for months and now she's smooth and silky as a baby's rear end, and heaps more tasty. Brazilian waxing is what these guys call it. But, Jay, are you sure you want to do this?' Her eyes looked up from the black hairs under discussion and the lips were posed in another delicious pout. 'The poor girl said it hurt like hell and hers was quite thin on the ground. With a growth like this one in front of me here you are going to be left totally, but totally raw.'

A door banged and Judith came to and squinted at the figures on the clock by her head. At three-fifteen in the morning that must be Zadia in. She turned over ready to slip back into a half-remembered dream, glad that in the end a reluctant Petra had been pushed out to the sororal bed. However, ten minutes later sleep had become a distant prospect. First there was the clomping about with God knows what kind of heavy boots on the kitchen floor and then after that there was the talk and laughter that came from the adjoining room. But what happened next was much worse. Just as she was planning to go and voice a complaint, it occurred to her that the giggling had turned to squealing and added to that were the sounds of a protesting bed frame. Plainly the sisters were back in full-on mode and while Judith told herself firmly that jealousy had no place in her fresh start, the memory of the young body was too vivid. She could imagine only too well its responses to the Amazonian caresses and her own lusted horribly for the girl's touch. But the relationship being enacted next door had a prior depth that absolutely ruled out her intervention, so Judith stuffed her head between two pillows and gritted her teeth. There was nothing for it but to wait the thing out. Eventually, of course, silence supervened, but the light was coming through the blinds before she was calm enough to sink into an exhausted sleep.

It was midday when Judith woke to sounds from the kitchen and in the bathroom she showered briskly, bracing herself to appear unruffled in front of the others. She need not have worried, however, for both were subdued and it took only a short discussion over coffee for her proposal to be accepted. While there could not be an advance on such a project, she would stick her neck out and recommend publication under the mooted NemArch imprint with royalties split between them to acknowledge the amount of editorial and analytical work she would need to do. A phone call to Grace at the Archive arranged for a contract to be emailed to Marissa at CatWork which Judith could collect later in the day for signing before she left. So business was done and Zadia announced she was going back to bed to nurse 'the sore head' after three days' gigging and boozing and Petra declared herself to be similarly shattered. Hardly surprising, thought Judith grimly, then looked up to find the provoking child-woman still in the dooorway.

'Duty calls. But Zee will be gone again tonight, OK?' Blowing a kiss, she disappeared from view and there was the sound of a door being firmly shut. Judith sighed: it was her first experience of a sexual triangle and she was far from certain she could cope. But two more pieces of telephone business helped restore a feeling of control. First she confirmed her return flight for 4 p.m. the following afternoon and then made an appointment with the beautician Petra had recommended for noon. That was it then. She was going to be 'done' and she was going to leave Seattle in little more than another twenty-four hours. That left just one thing: after picking up the papers there ought to be a last visit to the bar. Even if there was nothing happening it had to be a better option than sitting in the flat thinking of what was going on behind the door of the double bedroom.

There was no sign of Cal but once she ordered, the barmaid called through and Lolly appeared out of the back. 'Hey, Jude honey, you got here just at the right time. Now you sit and drink your beer while I go through and talk to the guys. Y'see, they were planning on doing a movie today but the model took one look at that cane and was out the door. And the idea is, it's all very *English*, so this is where you could come in. If you wanna play . . .'

An hour later Judith was togged out passably as a private schoolgirl of the 1950s standing before her icily angry Headmistress. The scene was perhaps slightly enhanced with both women showing more leg and the punishment instrument more weight than was histori-cally accurate. However, the producer pointed out that viewers these days demanded to see marks a real girls' cane was unlikely to deliver and since she offered a fee that easily covered the treatment booked for the next day Judith wasn't moved to object.

Her co-performer Geraldine was a willowy figure with fair hair and black-rimmed spectacles and she was good. The unscripted dressing-down, delivered in an accent worthy of a BBC announcer of the period, had Judith a touch weak-kneed at the memories it brought back. Not that a cane was ever used at her own school – though one mistress was rumoured to keep a strap in her rooms – but she had been subject to that kind of lecture distressingly often. This time it seemed her work was a disgrace, her manners terrible, her appearance slovenly

70

and, to cap it all, she had been caught with a packet of cigarettes.

'Since you will be leaving us next year, Margaret, you may think you are already a young lady beyond my jurisdiction. Well, let us see how grown up you are with your skirt up and your knickers down, bending over that chair. Get in place. At once!' It was the voice of authority and Judith obeyed smartly. Once bared she felt the cane tap several times across the centre of her behind. The position was a little different but it could be Miss James at her back poised to administer correction, and she shifted nervously at the thought. Two strokes were duly laid on, then there was a pause while the verbal message was reiterated allowing Judith to take a firmer grip of the chair seat. Thus far the severity was less than that of her boss, but there wasn't a lot in it: she was going to earn her money.

At five she leaped up and did a little dance, rubbing. It was only partly an act for Geraldine was warming to her task, and promptly decreed an extra three with yet more on top if 'Margaret' did not stay down until the end. What got into her Judith didn't know – this was anything but a fake caning – but she leaped up twice more and thus increased the tally to a full dozen stinging cuts. There was a small ripple of applause from the dykes squashed into the doorway and while Judith stayed down for some still shots of the damage, Geraldine spoke in her ear.

'The stripes are coming up beautifully, dear. And unless I have misread your condition, you would get off –' she said it *awf* '– if I gave you a good oiling. Are you game?' Judith swallowed, then nodded vigorously. To have come this far only to succumb to shyness was a bit silly. 'Super,' said the 'mistress' and turned to the crew. 'Right, gels, how about it? Let's get down to basics.'

Geraldine set to work and the camera came in close. The way her hands were lifting and separating the sore

71

cheeks Judith knew there would be plenty of open-cunt shots – and wet ones at that. So now she could claim a brief role as porn star to add to the weekend's activities. At first there was an inhibiting self-consciousness in the notion, but soon the bodily sensations rising in her made awareness of the audience and the camera recede. The massage and the after-effects of the caning were combining to make the conclusion inevitable, and when after much teasing the fingers found the stiff bud between her spread legs it was only seconds to the final explosion.

Judith eased into her seat on the half-empty plane with a sigh of relief: it had been a hectic leaving. First there was the after-shoot party at The Candy Bar kicked into hilarious life by Geraldine's experiences of running a New York dungeon, related in the received pronounciation English that seemed to be her native speech. The evening wore on and the alcohol flowed, with the result that Judith had no clear recollection of exactly what she might have done with whom when she woke up in the morning on a sofa in the club lounge.

At the apartment only Zadia was to be found, though the contracts had been properly signed for her to take away. Judith scribbled a guilty note for Petra which promised to send a tape *showing* some at least of what had gone on as soon as she had a copy herself. The tall skinhead still looked rather down but having learned of Judith's next port of call pressed on her a white halter dress that her stepsister never wore which flared out from the waist to just above the knee. 'It will hold away from the parts,' she had said with a grimace, 'and no panties, of course. I think you are crazy.' But she gave Judith a kiss and a hug who in turn promised to phone as soon as she had made progress with the manuscript.

When it came to the crunch, the depilation was like another bizarre sex act to round off five days containing more erotic activity than she had seen in the previous five months. But first there was a slight hiccup. She had stripped and lain back as instructed with legs up and knees wide only to feel a fingernail tracing the lines left by Geraldine's efforts of the day before.

'It's not my place to comment on your lifestyle, Ms Wilson, but if these bruises were even a fraction deeper I should have been obliged to turn you away.' The lady was coldly disapproving and Judith coloured. Part of her was ready to march out in a huff and another part wanted to try to explain how such usage thrilled her just as much as it hurt. And that the fact didn't make her an abused victim. But she had buttoned her lip, save to mutter, 'OK, OK,' and the beautician had carried on with the operation of applying hot wax to cover the whole area around the anus, genitals and the pubis itself.

Petra had exaggerated, of course, for the prior use of procaine served to dull the pain when the cotton strips were torn off. That was then, however; now she prickled and burned intolerably from the top of the bare mound right on down. On consideration, shortly before a long flight was not the best choice of time for such a procedure, but left to be done on home ground she doubted the thing would have got done at all. Once they were in the air and she was allowed out of her seat, Judith made for the toilet. After one more application of the soothing inhibitory cream she came back and arranged her borrowed clothing carefully to make minimal contact with the inflamed skin. She was just going to have to grin and bear it. At least there was beside her the remainder of Jana's tale: if it was as engaging as what she'd read so far it might help take her mind off the discomfort.

8

Cruel Pleasures

I have been telling of the dozen or so times over the winter months when I assisted the First Mistress to apply hand and strap to the bottoms of errant pupils, and how I looked forward to these occasions for their stimulating effect. But she has made no return visit to *my* room for any purpose at all, and I have to confess to being rather more disappointed than I am relieved. The spankings themselves are characteristically business-like affairs and as a rule once the culprit is plainly in distress the proceedings are brought to an end with the not unfriendly admonition to avoid the necessity of coming back. It is a foolish girl, though, who takes the manner of this as signalling any kind of leniency, for a second offence will not generally bring her *back* at all. Instead she is likely to find herself in the study formerly occupied by Dr Schermann, and once there she will, with the aid of the bench it still contains, acquire marks beyond anything inflicted in Mrs K's office. My help is not needed for this, of course, since the one to be caned is secured by the strong leather bands I know only too well at first hand.

Early in the spring term, however, Sophie Dvoreslova – a new boarder – is strapped twice in the space of ten days. Though it is unusual, I recall that the first punishment I took part in was a repetition, so I think little of it at first; but when she returns for a third spanking the following week I begin to wonder. I know what earned her the first one for she was in the company of another girl whose answers, right and wrong, in a class test had been identical to her own. Since they were sitting next to each other it was assumed one must have been cheating, and since neither would own up, both were treated as guilty and duly chastised. But this time there is no lecture (nor was there, I now remember, on the second occasion) and on entry Sophie goes straight to the table to take up position over the cushion on its top. She is slim and dark with a slightly withdrawn air, and she cooperates fully as I raise the blue tunic well up her back and lower the knickers to mid-thigh. The First Mistress likes the target area fully exposed and this one is revealed with traces of bruising from its previous encounters with her discipline. I move to the side of the table and take hold of the girl's torso, though if the earlier times are any guide I shall not have to contend with struggling.

The spanking begins with the customary methodical smacks to left and right and it is not long before both cheeks are blotched red. Sophie is silent though her body jerks a little and after a while Mrs K stops to flex her fingers. Surely it is time to move on to the strap for she is plainly feeling the effects of the blows herself. But no, after a pause she resumes though now the slaps are slower and after each one the hand lingers in contact with the burning flesh. It is remarkably like a perverse caress and I look at the chastiser with a quickening pulse. She is flushed and breathing hard, utterly intent on her task, and it hits me with the force of one of her smacks that what she is doing is a kind of love-making. It is, I understand with a shiver, what she was doing with me when I lay across her lap that night I cannot forget. The locks of her light-brown hair swing as she moves and her lips are parted. She is radiant and it is as if I am seeing her for the very first time.

I have, of course, been in her presence often – several times a week for more than a year now – and have always been aware that she is a handsome woman in perhaps her mid-forties. While not particularly tall or muscular of build, she exudes a strength which coupled with her power to deliver girls to the headmaster's bench made us all keep our eyes cast down while in front of her. The last thing any girl wanted was to do something that would attract the attention of Mrs K. Since then I have been in close proximity to her in my capacity as assistant and while I am still in awe of her, I do not quite fear her as I once did. Is this because I believe I shall be spared a future caning? Oddly I am half-prepared for that eventuality despite her promise. She will not force me, I am sure, but perhaps she will not need to. At the back of my mind I have the curious notion of being persuaded that it would be somehow to my benefit if I were to submit just once more to being buckled to the wooden frame.

Then the First Mistress glances up and I am caught in mid-stare. I drop my eyes and bite my lip: it feels as though I have seen too much. She stands back a little and says softly, 'Stay in place, Sophie,' then faces me with an expression that is reserved, almost cold.

'Thank you for your help, Jana. I shall manage the rest myself, for as you see our naughty girl accepts the necessity for her punishment.'

I leave embarrassed for it is as though I have been caught spying, and when the door has closed behind me I hear the sound of a key being turned in the lock.

While I dare not check I am sure of it, and go slowly back to my room wondering at the things I have witnessed.

The very next day two of the staff are struck down by influenza, and my stand-in duties occupy my attention to the exclusion of all else. Then, as the pressure begins to ease at the end of a second hectic week I find a note in my box calling me to Mrs K's office at 4 p.m. I have not spoken with her since I was dismissed from this same room but it seems there is no need for anxiety. She ushers me in cheerfully, thanks me for my recent hard work and explains that I am to assist her with the formal chastisement of the probationary mistress of physical education.

'Miss Weiss recognises that her performance initially fell short of what we expect at the Academy and she has agreed to accept correction at my hands. I have assured her that my official assessment need then make no mention of those early failings which have since been remedied.' I cannot quite believe what I am hearing: Mrs K is doing again what she did to Miss Werther and her manner contains no hint of recognition that it is an abuse of her power as First Mistress. Yet who am I to condemn? I was aroused by the sight of Magda's injuries and I cannot deny the stirrings I feel at the prospect of seeing suchlike inflicted on a new victim. Then comes a knock at the door and the young woman is there, a little flushed from her class in the gymnasium. As we make our way along the corridor I try to suppress the unworthy thought that she will be rather more so by the time Mrs K has finished with her.

'I understand that you are no stranger to corporal punishment, Miss Weiss.'

'That is correct, First Mistress.' We have arrived in the study and the trainee teacher stands squarely in her PE kit complete with plimsolls and knee-length white socks. 'At my senior school stripes were tallied on a daily basis and they were laid on while we were held over a vaulting horse. Bared, of course. I would say most girls took several doses each term. I certainly did.'

'In that case, you will be prepared to receive today the full twenty-five strokes that our regulations allow?'

There is a pause – this harsh sentence must be more than she was expecting – but in the end Miss Weiss says simply, 'I am.' Her face is set, though if she is frightened she does not show it. Mrs K moves to the other half of the room, gesturing towards its principal piece of equipment.

'Here, as you see, the headmaster had this bench installed for the purpose of administering discipline. Perhaps you would be so good as to remove your underclothing and position yourself for Miss Marlova to secure the straps.'

She obeys and I set to work, mindful of the instructions I have been given. First the wrists must be tied tight to make sure the hands cannot pull through when slippery with the sweat that is likely to break out. Next I fold up the pleated skirt into the small of the back and bring the leather band across it to pull the body hard to the slatted top of the frame. The buttocks are firm and muscular, and they make a broad area that should stand her in good stead for what is to come. Finally I crouch behind to buckle each leg to the apparatus just above the knee, and as they are pulled apart I see a glimpse of dark flesh between the tops of the thighs. A quick glance at Mrs K shows her to be busy selecting a cane from the corner cupboard, so I take the opportunity to study the nether lips in their nest of wiry hairs. Does our Miss Weiss too, I wonder, dip her fingers into these secret folds when she is alone in her room at night? But now the First Mistress is ready and I stand quickly back: the thrashing is about to begin.

Six strokes are applied, then another four. Ten in all and it is almost an anti-climax for the only sounds are the *whup!* of the flexible rattan and a kind of grunt forced out of the recipient at the moment of impact. Then at twelve she says, 'Dear God!' and Mrs K gives me a grim little smile. We are having an effect and I thrill to be a collaborator in this punitive exercise.

At fifteen it is a cry of 'God in heaven!' and the feet drum the floor in her anguish. 'First Mistress,' she gasps, 'the other side, please. No more on the left, for pity's sake.' Indeed the spectacular weals curve across into a blistered wedge that looks certain to bleed if it is struck again and a horrid sick excitement takes hold of me at what we are doing to this strong young woman.

'As you wish, Miss Weiss. But I have to warn you that my right hand is much less accurate.' So we change places and the affair moves to its conclusion without more incident, although each of the two last strokes lands just below the curve of the buttocks and makes her cry out again. As I release the leg-bands the welted flesh is right in front of my face and I am overwhelmed with the rich purple hues and the black swellings where the tip of the instrument has buried itself in the dimpled flanks. This thing puts my little caning – which I had thought the end of the world – into perspective and I am ashamed of how I have let it assume such importance in my mind.

When she gets up, the student teacher is breathing hard but there are remarkably no tears. She winces as the skirt falls back into place: plainly her energetic classes are going to be a trial for some days and it will be several more before she is able to sit on a wooden chair in comfort.

'Our business is done, Miss Weiss. I shall attend to your report forthwith and while you will appreciate that its contents are confidential I can tell you they will make a point of commending your strength of character.' Miss Weiss shakes the offered hand and next her firm grip is on mine. Then she turns, scoops up her discarded knickers and makes for the door. She walks rather stiffly, it is true, but her head is erect. I am overcome with admiration for this determined composure in the teeth of an ordeal that must be leaving her yet in considerable pain. Now I see the eyes of the First Mistress are on me, as they were after the first time I provided disciplinary aid. Again, though, she is inscrutable, merely bidding me to take an evening free from preparation since she will supervise the morning's classes. And once again I am left alone to digest the implications of my complicity – all too willing, I fear – in these increasingly cruel pleasures.

It is almost a month later, in the last week before the holiday, that I wake to find the First Mistress sitting on my bed. Tousled with sleep I make to rise on my elbows but she puts a hand on my forehead saying 'Hush,' and I lie back. I cannot see her eyes for the room is dark save for the first light of morning in the window at her back, but I feel that she is examining my face.

'Jana,' she says softly, 'will you come to my office after lights out tomorrow? I shall be waiting with Sophie.'

'Yes.' A kind of whisper is all I can manage but it seems to be good enough. She takes my arm and I kneel up beside her. Her robe is half open and I catch the scent from her body and in the gloom see the curve of a breast in a silk chemise. Then I am across her lap with my nightshirt raised, my thighs bare against hers, flesh to flesh. For an age she runs her hands over me, murmuring my name, nearly as much it seems to herself as to me. Then, at last, she begins what I have been waiting for, and, I now realise, pining for, most of the term.

It is not as before when I felt her holding back, perhaps unsure of my reaction. Now she strikes hard: six stinging smacks that make me gasp and then she is caressing me once more, squeezing and petting the hot cheeks before she slaps again. The cycle repeats and repeats: I become so exquisitely tender that the slightest pressure sends shivers running all over me; but still she does not touch me where I burn to be touched and where my longing brims over.

When I get up I know my seeping wetness is smeared over her skin but she pays it no heed and kisses me gently on the mouth. I am fit to swoon and she takes my shoulders in her hands. 'Sit,' she says and I sink weakly down on to the bed. Still I cannot make out her expression outlined as she is against the dawn light.

'It would give me such pleasure, Jana, more pleasure than I can say, one day to fasten *your* sweet body to the headmaster's bench. And then, and then –'

'Not, not like Miss Weiss, oh please.' I blurt out the words in sudden fear.

'No, child, not like Miss Weiss. Her youth notwithstanding, she is already a creature of steel. Whereas you, dear Jana, for you the butcher's dozen will suffice. But this time, you will *want* me to lay on every single one of them.' The First Mistress turns to go and for the first time I see her face: despite her buoyant tone she looks tired and the eyes seem troubled. When she leaves me at the door it is with a reiteration of her promise in words that carry the ring of fate.

'I said I shall not compel you, and I meant it. When you are ready, Jana, *you* shall come to *me*.'

PART II

9

Hardcore

The plane landed on schedule at eight in the morning but it was two in the afternoon before she was climbing the stairs home and Judith was shattered. The itchy tenderness of her groin had made sleep impossible on the long flight and to cap it all a missed connection had delayed her for two hours more in London – two hours that seemed an eternity knowing she must resist calling in on Harry at the British Library across the road while she was trying to bring herself to make a break. Inside the flat she ran a not-too-hot bath and stripped off thankfully for a soothing soak. After ten minutes and a fit of yawning she gave up calculating how best to minimise jet-lag and towelled herself carefully dry. There was just no way she was going to last until it was really bedtime so she gave in and stretched out naked on the cool sheets. When Judith next opened her eyes the clock said eleven-twenty and she sat up, wide awake. Pulling a T-shirt over her head she went through to the fridge which yielded up not only the makings of a decent size omelette but also a bottle of beer to wash it down. An hour later and much restored, she inspected the denuded pubes, a little awed at the way she had acted on what had been scarcely more than a whim. The inflammation was mostly gone but she decided that knicker elastic was best avoided and dug out a pair of old jogging pants. With a sweatshirt, socks and trainers the outfit was complete: she was ready to go out for an expedition into the summer night.

It was not far short of one when Judith rounded the corner of the old refectory and across the lawn she could see the roof of the Nemesis Archive outlined against the starlit sky. The space of the quadrangle was closed off from the sporadic late traffic on the street and as she stood quietly in the dark a shaft of light fell across the grass for a moment from the back of the building. She heard low voices and the sound of a door closing, then footsteps on gravel receding into the distance. There was no mistaking it: some people had just left from the entrance to the observation suite.

Resisting the impulse to chase after them, Judith crossed to the main entrance and inserted her key. If they *were* up to no good, what could she do on her own? More likely it was some legitimate use of the premises that had run late. In the entrance hall she entered her code into the panel by the lift and it flashed green indicating that the security system had not been breached. Up in the office she checked the wall chart but there was nothing entered in the period she had been away except for a regular booking the day before by the ladies of Strictly Uniforms. The semi-basement level of the stacks had been converted little more than a year ago into a central space in which disciplinary scenes could be enacted together with adjacent viewing and recording rooms. It was a self-contained area accessible from the outside through a double-locked door, or from within the Archive by Miss James – and latterly herself – only. Day-to-day running was overseen by Marjory Rowleigh of the nearby Business School, who maintained a database of clients and their predilections, and she would use the external door when necessary, though not usually in the small hours of the morning.

Well, she had better go and check the place over. It wasn't the most appealing prospect in the world, but Judith told herself firmly that as Assistant Director of the establishment it was her duty to investigate. Her footsteps echoed in the stairwell on the way down and she was glad to find everything quiet when she tapped out the number to let herself in. The suite was deserted and the back door properly locked, though there was an odd whiff of mild disinfectant that wasn't quite masking something else. The modified vaulting horse that was the most popular piece of heavy furniture stood as usual centre-stage and while it all looked in order she felt its fabric surface slightly damp to the touch. Or was she imagining it? It was difficult to be sure but the suspicion growing in Judith's mind sent her through to the cubicle that housed the digital cameras and processing equipment. Yes, it was as she guessed: while everything was in its place the central console was distinctly warm as was the DVD drive. Whoever it was had been making a state-of-the-art piece of recording but what they didn't know was that any input to the station here was automatically copied to the hard drive of the Archive's central computer. So however well they had covered their tracks – and Judith was prepared to bet they had used an eliminate program – she could access their efforts from her own machine at the top of the building any time she wanted.

Once seated at the keyboard, Judith had a momentary qualm about what she was doing, though it was soon dismissed. If it looked like Marjory was involved then she would close the file pronto and go home, but if not, then people who had helped themselves to the facilities were surely fair game for a bit of snooping. So she logged in to the internal network and brought up a list of recent acquisitions from the observation suite. Aside from the official session there were three, on the Friday she'd left, then on Sunday and the one she had almost interrupted earlier. All recorded late at night and all a mere ten minutes in duration. What on earth were they? Well, there was only one way to find out, so Judith went to the first, clicked File Open, and as it loaded settled back to watch.

Her first thought was what a pity she had woken with the decision to stop fucking Harry – any man – before she had taken the chance to study *his* right up close. For filling her screen was a penis rampantly, triumphantly erect, a thick and heavily veined rod of obscenely raw meat. The shaft glistened as if newly bathed in vaginal secretions and when a fingernail the colour of fresh blood was drawn along its length clear liquid oozed from the tip of the glans. Judith thought of such a thing working between *her* legs and squeezed them together, heedless of the residual tenderness of the depilated folds. Damn these resolutions. But there was no going back: her mind was made up.

Then fingers took hold of the slippery organ to ease the foreskin fully back from the head and a tongue appeared from the left, catching the dribble of fluid just as it fell. Lapping up and over the head again and again in a weird persistence of motion, its action had the viewer fixed to her seat. Eventually, scarlet lips came fully into sight encircling the purple dome, and when they closed and began to suck with a slow sustained energy the stem – incredibly – bulged yet more. It didn't take a brilliant mind to work out that a conclusion was in the offing and after the almost hypnotic foreplay it was brief and dramatic. The elegant hand closed tight on the shaft, the mouth drew back in a wide O and a series of rapid contractions pumped thick mucus on to the hollow of the waiting tongue. The camera closed in on the collecting pool of semen which began to spill over the bottom lip. Then a single trickle ran down into a freeze-frame that kept it hanging suspended in time from the chin until the concluding cut.

Wow. Judith was no expert but this was of a different order from the crudely staged and badly filmed stuff she had seen, managing to be both classy and lewdly in-your-face at the same time. However, the second clip of the three was a disappointment. While it was photographed with the same attention to detail as the first, it was little more than a standard penetration number beginning with a close-up of the model's fingers spreading and stroking her genitals. When the male erection came into frame it seemed somehow diminished from its earlier glory and after the obligatory thrusting pulled out for the 'cumshot' designed to show that it was all for real. But there was one thing that lifted the sequence out of the mundane: Judith was able to identify the cunt that was on display as that belonging to the Archive's secretary Grace.

While she had not examined the said piece of anatomy in over a year, there was no mistaking it. The sprinkling of fine hair allowed a clear view of the idiosyncratic labial twist which shaped the opening into a shallow 'S'. For a while after her arrival it had looked as though Grace might step into more than her predecessor's work shoes, and there had been two memorable close encounters. But Judith feared that bedding the secretary the boss fancied twice in a row was decidedly undiplomatic so she backed off and then got involved in London. Latterly, her promotion seemed to have set the seal on the distance between them and although Grace had tended her after a caning a mere ten days ago she had remained cool and businesslike throughout Judith's vocal and rather messy orgasm. Now she blushed to think of the occasion, but the fact of the girl's involvement in this rather elegant hardcore was an eye-opener. It was high time to sample the third and final piece of work.

The opening long shot of a naked figure across the basement horse allowed a glimpse of the trademarked coil of hair at the back of the head. It was Grace all right and when the camera zoomed right in to the rear of her Judith sat forward with quickening interest. Although the buttocks were well-fleshed – and she remembered with a pang the luscious feel of them – the splayed legs gave a clear view between. The knot of the anus was eased apart enough for the contents of an eye-dropper to be inserted and the finger to work them in. The whole process was repeated twice and in the relentless close-up, the tight, puckered hole could be seen to slacken and expand. After these preliminaries the cock that nosed into the picture to do its job was already wet and Judith realised that she was too. Pushing a hand inside the waist of her joggers, she steered carefully over the sore mound and located the source of her own lubrication. May as well make the most of the occasion.

On screen the thing was a configuration of piston and cylinder become weirdly flesh. The shaft sank deep and when it pulled back the outer sphincter gaped wide to reveal an inner wall of glistening muscle. Between each full stroke the head circled round the opening, at the last leaving a glutinous trail of urethral discharge: the guy must be getting as close as she was herself. Indeed, on the next withdrawal he held right at the rim while the pent-up load jerked out and welled up around his organ. Then, still ramrod hard, he set up a rhythm of slow deep thrusts into the welter of secretions which persisted through the long fade that saw Judith's own spasms peter out in front of a blank screen.

Although it had been well past three when she had reached her bed and another full hour before sleep came, Judith was up at nine showering with a sense of anticipation. She was going to see Marsha, tell all about the dalliance and its impending termination and pass on the new manuscript for an opinion. If anyone could smell a rat it was the wily American lady, so if she was satisfied then they could go full-steam ahead. But first, there was the small matter of the illicit filming and Judith grinned to herself as she selected a black shirt and tight flared trousers from the built-in cupboard that was the principal storage space in her small flat. The night before she had ended proceedings by copying the movie files to CD, and it was going to be fun watching Grace's expression once she had started it playing on the office PC.

However, come the time Judith found herself rather uncomfortable. When she brought up the first image there was a shocked 'Oh' followed by a silence in which they both faced the startlingly engorged piece of manhood that filled the screen. It was all a bit much for the time of morning and Judith snapped it off with a curt 'Well?' The story came tumbling out of her friend Mo who was a wizard with the camera but of course because she was a woman had loads of trouble trying to get into the hardcore business and if she could get a go with really ace equipment it might just give her the breakthrough she needed. And Grace hadn't *dared* ask Mrs Rowleigh because she'd *never* have said yes without clearing it with Miss James and then she was off in France . . .

So Judith's impromptu absence had provided an ideal opportunity to slot in three late-night sessions with a couple of days between to allow the male body to regenerate its crucial supply. It couldn't have worked out better Judith thought with a wry smile. But now a very contrite Grace was looking up at her through long eyelashes asking what she was going to do. She had to make a decision.

'I don't honestly know, Grace. I suppose we should ask ourselves what Miss James would do if she were here herself.'

'Er, well, I think it would take a bit more than the strap she's so fond of, wouldn't it? I don't like to say it because it makes her sound a terrible ogre, and she isn't at all really, but I'd have to expect to be striped good and proper. And then she might give me the boot on top.'

Judith shook her head. 'She'd make you pay all right for helping yourself, but I'm pretty sure being sacked wouldn't come into it. Not for using the equipment as it was meant to be used.' She saw the troubled expression lift at her words and the young secretary stood up.

'I know where she keeps the special rattan. It might be just what she'd want and I can get it for you right now.'

For one proposing to bring upon herself a very painful experience Grace was looking cheerful, even eager. But Judith was reluctant to take up the offer. Spankings she could give as well as take, though she lacked the cast of mind to hand out the more severe formal punishments her boss took such delight in. She had performed when there seemed no other option but it took real anger to rouse her to effective action and that was something she could not possibly feel towards Grace. What she *was* feeling was in fact decidedly peculiar. This fresh-faced English rose in the skimpy cotton dress, all modest ingenuousness, was the stuff of lesbian romantic fantasy and yet Judith's head was full of pictures of the juiced openings captured so vividly on disc. Somehow the combination was the most potent thing in the world and she felt quite faint. But the idea of the girl receiving a stinging punishment was too exciting to forgo and Judith had a sudden brainwave.

'Hold on, Grace. Since it seems to appeal to you, let's agree that's how to clean the slate, but punishing you isn't *my* job.' She tried to sound as if it were a mere executive matter with no connection to the emotion churning inside her. 'However, I'll tell you who might consider it hers. In fact I'm prepared to bet she is going to describe it as a duty to give you a damned good hiding.'

'Yeah, I arranged for her to go to Marjory's tonight, and I've given her tomorrow morning off. Even then she'll be lucky if she doesn't have to stand at her desk. The lady was not impressed to learn of unauthorised entry into the premises she's responsible for.'

'I see the Assistant Director is taking after Samantha in more ways than one,' said Marsha, with eyes directed at the unrelieved black of Judith's outfit, 'though I guess it's in your favour you're not actually beating the poor girl yourself.'

Judith exploded. 'Marsha, you have got one fucking nerve! The things you do to some of your paramours . . .'

'That's the privilege of the older woman, and they always come back for more. Well, most of them. But what's all this about making a clean breast? Would it be anything to do with visits to the capital city, perhaps? And I thought it was just the appeal of all those dirty books . . .' Marsha put up her hands in conciliation as Judith made an infuriated fist.

'OK OK, I'm listening. You do so rise to the bait, Jude, I can't resist teasing. But I know this isn't a joke.'

'And you know what I'm going to say, don't you?'

'Well, honey, I can't answer that until you say it, can I?'

It was confession time and Judith spoke about the cataloguer she had met while researching flagellation memoirs from early in the last century. She related, with blushes, how she had more or less volunteered herself across his knee and then made herself available for more than the palm of his hand. And not just a one-off either. But that he wasn't what you could call straight since he had a dishy boy of an assistant who was also favoured with Harry's disciplinary and sexual attentions.

'So I didn't think I was really selling out or anything, and I *have* decided to call the thing off.' Aware that the logic of her little speech was anything but watertight, Judith looked up, bracing herself for a sarcastic quip, but Marsha's expression was quite serious.

'I heard about this man from the British Library who organised some kind of rescue party last summer so I did kinda put two and two together. I'm just sorry you didn't think you could tell me what was going on. Not that I gotta be privy to every one of your sins, honey, it's the thought you were keeping away because of it.' She went behind the bar and opened a bottle of wine from the cold cabinet while Judith watched the neat movements of her trim figure in the uniform of white T-shirt and faded denims. Then she sat down and poured out two glasses.

'I know I come on strong about men and their evil ways, but I'm going to tell you something now, Jude, so long as you promise it stays between us. OK?'

'Promise. But –'

'From time to time – and it isn't often, though that's kinda beside the point – I go to a guy I've known for years to get myself laid. Royally fucked, not to put too fine a point on it. So go ahead, tear me off a strip for being a prize old hypocrite.'

Judith took a sip of the cold liquid, trying to get her head round this piece of information while her normally voluble companion sat in silence, waiting. Then she began to chuckle and in an instant they were both convulsed with helpless laughter. When it had run its course she remembered the CD in her pocket and slapped it down on the table.

'I told you what's in these three clips, and I reckon you'd better have a look. But don't blame me if it sets you off to make a date with your man sooner rather than later.' Judith leaned forward and squeezed her American friend's arm. 'Thanks, Marsha, and I won't breathe a word. Got to keep the side up now I'm going to be back on it.'

'Any time, honey. And now we have a space before I need to open this joint for you to tell me exactly what was going down stateside that's brought you back *onside*, as you put it.'

On the street half an hour later Judith was feeling buoyed up by a conversation in which the recounting of Cal's throwaway remark and how she had acted on it had been crowned by the demand to inspect the results of Brazilian waxing. But while she had unburdened herself to general applause there was one thing that had not been mentioned at all. Light banter about Grace's punishment had been an effort and now that she was alone Judith couldn't help thinking of that behind being bared and then . . . Fuck it. She couldn't help thinking about Grace full stop: the long fine hair she'd only ever seen down once and those unusual slate-blue eyes that were so serious yet so open.

Judith shook herself mentally. This was the stuff of adolescent crushes and she had to get a grip. Besides there was work to do: she needed properly to digest the bits of the manuscript she had struggled with in adversity on the long flight. Now that she'd given Marsha a copy it would not do to be caught out having shirked her scholarly duty. But Judith nonetheless sighed at the prospect of the evening's reading for its topic was hardly going to take her mind off what would be happening just a stone's throw away in Marjory's well-appointed Georgian terrace house.

10

Sophie's Lot

This morning there are three candidates for the bench, which has stood unused since Miss Weiss was fastened to it for her rigorous correction a month ago. I meet Mrs K whose formal manner has been resumed since the nocturnal visit to me and accompany her to the classroom. There the culprits are lectured in front of their fellows on the persistently skimped preparation of which they are guilty and informed of the fate that awaits them. It is clear, they are told, that spankings have been insufficient to induce a change in behaviour, therefore recourse will be had to sterner measures. Two of the girls are plainly stricken at the news although the third seems anything but contrite. Greta Lerner, whom I know as one of our few boarders, is a thick-set girl whose build will be to her advantage under chastisement, so I wonder what steps the First Mistress will take to deal with her unusual truculence. It is a question worthy of attention, though as I follow the small party down the corridor my mind instead leaps ahead to what I shall see happen to Sophie after dark.

Once we arrive I am occupied with straps, buckling and unbuckling as the woebegone pair are each taken without ceremony through their twelve plus one allotted doses of pain. The howling they set up may have made the waiting Greta turn a shade more pale but her mouth is set in a stubborn line as she watches Mrs K go to the cupboard and return with a cane perceptibly longer and thicker than the one she has just used.

'Your manner leaves something to be desired, Miss Lerner. We shall have to see if a slightly heavier instrument can bring about a change for the better. Remove your underwear and take up position, please.'

Greta lifts her frock to comply and when she goes down I do my part to ensure that the bared hindquarters will remain a fixed target by fastening the bands at waist and knee a notch tighter than before. And it is as well I do, for once I stand clear the girl's body jerks as in an epileptic seizure under strokes – all thirteen of them – applied with a force and rapidity beyond anything I have yet seen. The First Mistress is breathing hard, her eyes fixed on the welts she has raised in short order and for an awful moment I think she intends to continue. It seems plain that she would *like* nothing better, but then she drops the cane on to the desk and signals me to release the victim from her confinement.

Greta starts up at once and cradles her injured parts with a moan. I see a struggle for composure cross her features but her mouth crumples and she clutches at me, bursting into tears on my shoulder. I hold her – what else can I do? – but Mrs K gives no sign of the disapproval I expect. Instead she dismisses the wide-eyed pair who scuttle out, no doubt to recount the drama to their classmates at the first opportunity, then waits until the crying begins to subside.

'Now, Miss Lerner, you have taken your punishment and it was a sharp one. Am I right you will do what you can to avoid a repetition?'

'Yes, First Mistress.'

'Very well. If you go with Miss Marlova, she will apply a salve that will help restore you. I hope you don't mind, Jana: you will find a jar on the shelf in my back office. I shall stay here to make the appropriate entries in my disciplinary log.'

'Please, call me Jana. It's not long since I was in my final year too.' I am prattling a little nervously as I place the cushion on the table and Greta goes over it for all the world like one about to be spanked, although the thought of even a playful pat to her ill-treated bottom is enough to make one wince. Thick purple bands stand out on the olive skin and my first efforts with the aromatic cream make the patient wriggle and complain.

'Ow-ow-ow. She should not have beaten me so, not with *that* cane. And all because I would not cringe and grovel like the other two. Ow, Jana! I know this is good for me, but it *hurts*.' Greta is still indignant and assertive and I can't resist voicing the opinion it is as well she did not show it in the study.

'Well, I suppose I have learned something, if only not to let Mrs K see what one thinks. With a bit more sense I could have saved myself these awful stripes.' She speaks rather emphatically and I know she has been mocked by some city girls for her supposed 'country' origins. But when she turns her head to me with a rueful smile I am struck by the jet-black hair and the dark eyes and think her quite a beauty. 'But what of you, Jana? I have seen the way she looks at you. Do you not fear the bench even as her assistant?'

I explain that I did make its aquaintance in the headmaster's day and that the First Mistress took her part in the castigation. I mention too that I *know* that she wants me back there for she has told me as much herself and that she expects me to put myself forward when I am ready. 'Can you imagine it, Greta, that anyone would volunteer for the privilege of such a thrashing?' I fear I am letting my tongue run away with me under that soulful gaze.

'Oh, be careful, Jana, do. She is a dangerous woman. I feel it myself, though I don't know her at all as well as you. She could get you under her spell, and then –'

'Come, Greta,' I say interrupting briskly, 'I must finish off my job here.' All of a sudden I think I may have said too much and wonder at Mrs K's purpose in having me do this intimate thing. The broad cheeks I am soothing meet in a tight crease that reveals nothing of the girl's secret parts, though from her movements I judge that she is responding in the way my friend Magda once did, as indeed am I. But I dare not risk a move when we might be interrupted at any time, so I break off saying that I have done what I can and that I shall go with her to class to make sure she is allowed to stand at the tall desk.

'Oh but, Jana,' she cries, letting her frock fall back into place, 'I have left my knickers in the study. Hadn't I better –'

'No,' I say quickly, 'you don't want to meet the First Mistress again, do you? Just tell me which is your bed and I'll deliver them there before lunch.'

At last it is late evening and the appointed time has arrived for me to steal out down the black gloom of the corridor. The air is oppressive with the threat of a thunderstorm and I am prickling with sweat in just my cotton shift. Outside it is no cooler as I cross the yard under the still lighted windows of our three live-in teachers. While they are not likely to stir at this hour I am glad to turn the corner and reach the door of Mrs K's quarters. I ring the bell and she comes at once to usher me into the sitting room where Sophie is waiting. She is flushed, holding a hand to the back of her dress and I guess that the proceedings have started without me.

'Yes, Jana, you suppose right. Our little entertainment is already begun and I think it only fair that you at least receive the same, if nothing more. Is that acceptable?' Of course it is, though I am troubled by the ambiguity of the statement that seems to leave 'more' as an option. It is a strange feeling to go over her knee in the intimate fashion I have known with another girl watching, and perhaps in recognition of this the First Mistress leaves my underpants in place for the brisk spanking that follows. It is hard enough to make me gasp and squirm but it is soon over and I am told to stand.

'Now I am going to change into more suitable wear and I should like both of you to disrobe completely before you join me in the bedroom. There is no call to be shy; we are all women together.'

We do as she says in a rather awkward silence but when Sophie bends to take off her shoes I see that around the pink of her freshly smacked bottom the flanks and thighs are thickly marked with discolorations, some recent and some not so recent. The sight makes me catch my breath and she turns round to see me staring.

'Oh, do not look at me like that, please.' I lower my eyes, embarrassed. Questions fill my head yet I am tongue-tied. What makes her submit to such beatings? Could I ever do that too? However, she says simply, 'Jana, I am not compelled to be here. It is my lot and I am content with it. But we must not keep the Mistress waiting. Come.'

When we enter Sophie kneels up on the bed at once as if the action belongs to a practised routine. The lamp at its head which is the room's sole lighting throws the contours of her body into sharp relief, and

100

with her shoulders pressed down into the covers the private parts stand out in a startling display. Dressed in a blue silk robe that sweeps to the floor Mrs K takes up a cane and swings it through the air with an evil whirr. Then she motions me to a chair to the girl's right and as I sit she inserts the tip of the instrument into the fat little purse at the top of the girl's thighs. It is a shocking gesture and I gape at the pink lining thus exposed between the outer lips. Sophie makes a whimpering noise but she must be feeling more than fear for when the rod's end is removed it gleams wetly.

Then the chastiser draws back to strike and I see through the clinging layer of material the outline of a nippled breast and on the downswing the curve of the buttocks. I wonder how often she was stripped and thrashed when young, for I cannot imagine that her present behaviour has no such foundation in her own past experience. The slight auburn tint of her hair is accentuated in the yellowish light and her tongue protrudes between the teeth in her complete absorption. The First Mistress is not striking with the angry force of the morning; instead her demeanour reveals a disturbing combination of relish and solicitude. While the weals multiply on the girl's buttocks she feels them from time to time with a cupped hand as though she wants to savour the heat and swelling she is causing and at the same time check that she does not inflict excessive damage. In addition, there is a running of the back of the hand – so much more sensitive than the palm – over the white skin of the upper haunches with a delicacy that will allow her to register every palpitation of the body she is subjecting to such intense treatment.

At length the cane is laid aside and, in a move that makes me shiver, her tormentor smooths aside the girl's hair to kiss the nape of her neck. After a pause

101

she begins to stroke the hindquarters all around the edge of the long weals that are darkening in colour by the minute. Her efforts are soon rewarded when the dark meat of the nether lips glistens, whereupon Mrs K dips two fingers inside and moves them up and down. At once the whole area is slick with juices and she works then on the tight hole until that too will take easy penetration. All the while Sophie trembles, and little breathless squeals have replaced the sobs of before as she rocks against the manipulative hand. Following the initial shock, I am now so drawn into the sight in front of me (and all too aware of what is happening between my own legs) that I start when the mistress speaks.

'Jana: please fetch me what you will find in the top of the chest. I feel there is some more work to do here.' Work? What does she mean? Surely not more punishment, I beg silently, but the opened drawer's sole occupant is a slim malacca cane that allows no other interpretation. Thus am I left to hand it over in a flutter of concern for poor Sophie's fate – however she may feel it *chosen* – and watch as it is tapped against the thighs that have so far escaped attention.

'Now hold still, my angel, while I give you six more. I do not need to tell you how the release will be all the greater in the end, the greater the trial that has gone before it.' So saying she strikes and while the victim stays in place the cries are piteous as the thin scarlet lines spring up one after another on the previously unmarked flesh. More lewd caresses follow, then more cuts; after which the pattern is repeated one further time. Sophie is bathed in sweat and her whole body is alive with tremors and spasms that are making me itch with desire to take part in the spectacle. I want more than anything to feel the hot bruised cheeks and the slippery openings between them, and I am desperate too to delve into my own wetness. That I can – indeed must – do later; for the present I struggle to master the overpowering urge to reach out and, and –

'Very well, Jana. It is time for you to leave: the remainder is between Sophie and me.' The utterance comes just in time to save me from an act I am sure would be judged unpardonable and I bow out at once from the room more relieved than disappointed. It is the work of a second to pull the shift over my head and I am outside breathing in great gulps of cooler air. What is happening to me? Mere months ago I was an ingénue in matters of the body; now I am driven by such desire that it threatens to disgrace me in even Mrs K's eyes. And, as if to underline what I am thinking, an idea has occurred to me that I know already I shall be unable to resist. In the stillness of the night my own need is pressing as is the impulse to go where it might be reciprocated, to a bed I visited earlier on an errand with an undergarment. Immediately inside the entrance to the dormitory, in the morning it was empty; *now*, on the other hand . . .

At a touch Greta starts up and whispers, 'Jana, what are you doing here?' but she allows me to take her hand and lead her away from the other sleepers. Outside I close the door quietly and kiss her mouth. She responds at once and we stand locked together in the passage until I collect myself and hurry her down across the yard. In my room I make to inspect her bottom again but she pushes me on to my back and lifts up my cotton nightdress.

'Listen to me, Jana. Last summer I went with a boy for the first time who lives with his older sister. Then he was called away for training for a month so she took me in hand and taught me about women. I got to taste her strap because she was quite a tartar, but more important than that I got to taste *her*. Like I'm going to show *you*.'

Amazed at this turn of events, I lie back obediently and open my legs wide.

'Oh, Jana, I don't know what you have been up to but I can *smell* from here how much you need me to do this.' Greta gives a slow chuckle and I blush at the thought of what I have in fact recently seen and what this girl might think of it. But once her head goes down and I feel the first touch on me embarrassment is soon left far behind together with all sense of place as the small hours of the night become clothed in ecstasy.

'OK, JM, I get the idea. You don't have to fucking rub it in.' Judith snapped the file shut in annoyance. For a lady who prefaced her story by bemoaning her perverse tendencies, she was having a lot of fun acquiring them. And it was all a bit near the bone for a reader trying not to think of a certain young secretary who was – in all probability at that very moment – having her bared bottom painfully warmed. She swivelled her chair round and keyed in the password to log on to the main computer: although Marsha had the disc she could still access the original files. Judith grimaced at the irony of the situation: while the naïve Jana was romping with her new girlfriend here *she* was having to make do with screen images of the object of her unrequited lust.

She had up her sleeve a trick shown her by the erratically knowledgeable Petra during their one long night together. If you took a mirror propped at a shallow angle on the floor and squatted over it, you could study your own vulva while you brought yourself off. A perfect diversion for the girl unhappily without sexual company and one Judith was promising herself before bed at home. However, for now she was going to do a little priming courtesy of the close-up camera work that was, unfortunately, as close as she was going to get to Grace herself.

11

Grace Notes

'Sorry, honey, I just didn't get a chance to read those chapters. I had an unexpected visitor – that's *female* visitor, OK? Nothing at all to do with that *thing* on here, right?'

'I believe you, Marsha.' Judith grinned at the older woman as she put the disc down between them.

'But these movies gave me an idea. That's an ace woman behind the camera and I plan on hiring her myself to shoot a couple of girls in action, even though I rate the pussy number as definitely the weakest link. Would you go along with that, Jude?'

'Yeah, I suppose.' Objectively she had to agree, though it hadn't exactly seemed weak to her late the previous night. However, this wasn't the time to let Marsha in on what seemed to be growing into an infatuation. 'But I don't know quite why.'

'Well I think I do, and I have a suggestion to make if you'll hear me out. No disrespect to your secretary here, whose other assets are beyond praise, but what that organ needs to show it off is a naked cunt where you can see every single fold as it thrusts in and out. One just like that sweet thing you have there, honey.' For a moment Judith stared, uncomprehending, then the penny dropped.

'Oh, now, wait a minute, Marsha –'

'Look at it this way, Jude. If you are gonna rejoin the local sisterhood – which these days admits to being ever-so-slightly tarnished itself – then there really ought to be a last ritual fuck. And what better way to do it than on camera for posterity to marvel at? Grace sure owes *you* one on top of penance paid to Marjory, so what do you say?'

As two o'clock approached in the office Judith was getting distinctly edgy. What on earth was she going to say to the girl when she arrived? A cheery 'How's the bum?' was hardly going to fit the bill, and heartfelt commiseration would not come well from the instigator of her punishment. However, when at last the door opened, Grace took charge of the situation herself.

'You'd better have a look,' she said briskly, peeling down an uncharacteristic pair of trousers and sticking out her knickerless behind. Judith gave a silent whistle at the purple swellings thus revealed: their tenderness had no doubt ruled out the underclothing that the more usual choice of miniskirt would have required.

'If you want the details, Mrs Rowleigh used a paddle and then went on to a long thick piece of leather I've never seen before. It was awful. And then afterwards she was so nice –'

Aghast, Judith watched the huge sob rise and choke out the rest of the speech, but before she could do anything the girl bolted into the bathroom and slammed the door. It seemed much longer than the five minutes on the clock before Grace emerged again, eyes downcast.

'I'm sorry,' she muttered, 'I don't know what you must think of me. Some kind of baby who can't take a well-deserved whacking.' Judith longed to reach out to stroke and comfort, even just to touch, but she feared to add insult to the injury she had already caused. 'Thing is, it brought it all back – what it was like at the

Hall. The punishments were never enough and I couldn't say stop. No! That's not it. I mean – I mean she was so angry I thought *she'd* never stop. I *did*, really. But then she threw the belt down and cuddled me . . .' The curious sentence tailed off but it was no time for questions. Afraid of more tears Judith jumped in.

'Look, Grace, I shouldn't have had you come in today at all. Go home and I'll cope with anything here until tomorrow. All right?' The small motion of the head was interpretable as a nod so she went on. 'There is one more thing. You know Marsha at the Phoenix? Well, she wants to pay your friend to do some girls.'

'Do some girls? You mean downstairs?'

'Yeah. But all official this time.' She tried a smile but Grace was staring over her shoulder, poker-faced. 'However, part of the package is that I get a taste of that cock too. I mean, er, not a taste exactly but, er . . .' God, this was ridiculous: the Assistant Director of the Nemesis Archive unable to string two words together in front of its secretary. Judith pulled herself up sharply. 'What I am trying to say is that along with Marsha's stuff I want a good close-up sequence of my vagina being penetrated, just like in the clip of yours. If, that is, the owner of the phallus is available and willing.'

'Oh, he'll be *willing*.' At last Grace met her eye and there was the hint of a smile. Then she frowned. 'So it's true, you're not . . .'

'Gay? I certainly am. Apart from a bit on the side. But now I'm firmly back in the fold and we thought what better to mark the fact than a final impaling on camera. Well, it all seemed like a great idea after a few beers . . .' Judith looked up but the moment of rapport was gone. Grace had turned away and was writing on a notepad at the desk.

'Here's Mo's number and email. Your Marsha can arrange it all direct, right? You won't be needing me this time.'

'Oh yes we will, Grace.' Judith made a sudden bid to get some – any – reaction. 'I don't suppose you care to see *me* getting fucked, but the girls could do with someone to look after them and show them the ropes. In return for an appropriate fee, of course.'

Well, the offer hadn't elicited anything you could call a show of gratitude, but Judith fancied she detected a slight thawing of the atmosphere before the enigmatic young woman took herself off. While tempted to put the coolness down to a sense of injustice – Marjory's hand had proved heavier than she suspected Miss James's would have been – Judith guessed there was more to it than that, if for no reason other than the odd incoherence about what had actually happened the night before. However, before indulging in her own speculations, it would be as well to find out what the chastiser herself had to say, so she picked up the receiver and dialled the number of the Business College.

'Can I speak to Mrs Rowleigh, please? It's Judith Wilson from the Archive here.' After several seconds on hold, the secretary relayed the message that the Deputy Principal would call her back, and indeed the phone sounded almost at once.

'Ah, Judith. I have to say I was expecting you to call and I thought it better if I spoke to you on my, ah, direct line. Nobody else listening, you know, unless MI6 are interested in me.' The plummy tones were more obtrusive divorced from the impeccably suited slightly matronly figure and Judith made a face at the heavy-handed attempt at humour. 'I'm afraid that I became a little carried away last night dealing with Grace. I do hope the poor girl is not too much the worse for wear today?'

'Well, Marjory, let's just say that I thought it better to send her back home as soon as she came in.'

'Oh dear, that's terrible. What was I thinking of? It's just that in Samantha's absence I felt I had to come

down hard on anyone making free with the facilities . . .'
She sounded quite stricken and Judith's irritation eased.

'She'll live, don't worry about it. I've suffered worse
and I know you have, Marjory. In fact, I reckon her
reaction's a bit over the top, really, and that's why I'm
speaking to you now. She's mentioned this hall place
once before and now it came up again in amongst the
tears. Do you know what that's all about?'

'Well yes, I do actually, though I rather wish it hadn't
been mentioned. With my position here, the connection
with the Archive can be embarrassing at times but if the
business of the Thomas-Halle were to come to light . . .'

'Marjory, I promise you I won't breathe a word. Not
to a soul. I'm thinking of Grace, really, and if I knew
what had upset her back then that seems to prey on her
still, well –'

'She might be able to confide her feelings to you. Yes,
I can see that. Someone near her own age providing a
shoulder to cry on.' And in time, with any luck, rather
more than a shoulder, thought Judith, suppressing a
pang of guilt at her own deviousness. 'The girl does
rather need someone to talk to. You're aware of course
that at first she was very much Samantha's pet but then
she was displaced by that chambermaid –'

'Penny.'

'Yes, and I think it left Grace feeling out in the cold.
To tell the truth Judith, I even thought at one point she
was developing an attraction to *you* but –'

'Oh, I don't know about that.' Damn the woman's
sharp eyes. They had caught her out once before and
now it would be better to make a clean breast of it.
Especially if she was going to get Grace's story. 'But if
I'm honest with you, Marjory, I have to admit to recent
inclinations that way myself.'

'Capital. You would make a good pair, though she is
a strange, deep girl. Well, I can at least arm you with
what information I have. How about calling round to

the house this weekend for a drink, say tomorrow night?'

'Now, Judith, I hope you don't think this is all *too* disreputable. I suppose I see it now as a kind of last fling before settling into the job here. And of course I did need a new assistant-cum-housekeeper, though I realise that does not justify going for all the, ah, trimmings.'

That sexual services paid for could be called 'trimmings' was one thing; it was rather another that Marjory had been prepared to have dealings with such a doubtful establishment. From what Judith could make out it functioned to provide employers of a sadomasochistic bent with a supply of largely menial employees, many of whom had been siphoned off from the juvenile justice system. How this was done wasn't explained – the lady's characteristic clarity of expression seemed to have been swallowed up in her embarrassment – though the picture that sprang to mind of bent officials and exploited girls was not an agreeable one. But what exactly had happened to Grace?

'Well, I can't tell you that because I came in only on the end of it. I was shown two charming young creatures with quite adequate secretarial skills for my needs and both, I was assured, were more than happy to submit to regular discipline. All I had in mind, of course, was old-fashioned spanking of the over-the-knee variety – you know, Judith, I hope, that I would take no pleasure in causing any real hurt of the sort I sometimes require myself. And I didn't have to take anyone's word on the matter for the older girl promptly downed knickers and arranged herself across my lap there and then to be sampled. I was quite bowled over, I can tell you.'

'And Grace . . .' Marjory seemed to have found her voice again just as Judith's mixed feelings about the whole operation were making her impatient to get to the point.

110

'Bear with me, Judith, I *am* coming to her. But you need to know something of what the institution was like. You see, there was no way I could afford the hiring fee they charged but I was given to understand it was possible to obtain a substantial reduction by submitting oneself to the public ritual chastisement each girl had to undergo before being judged ready for release. Its essence was that the recipient was required to specify her own punishment in stages as it took place.'

'How do you mean, specify?'

'Just that. One had to select from an array of instruments laid out on a side table, name a number of strokes, then go to the horse and take them: the sequence to be repeated *ad libitum*, though there was obviously little pleasure involved. But you see the point, Judith. The rigour of the experience was entirely in the hands of the one undergoing it and had to be nicely tailored to the expectations of the audience. They wanted severity, of course, but not to a degree that would render the victim of it incapable of a dignified withdrawal at the close. So the choice of cane for the finale needed to be finely judged.'

Judith shuddered at the thought of trying to focus the mind on such a calculation as the body shrieked for the pain to end. 'It sounds quite fiendish. I don't reckon I'd get very far in such a test.'

'Oh, I think you would, Judith, you shouldn't under-estimate yourself. If you had sufficient reason –' Marjory's earnest expression turned into a frown as she broke off and shook her head. 'Grace,' she said firmly, 'we are meant to be talking about Grace. And in fact that session was the occasion when I first saw her. Towards the end I caught a glimpse of one face that stood out from the others watching, for it looked like nothing so much as a Botticelli angel. And it bore the most haunted expression, as such a creature well might having found itself cast into a place of torment.

'I might have discounted the image as the product of an overstimulated imagination but for the fact that no sooner had I collapsed on my bed than there was a tap at my door and the girl herself was in my room begging to attend to the damage. I was doubtful at first, thinking that I could not bear even a touch to the marks acquired in the last minutes on the horse but she insisted and her way with the cool cream was as promised exquisitely gentle. Then, just as I was becoming somewhat restored, I heard an unmistakable sniffle and looked up to see the poor girl's face creased and streaming with tears. So I had her stop and sit beside me and the whole story came spilling out.

'Not that it was much of one really. A teenage runaway living hand to mouth in, well, let's just say an old European city, she had been rounded up by the police and sent out to the Hall. While most of the inmates were native speakers of other languages, its day-to-day business was conducted in English. She seemed not to have been charged with anything, but no doubt her looks would have earned at least one officer a handsome backhander. I had half-convinced myself that the set-up might serve to provide a girl with better prospects than she would have with a criminal record, but the state Grace was in quite shocked me. It seems she had been unable at all to adjust to the regime and was due to be transported to an official penal institution at the end of the week. When I wanted to know how, exactly, couldn't she cope her only reply was to lift her dress and show me an array of discolorations the like of which I had never seen before. Not only were there fresh weals as extreme as any I bore, but they were merely the most recent additions to the traces of a succession of similar mistreatments. I recall staring at her as I tried to comprehend: unless I had misconstrued the system Grace must have brought it all on herself, must have pressed to be treated with such severity. But when I tried

112

to ask how such a thing had come about her face crumpled again so I shut my mouth and comforted the girl as best I could.

'Well, that was it, Judith. In the morning I went straight to the woman in charge and told her I was going to employ Grace. She was naturally rather bewildered that I should choose one of their failures, but when I made my resolve apparent her attitude changed to one of gratitude that a problem was being taken off their hands and insisted on waiving the remaining charge.'

'Let me see if I've got this straight, Marjory. You're talking about some kind of neurotic *compulsion* for punishment that was way beyond what anyone in the Hall expected.'

'Or could deal with, it seemed. I believe I did the right thing to take Grace away, but any hopes I may have had of playing the therapist were soon dashed, for from that day to this she has never spoken of her problems again. Once we reached home she simply wouldn't discuss it and settled in to becoming a quiet and very organised secretary. I did summon her to my bed a few times and even had her across my knee – this was after all what she had been on hire *for* – but while she was sexually responsive it was all very, well, efficient. She was, and has remained to this day, somehow locked up inside. I have to admit to trying to re-open things, as it were, by sending the girl to Samantha in the full knowledge of your Director's predilections. Perhaps that would have worked, in time, for I know that Grace rather relished her use of the strap even when it was quite sharp.'

'I suppose there would be no question of who was in charge there. All she had to do was submit.'

'Well, exactly. No call actually to engage with the situation. I must say, thinking about it afresh, you are going to have your work cut out to break through that shell.'

'In fact, Marjory, the last time I saw her she was actually rather raw and upset.' The clinical edge of these remarks about the object of her own desire was too much and Judith hit out. 'How could you,' she snapped bitterly. 'You knew about Grace's fucked-up history and yet you beat her like that yourself.'

The older woman got up from her chair and circled round the back of the large chesterfield until she faced Judith once more. 'Well, I suppose I'd better tell you what actually happened last night though it will only make you think worse of me than you already do. I had planned to give her no more than a sound leathering, but as soon as I eased off she began to mutter, "Not enough, that's not enough," on and on like a mantra. I told you how irate I was that such a thing should happen while I had sole charge of the basement and I'm afraid I lost control. All the past frustration about her irrational behaviour joined with it and I struck and struck while she gasped out those terrible words, over and over. "*Not enough?* – I'll give you *not enough*," I recall shouting at her before I came at last to my senses. So there you have it, I'm afraid. To my shame, there you have it.'

With her own anger mounting, Judith let the picture of the desperate Grace being thrashed by a powerful woman in a rage take full shape in her mind. Not trusting herself to speak she sat with clenched fists until the heavy silence was eventually broken by Marjory's tentative words.

'Can I make a suggestion, Judith? I can't undo what I did, though I shall make a proper apology once the girl is more herself. But how would you react if I offered to, ah, atone? Do penance here and now, at your hands, in the manner we both understand.'

Judith looked sharply at the expensively tailored Deputy Principal but her expression was fully serious. Hard corporal punishment was something she could steel herself to take only rarely – the thrill the idea of it held for her being liable to dissipate in the grim actuality – however, Marjory was by contrast notoriously robust. So how real a 'penance' would such a thing be? And her own inclination was not in general to dish it out, not unless she was really in the mood . . .

'I can guess what you're thinking, Judith, but don't worry, I'm not looking for any perverse enjoyment. While I may have a *need* to be chastised from time to time, I can find you an instrument downstairs that will cause me nothing but pain. I can't of course deny wanting to purge some guilt but that will be at a price as high as you care to make it. So what do you say?'

12

Moving On

Running the length of the house from front to back, the room was laid out in two contrasting halves. At the street end was a book-lined and carpeted study complete with leather armchairs and a heavy wooden desk while the plain parquet floor of the remainder was furnished with a mere three items. Against one wall was a long narrow table, on the opposite side a large old-fashioned press and between them a rough-hewn trestle to which a padded top had been attached. French windows at the back gave on to a walled garden just visible in the gathering dusk of a summer evening and Judith stood in front of them while she looked over the object in her hands with a touch of awe. It was a cane around three feet in length and some three-eighths of an inch thick, but there the resemblance to the once-standard piece of school equipment ended. This instrument was made out of a rubber sheath bonded to a synthetic core and in combination they gave it a weight and tensile elasticity palpably beyond those of its rattan counterpart.

Judith closed the curtains and turned back into the warm light. It had been decided that her tight trousers and heeled boots might detract from a fully energetic performance and the spare room had yielded up some sportswear that Grace had abandoned. Thus she was kitted out in trainers, singlet and shorts, whose snug fit made her think at first lustfully of the peach of a behind that had once filled them. The gear was appropriate enough for the quite athletic activity she was to be engaged in for the next several minutes but any sexual frisson attached to it had since vanished. The thought of the bodily harm she had agreed to inflict now weighed on her and she was glad to hear the sound of Marjory's step on the stair. The sooner the punishment was underway the sooner she could be finished with it.

The procedure had been discussed in detail before-hand so when the door opened, the figure in a light cotton jogging suit moved straight to the trestle and lay across it without a word. The breasts bulged to the sides under the thin material and the elasticated waist pulled it up around the rear cheeks in a way that emphasised their fullness. Visible was a *depth* of buttock – to use a common nineteenth-century term – capable of absorb-ing quite stringent discipline and Judith found her resolution hardening. It wasn't just the beating of Grace: this woman had taken on a vulnerable, damaged girl and treated her with too little care. Her own boss was guilty as well, but she was unlikely ever to have Samantha James in this position and, fair or not, Marjory was going to suffer for both their misdeeds. The thought threatened to formulate itself that she too had played her part in Grace's misfortunes but she pushed it firmly to the back of her mind and measured the cane against the prominent hemispheres.

The number of strokes was hers alone to determine but it had been agreed Judith would begin with some preliminaries across the clothed seat. Her first – and only – lesson of two years past had stressed the need to get one's eye in before striking hard and after six increasingly forceful blows she felt ready to proceed to the punishment proper. Stooping, she drew down the jogging bottoms and removed them and the canvas mules completely. Then, as instructed, the ankles were

placed each side of a central block and a bar slotted in
tight at the back of the calves to hold the legs fixed in
an inverted-V shape. While it was the duty of the
chastisee to maintain position by gripping the front of
the frame, connoisseurs of discipline apparently recommended this concession since even with the best of
efforts control of the legs was likely to fail *in extremis*.

Now the hindquarters had been bared it was plain
that Marjory had been leading a quiet life of late. Save
for the fresh pink imprints of the warm-up cuts there
was not a single mark, new or old, to be seen. *You'll
soon change that*, said a voice in her head as Judith took
up position to the right and a little forward of her
target. Three blows with the full swing of her arm and
three more with the added weight of her shoulder
behind them may have produced no response from the
recipient (*yet*, went the voice again) but the broad
posterior was already startlingly laced with blood-red
stripes. Ten, eleven and twelve were each met with an
audible grunt and Judith saw with a grim satisfaction
that the double-edged welts were darkening to purple as
they multiplied. Under another six strokes given at full
stretch the buttocks bounced and rippled and the body
jerked but there was no increase in vocalisation. *You can
do it, make her cry out*, and obedient to the internal
prompt Judith rose on to the balls of her feet and
slashed with all her might.

'Oh, I say!'

The recoil of the black rod stung her hand and the
thought of the pain being inflicted at its other end made
her scalp prickle. However, try as she might, the only
response to the next five strokes was that noise from the
back of the throat of air being expelled from the body.
It was as if having weakened once, the penitent was
determined to keep her silence to the bitter end. And
that could not be far off. Two dozen of her best with the
vicious weapon had turned the pristine rump into a

swollen mass of raw contusions some of which must soon break. *Six more*, counselled the inner demon and Judith steeled herself. There was indeed no point in this exercise unless it went to the limit so she moved back, took a deep breath and delivered each of the further half dozen at a run.

Twenty-eight, twenty-nine, thirty, and still no screech of anguish. *Again!* Almost in a reflex she whipped the cane into the black blisters at the base of the right buttock and at once blood flowed down the thigh. The torso wrenched upright with a feral howl, back arched, then slumped forward to lie silent and still. Feeling suddenly sick Judith drew back. The thing was done. She dropped the instrument on to the wall-table and made for the door. Marjory could release the leg restraint when she was able and Judith was glad to make herself scarce. However much the thrashing was merited in theory, it was going to be a while before she could look the woman in the eye. Upstairs in the hall she found a carrier bag containing her clothes and with a great sigh of relief she headed down the front steps into the quiet cul-de-sac of the residential street.

Back in the flat Judith studied her appearance in the long hall mirror, turning this way and that. Grace would look a treat in these shorts with her narrow waist and sloping hips though she suspected the discarded item dated from at least her later schooldays. A hand to the crotch found the light polyester material slippery wet to the touch and while it had been warm work in the basement Judith guessed that more than sweat was involved. She peeled the garment slowly down clear of her bottom picturing herself doing the same to Grace before planting her lips on her labial folds. The jolt of desire this image evoked took her aback. Fuck, she was getting it bad. And the irony of the situation was that she had done just that last summer and then tossed it all carelessly away. Well, if she had turned the girl on before, she could surely do it again, even through the weirdness going on in her head. But for the immediate present there was only one remedy to hand and Judith took a last look in the glass before she turned into her bedroom. Good old self-help: it was quite literally at your fingertips and it never let you down. How people had been conned into calling it abuse she had always found difficult to understand.

'I just *love* these stories where a naïve young virgin gets seduced into deep and dark perversions.' Marsha was speaking over her shoulder as she pulled a bunch of beers out of the cold cabinet at the back of the bar. Her voice was raised over the Sunday lunchtime hubbub of The Phoenix and Judith was amused to see the slightly startled expression on the baby-face of the youth holding out a ten-pound note. 'But it kinda peters out with no proper end.'

'Does it? I haven't got to the last bit yet.'

'Well, you'd better take it back and see for yourself, Jude. I'm sorry to have been so long getting to it but I've been run ragged with all this preparation.'

'Preparation?'

'For the videoshoot on Wednesday. Aren't you in training for stardom too, honey?'

'Marsha, I don't believe it. With all the practice they get, how could your girlfriends be needing *rehearsals*?' Judith couldn't help smiling at the thought of the American selling them the idea, though she was underneath envious of the continuing ability of her forty-something friend to draw nubile youngsters to her bed. 'I'm just going to do what Mo tells me to do. I mean, mine is merely the supporting role in which I lie about legs suitably spread. I'll be relying on the stud to make the, er, seminal contribution.'

'For that you don't deserve your weekend freebie,' said Marsha with a grin, plonking the uncapped bottle on the counter between them, 'and in any case that gorgeous bare pussy is going to be the scene stealer and you know it. But seriously, girl, Kitty goes off in five so I can't stand here yakking for long. I had an idea, though, about this memoir, if that's what you call it. Do you know where the place – the school – is, or was?'

'Yeah, there's stuff about it in the notes. I can't remember the name of the town it's close to, but it's in the Czech Republic, not far from the German border.'

'Well, it's just a thought, but that bench thing: do you suppose it might possibly still be there? What you've got here in these papers might not amount to a lot, but if you could put your hands on the actual article . . .'

Judith stared as the implications began to sink in. 'You mean if we could find it – and bring it back –'

'Imagine a thing like that set up in your basement over there. I know a few of my own countryfolk who'd pay to get their rich asses fried on an authentic old European flogging frame –'

'And what about the crowds who'd flock to the Archive to see such a sight? Marsha, you're a genius!'

'Hold your horses, girl. The thing was probably turned into firewood long ago, but it may be worth trying to find out. And there is something else, too. Maybe it's nothing to worry about, but didn't you say your old sparring partner had fled the country with a copy of this precious manuscript? Well, honey, what do you suppose *she* was thinking of doing with it?'

Judith came to and squinted at the illuminated figures on the bedside alarm. Fuck it, seven o'clock. The single beer on the house had been followed by several more out of her pocket and then a terse interchange with Marsha on the subject of her use of young women. *Ab*use, she had come close to saying, and at the recollection of spitting out the word 'bimbo' Judith sat up and groaned out loud. The constant interruptions to

121

their dialogue as the bar manager dealt with customers hadn't helped her temper, but sober she couldn't duck the plain fact that she was jealous. How long it was since her own bed had been graced by a visitor didn't bear thinking of and the previous weekend's frolics only served to underline the emptiness of her love-life at home. And she had decided to cut Harry out before she had hit on a way of drawing Grace in.

However, there was no point moping. Judith got up and splashed some water on her face in the bathroom, pulled on an old pair of jeans and went through to the kitchen. Tomorrow she would grovel abjectly before her American pal and have another go at the coy secretary; but there was one thing she could do right now, or as soon as she walked round to the Archive. She would phone Seattle and, fingers crossed, get one of the girls in. As if to confirm her resolve she found a piece of Brie at just the right stage of ripeness lurking in the fridge and half of a still-fresh loaf in the breadbin. With a feeling of virtue she left untouched the half-full bottle of wine and settled down to eat in a slightly better frame of mind.

'Hallo, yes. Who is this, please?' There was no mistaking the accent and she warmed at once to the German woman's idiosyncratic speech.

'Zadia, hi. It's me, Judith. I hope I didn't get you out of bed.'

'Judith! I am only in the door, just. The party after we play. I am sorry, I –' The voice broke into giggles and Judith gave a sigh. Clearly drink had been flowing and she regretted her own recent abstinence. But it was important to get an answer.

'Look, Zadia, I won't keep you. I just want to ask you something.'

'Oh Judith, is it the writing? My grandaunt's writing is no good for you?'

'No, no. It's fine, just fine. No problem.' It was clearly not the time to broach the idea of trying to locate the infamous bench. 'Just listen, Zadia. You know you said Cate had gone off with a copy of it. Well, we never got a chance to talk about that last weekend. Do you know what she's up to?'

There was a silence and the voice that broke it sounded rather more sober. 'I have been bad, Judith, but I confess it now. I make up the story. Cate read the papers and then she went away like I said. But not with them.'

'Let me get this right. You're saying that Cate didn't take a copy of the manuscript? So why –'

'Why do I say she did? I must get your attention, Judith, and the name of your lover, I mean ex-lover –'

'Oh, Zadia, you didn't need to do that. I would have been interested anyway.'

'I am sorry, Judith. Telling a lie like that is bad.'

'Don't worry about it. That's fine. I just wish you'd given me the truth when I was there.'

'I mean to but I put it off, you know how it is? But I shall make amends and tell you something else, yes? Something about Petra?'

'Er, OK.' She could hardly say no, though mention of the name made her apprehensive. How much did Zadia know or guess about her sister's visits to Judith's bed during the last weekend?

'Do not be alarmed. No longer do I ask about what she does. If she stays with me it is good and that is what I hope for. No, it is to warn you she goes to London and I guess she will come to you for – how do you say it? – a flying visit. It would be the big surprise, yes? And maybe you do not want to be surprised. If there is another . . .'

Oh God. Not only was the woman apparently resigned to Petra's voracious promiscuity, she was taking the trouble to make sure Judith had the decks cleared ready to have sex with her. Not that *that* was a problem in her present deprived state. But it was all a bit too much and having established that Tuesday was the day in question she brought the call to a close as soon as she decently could. Under the hard muscular exterior Zadia was so vulnerable it hurt to think about it, expecially when Judith herself was implicated in her sister-lover's disloyalty. The fact that it was by invitation was no excuse.

Judith swivelled round in her chair and stared moodily at the lines of the old rooftops across the silent quad. Resolving to give the girl the cold shoulder was pointless: even the mention of the name made her tingle while the thought of the eager mouth between her legs produced a pang of pure lust. Fuck it, it was up to Zadia not to be a doormat. After all, such an Amazonian figure could have the babes lining up for the privilege of her bed if she would only stop moping over the plainly doomed incestuous relationship.

But who was she to talk? It was barely more than a week since she had broken down about the lost Cate who had stalked her innermost thoughts for a whole year. Rationality didn't get much of a look-in in this territory. And then it struck her. Cate. *Cate.* She had been phoning specifically to ask about what the woman was up to and it hadn't meant a thing. Not a damn thing, except that she might cause problems with the manuscript. As if to confirm her thought an evening shaft of sunshine caught the clock tower opposite and she felt a sudden surge of liberation. Something had shifted inside and she was free of the ghost that had haunted her for too long and placed a hex on affairs of the heart.

Judith sat up and straightened the papers on her desk. It was early yet and she decided to go and abase herself before Marsha. It was better done sooner rather than later, before the lady had had a chance to sleep on her indignation. If the past had let her go, she could move on at last. All that was needed now was to engineer a present that included having loads of totally raunchy sex with Grace.

13

Wet Lips

On Monday afternoon when Judith walked into the office Grace looked up with a smile. It might have been diffident, but it was unmistakably a smile.

'Hi, Judith. I just had a call from Mo and she's dead chuffed to get the commission.'

'Great. It's for Wednesday, yeah? And you'll be there too?'

'OK. Er, is it really true that you're giving up men? I mean, I didn't know if you were joking or not.' Judith nodded, uncertain how to respond to the sudden burst of chattiness.

'Sure am. So I'm available for any propositions from our side, right?' What *was* she saying? But the answering blush went straight for her loins and then Grace had more.

'Mrs Rowleigh came in this morning and she, er, apologised. To *me*. And it was funny the way she was walking, very stiff. Didn't you go to see her the other night?' How did the girl know that? Later she would dig, but questions could wait. Now seemed like the time for action.

'That's good she said sorry. It was way over the top what she did.' Judith forbore to add that Grace's compulsive demand for more had made a bad situation worse. 'But what about you? Are the bruises on the mend?'

'Have a look.' Without so much as a moment's hesitation the minidress was hoisted to the waist and in another single movement the secretary presented herself pants-down for inspection. Judith cleared her throat and tried to ignore the thumping in her chest.

'You know, there's still quite a lot of dark round the edges. I'd say a good massage could help even after this time.'

'Um, is that an offer, Judith? I've finished those publishers' letters and, er . . .'

Things were moving unexpectedly fast and Judith had to quell an impulse to back off. Shit, this was no time to be having an adolescent panic attack. 'Yeah. I've got the very thing next door, so if you just hang on there . . .'

She bolted for her office before the firm tone could waver and opened the lower drawer of the desk. Over her time at the Archive she had built up a small medicine cabinet of palliatives for the residual effects of corporal punishment. Among the items was a jar of witch hazel contributed by the secretary herself but Judith passed it by judging that in the present circumstances a simple herbal oil would best fit the bill. On the way back she scooped up a small square cushion and placed it on the empty corner of a table in the main office.

'May as well be comfortable,' she said with what she hoped was a no-nonsense air, giving the cushion a pat to indicate where Grace should take up position. Still holding up her dress the girl lay obediently forward and it took only a moment to take the wisp of black underwear right off over the patent leather pumps and begin to apply the contents of her bottle. It was heady work for the sheen the bottom-cheeks acquired beneath Judith's gaze accentuated their already ripe curves while their soft weight moved deliciously under her fingers. The thought surfaced that anyone who began to lay a belt across these beauties might find it difficult to stop but she pushed it hastily back down. There was guilt enough in her head from the viciousness that had overtaken her in Marjory's basement without finding more excuses for what the woman had done. After all, the traces of her severity were there in front of her in the heavy purple smudges right in the cleft. To make such imprints the strap must have been aimed with a repeated cruel intention to bite into that sensitive place.

Fingering the marks with care, she parted the globes and trickled a little oil between; then, with quickening pulse, she pressed a wet fingertip firmly into the tight knot of the anus. The body pushed back to meet her with an audible 'ah' and emboldened by the reaction Judith turned her attention to the vulva below where the outer labia formed a neat, almost prim line under a sprinkling of fine curls that grew denser toward the pubic mound. The massager took a deep breath and inserted an index finger between the lips.

'Oh, yes . . .' sighed the secretary and what Judith saw made her gasp. Like some exotic plant the dun exterior parts opened at her touch to reveal fold upon fold of a startling oyster-pink that swelled glistening before her eyes. There was a dribble of fluid that begged for a tongue – *her* tongue – to lap it up and then curl its tip deep inside but Judith forced herself to resist. One step at a time. The girl was visibly turned on and for now the hand would be enough. If she could just apply the right kind of pressure to the nubbin that must be throbbing like her own –

'Jude – aaahhh – Ju-u-u-de!' It ended as a yell and was followed by three sharp cries that rang in her ears. For a long moment she stood awkwardly over the figure that lay prone in the wake of its spasm before reaching out to fondle the back of the neck. It was a mistake for the girl twisted away and was on her feet in a trice, smoothing the rumpled dress down over her crotch.

'Er, thanks. That feels heaps better.' The expression was hard to read and there was no eye-contact. So that was the way it was going to be. One orgasm had worked no miracles, but what could she really expect? Judith sighed inwardly. It looked like being a long haul to the desired 'therapeutic' outcome.

The following morning she was at her desk early after a restless night and when Grace appeared her manner was again cool. OK, that suits me fine, thought Judith as she dispatched the girl to the leather goods warehouse with a list of items added to their advance order. That would tie her up for some time and then she could take the rest of the day off. Judith was absolutely not going to feel guilty about keeping the secretary out of the way should Petra indeed put in an appearance. It seemed unlikely on the face of it since she could hardly pop down from London in a lunchbreak, but what was unlikely for most Judith knew – even on her limited acquaintance – to be just what Petra might pull off. However, as the passing minutes turned into hours while she began and abandoned one job after another from the in-tray, Judith's conviction began to waver. And when the the time reached and passed three-thirty she became resigned to disappointment. Now if only she had put her efforts into sweet-talking Grace instead of sending her off on an unnecessary errand –

The angry beep-beep-beep of the rarely used buzzer made her jump and she leapt across the outer office to the intercom. 'Petra, is that really you?'

'Sure is,' came the crackling voice through the receiver. 'Now how the fuck do I get into this place?'

'Stay right where you are and I'll come down for you.'

Judith hit the stairs at a run and yanked open the heavy door into the entrance lobby. Lounging against the wall in a nonchalant fashion was a woman in a silk suit of a muted terracotta colour. A subtle perfume hung in the air and there was not a hair out of place on the immaculately coiffured head. Then she turned and the studied impression dissolved in a wicked grin that took her straight into Judith's arms.

Once they were through the door marked Assistant Director, Petra pulled a wooden paddle out of a bag and tossed it into the armchair. 'For the collection: an implement that has brought colour to the cheeks of many an all-American miss.' Then she sat Judith down and removed her boots. 'It would be ace to give a demo, but I really need to cut to the chase, if that's all right with you. There's a driver outside waiting to whisk me away.' Judith's mind boggled at the idea of the hours of chauffering needed to allow Petra to perform a fleeting sexual act. But that was her way: the world ever revolved around her and Judith was happy to be its current focus. Back on her feet she was turned round and instructed to unzip.

'OK, I was gonna say "drop them" but these pants need help. So the warning from big sis didn't make you run.'

'No *way*, girl.' Firm hands were drawing the tight material over her thighs and Judith felt the telltale seep of desire between her legs.

'Hmm. Not a single new mark that I can see. It seems Madam has no one currently taking her in hand.' There was a kiss to each buttock and a tongue poked lasciviously between before the thong was removed and she was turned to face the kneeling Petra.

'Oh, wow. Wow.' She breathed the words then placed her lips softly on the bare pubes. Judith shivered from head to toe. 'It would have been worth the whole journey just to see *this*.' She stood up on her feet and pointed. 'I just adore the big desk: totally VIP. And exactly what we need. So get up on it now, lover, and *spread*.'

* * *

Judith was on the point of stooping to pull on her discarded clothes when the door of the main office flew open and Grace backed in struggling with a large box. 'They pulled all the stops out seeing it was us so I thought I'd just bring this in on the way home.' She set the article down with a bump and looked round. 'You know there's a big Merc parked at the back with a guy in uniform . . .'

The eyes fixed wonderingly on the sight of Judith wriggling back into her trousers and at that moment Petra came out of the bathroom displaying a freshly glossed pout. Grace's mouth set at once into a line and turning her back she began ostentatiously to unpack the items from the container.

'I'll see you out, Petra, OK?' In haste Judith led the way to the stairs and clattered down them. Outside it was the American who spoke first.

'I guess Ms Frown thinks she's the only one who has a right to you bare-assed. Don't worry, Jay, I know the type. You'll soon have her eating out of your hand or, better still, your you-know-where!' She gave a lewd wink and with a burst of giggles she was in the back seat of the car and away, leaving Judith leaning weakly against the Archive wall. Jesus, talk about *attitude*. The girl ought to be downright infuriating, but somehow she could manage only to find her irresistible.

Back upstairs there was no sign of the aggrieved secretary until Judith noticed the bathroom was set on ENGAGED. She tapped on the door and put on her best cajoling tones.

'Grace, are you there? Grace, I'm really sorry about that. Please come out and I'll try to explain.' There was a silence while she waited. What with Marsha at the weekend life was becoming one long round of eating humble pie. Then the latch clicked back and a decidedly sullen face appeared.

'Look, Grace, that was Petra from Seattle. The one who translated the manuscript. I'd have put her off if I'd been able but I couldn't get in touch.' Well, she *couldn't*, but the first bit was simply untrue and Judith cringed inwardly.

'You mean you knew she was coming? So that's why you got me out of the way. Judith, you just can't keep your knickers on, can you?' The last words were delivered with a snarl, but even as she flinched from it Judith surmised that this real anger was a lot more healthy than cold distance. Maybe – just maybe – she could capitalise on the change of mood.

'OK, OK. You're right. It was an awful sneaky thing to do and I'm sorry. But will you let me show you something? Through here.' She led the way to where Petra's paddle still lay on the chair and held it out. 'You see this present she gave me? Now if you're really cross with me – and you are, right? – why don't you get a grip on the handle and apply the business end to my bum. As hard and as long as you think I deserve. A kind of poetic justice, yeah?'

Grace looked doubtfully from Judith's face to the slab of polished wood and back again.

'So is that, like, an order?'

'Er, yes. It is.' Again there was a pause as Grace visibly weighed up the situation then she took the instrument and smacked it twice against the palm of her hand.

'Right, boss lady. I think you'd better get those trousers down one more time.'

The spanking took a full fifteen minutes and it was another fifteen before Judith felt able to trust her blazing behind to the padded seat of the deskchair. Well, she could hardly complain of the treatment having quite literally asked for it, though how the relationship with Grace was going to develop as a result had to be anybody's guess.

Then the door opened quietly and the young woman in her thoughts sidled in and stood facing her, a vision in a tiny yellow dress with matching strap shoes, hair drawn back from the perfect heart-shape of the face. And in her hand was a white porcelain jar that Judith recognised at once.

Things were looking up, thought the Assistant Director of the Nemesis Archive ensconsed in her eyrie above the summer dusk of the quad. The orgasm had been quite sensational. Far from the routine exercise of cool fingers she had come to expect, after the soothing cream it had turned into an affair of eager secretarial tongue, lips and, in the end, teeth. The thing had been marred at the outset by Grace's demand to be told that her perform-ance outshone 'the Yank's' which Judith felt obliged to confirm. She could do little else, even though doubting at first that Petra could be outclassed in the art of giving head. However, it had been very much a white lie at the time – compared to the other of the day – and then it had rapidly become no lie at all.

Now she sat cocooned in the afterglow of it all, trying to remind herself of the jobs that were lining up. The next day was the porn-clip session with Mo (how was Grace going to react to *that*?) and as well she had to do some groundwork on Marsha's idea about tracking down the old punishment apparatus. And then there was Harry. Being fucked on camera was supposed to mark the end of fucking the librarian at the British Library, so she had better tell him about it – and sooner rather than later. He was hardly going to be thrilled by the news, but perhaps he could be enlisted in a search for the bench, and if she were still on offer for the occasional heavy hand . . .

Judith leaned over and pulled towards her the folder she had brought back from Seattle. Harry deserved better and these devious speculations were out of order. She would play it by ear with him the way she always had once a meeting had been arranged. That night there was the manuscript to be finished and in her present state Judith was rather looking forward to continuing Jana's excited account. Delving into the papers she scanned for the passage that had made her declare enough is enough and cast them aside. Yes, there it was: not only had the girl been introduced to Mrs K's intense s/m relationship with young Sophie, she had afterwards secretly bedded the surprisingly eager Greta. The last time round it had all been too much for Judith's dissatisfied yearnings: now she was rather looking forward to more of the same. You go for it, girl, she said to an image of the narrator in her mind and settled down to read.

My first lover! Of course I know she is a woman and I am not supposed to go with her in that way. But she has a boyfriend she lets do what men do to her, so surely I could go and get one as well. *If* I wanted that of course, and I must admit I am far from sure.

I go for Greta every night now. I know it is reckless but I am horribly aware that the holidays are upon us and in a few short days she will be gone for long weeks. When we reach my bed I lay her first on her face. The marks from the session over the bench are still clear and I love to kiss and stroke them. When she is hot and squirming I turn her over and suck her nipples before I move my mouth down between her legs. The first time she took charge completely, but now she seems to delight in giving herself up to me. Knowing as I do that Greta is to leave in such a little time makes me greedy to have all of her, to probe every nook and cranny of that sumptuous flesh.

During the daylight hours between I think about her with the boyfriend's mother – for that is where she is returning – and the idea of her strap smacking across the broad cheeks excites me. Even the thought of the older woman enjoying Greta's private parts as

I do does nòt disturb me: what I wish is only to be there to watch and then of course join in. But I do not like the thought of *him* with that *thing* (I am told one of them stands up like a pole when a man is ready) poking roughly between those wet lips that I love to taste with my tongue.

However, I must push the thought aside for all too soon the term is over and she has left. One or two of the staff remain for a while but the First Mistress herself has gone away and, so I heard it rumoured, taken Sophie with her. So I must content myself somehow and hit upon the idea that I should try to put together an account of how I have come to develop these longings that conventional folk find so repellent. Thus I bide my time and go out into the country on my own. While I can dream of Greta's return and anticipate, albeit nervously, what Mrs K may demand of me in the future, the days and hours pass acceptably. But then the blow comes and it is as if I had been secretly fearing such a thing without my mind daring to recognise it. When I return late from my walk a letter has arrived in a hand I at once recognise. We had agreed not to write for fear of arousing suspicion so I suspect it cannot be good news and open it with dread.

Oh Jana, Jana, it reads, the worst has happened. I am going to have a baby and I must marry and become a proper wife. I guessed at the end of term but could not say to spoil our times together. But they are finished and I am so sorry. Do not reply, please, there must be no trouble for you. I shall never forget. Greta xxx.

Stiff with shock I see myself as if from the outside: a creature who sits head bent over the note. She appears to read it again and again – for how long I do not know – as though by force of will she can change its message. Then she tears it slowly into strips and the strips into tiny pieces that she scatters on the floor. 'No, no, no!' she cries and the shriek brings me back into a body whose loss has the fierceness of physical pain. I collapse sobbing on the bed and cry myself eventually to sleep.

14

Desperate Measures

It is not possible for me to tell of those two weeks –
no, it was nearly three – that I was alone with my
grief and rage and despair. The last is the hardest to
bear when it seems to be a judgement on my newly
awoken desire to have been barred with such cruel
abruptness and finality. The academy is at present
deserted in the last part of the holiday except for the
elderly janitor Thomas who appears in the morning
and afternoon for a short spell to check over the
premises. During term he occupies a small room with
basic facilities which is available at other times for the
few of us who stay on. One evening there is a knock
at my door and he is there with bread, a steaming jug
and a bowl and spoon. His wife was asking, he says,
and he told her that he had seen me only once in
days and I did not look well. So she made soup and
he was to make sure I took it. The simple kindness of
the gesture brings my tears on at once and the
caretaker is glad to make an exit when I assure him I
will eat. And in a while I do, suddenly ravenous, with
concentrated attention.

The food fills the body and I am grateful for it,
though there is a hollow emptiness it does not reach.
The next day I ask Thomas if he will open Mrs K's

office and the old Headmaster's study on the pretext that she left me the task of copying the punishment records. As I hoped he seems happy that I am once more active and does not query my request. First I take out the paddles and straps I have helped the First Mistress use and weigh the leather they are made of in my hands. It is indeed thick enough to sting and to mark if applied repeatedly but I do not think these articles will serve the purpose that is beginning to form in my mind. So I make my way down the corridor to the room equipped with the article that has acquired a special significance in my mind: the Headmaster's bench. For me it has come to encapsulate the horror and the perverse thrill of corporal punishment that between them hold me in a strengthening grip.

For a minute I stand before it leaning on the wooden slats that form the upper surface. Deprived of the squirming heat from an afflicted body they are cool to the touch and the bands that sprout from the sides are deceptively soft. However, it is not principally the bench I have come to see but its accessories. Four canes are held in a wall-rack ready for use once the victim is tied securely in place and I take them down one by one for examination. The heaviest has the breadth of my thumb with still the flexibility to curl in at the tip and inflict deep bruising to even a well-padded behind. I realise with a lurch that it is in fact the one Mrs K chose to teach Greta a special lesson. *My* Greta, now no longer mine! The appalling thought will not be suppressed and I have to sit while the storm of weeping abates. Resuming my inspection I handle the rod that is no thicker than a pencil and slashes through the air like a whip. A cut with this will wrap round the hip and burn like a red-hot wire: with it a skinny culprit can be thoroughly punished with a minimum number of strokes. In between the

138

extremes are more commonplace specimens designed for the routine beating of unexceptional schoolgirl bottoms, though the idea I could think such a thing *routine* at all shocks me a little. I have come a distance in the past twelve months.

I return the items to their places for what I have seen confirms my intention. An expert application of any one of these fearful weapons must surely make me *feel* again, must in the searing pain it inflicts on the body bring the emotions back to life. It is time. Mrs K predicted it and she will be proved right. When she returns towards the end of the week I shall request that I be fastened down and chastised on the bare buttocks to the degree she thinks fit. I know she will not spare me and in my black gloom the thought gives me a grim comfort.

However, the following day there is another shock. Miss Prinz is the first of the teachers to return before the start of the term and she brings news with her. The scandal of it lights her face as she tells how her police inspector uncle was called to a country hotel over the weekend when a chambermaid came across a case of whips in the room the manager had at first thought to be occupied by a mother and daughter. But with suspicions aroused, he found that one of the two beds had not been used and there were traces of blood on the sheets of the other. I am only half-listening to this notorious purveyor of tittle-tattle when I go cold with the apprehension that she is talking about Mrs K and Sophie, and I puncture the woman's relish with a flow of sharp questions. It seems that the hotelier's wife had examined the girl and, horrified at the marks on her body, had contacted the police. However, Sophie was not a minor and insisted she had assented to a dose of extra-curricular discipline that would not have been thought out of order within the school bounds. So no charges were to be preferred but in view of the signs of an 'irregular relationship' between teacher and pupil, the inspector had decided to send a report to the school board. And its members will take the view, I realise with a sick feeling in my stomach, that while the whipping of a girl out of school by her mistress may be pardoned, even condoned, the bedding of her is beyond the possibility of sanction.

I know she is back because I see one of the station taxis leaving and later there is a light in her quarters but I keep away for the rest of the day. In the morning I dress carefully, choosing a short fitted blouse with stockings and shoes. On top of these I wear only a long grey skirt, so that when it is removed I shall be bare from waist to knee in readiness for my imminent castigation.

Mrs K is sitting in her office, elegant in a cream linen suit although I see her face is drawn. She hears me out in silence then asks if my decision has anything to do with the letter of notification of Greta's withdrawal she has received. I am disconcerted that she appears to know so much, but when I own that it does she seems content and stands up to face me with a grave expression.

'You come not before time, Jana, since my tenure of the post of First Mistress may soon be at an end. No doubt you have heard tell of last weekend's débâcle, and given what you have seen with your own eyes it will not have strained your credulity. I fear I have been very foolish and must take the consequences. So while I am more than happy to do as you wish, there is a need to act without delay. I take it you came prepared for that eventuality.'

Over the summer, the hair has become long enough to fasten back in a clasp that emphasises the cheekbones and the line of the chin. Her eyes are very bright and once again I am struck by how handsome is this potent woman who is shortly to subject me to a rigorous thrashing. For a moment I am appalled at what I have done and as she makes for the door I look wildly about as if for escape. But of course there is none, nor could there be any. I have willed on myself what is to come. With this thought the spasm of fear passes and I am able to turn and follow the firm steps down the passage to meet my fate.

In the study Mrs K selects the medium cane I had hoped for, takes off her jacket and sits in the centre of a wide leather couch against the back wall. I stand in front of her while she unfastens my skirt and drops it to the floor, nodding with approval once my nakedness comes into view. Then I am drawn down across her lap with the material of her skirt cool against my thighs. She begins at once with full-blooded slaps that make me draw in my breath as they fall in a steady progression from left to right. After a while there is a palm that cups the cheeks as if to test their heat, then the spanking continues until my whole posterior region is aglow.

'Come, Jana.' It seems the preliminaries are over and we move at last to the bench. I am secured at wrist and knee then the broad band is pulled into the small of my back pinning me tight to the frame. I feel the rod tap my exposed hindquarters, then there is the swishing impact and hard upon it a searing pain that makes me gasp and cry out. It is a lesson that however prepared for it one may think oneself, the first stroke is always so much fiercer than any impression the mind has retained. I am trying to steel myself for the second when there is a hurried knocking and the door is flung open.

'First Mistress, I'm so sorry. Please forgive the intrusion, but it's Dr Hobel. From the Board. He was so insistent –' The diminutive school secretary's flustered speech is interrupted by the figure who sweeps past her into the room.

'Ah, Frau Kästner, keeping up the good work I see!' Screwing round my neck I can just see a tall man of around forty, clean-shaven in a dark suit. His eyes are fixed on my nether regions and I lower my head to hide the colour rising to my face. 'Is this another of your *special* girls, dear lady?'

'You may leave us now, Dushka. I shall attend to Dr Hobel.' The tone suggests that Mrs K would like the cane in her hand to play a part in any such 'attention', and despite the indignity of my position I smile to myself. But the unwelcome visitor is impervious and rattles on.

'What was it with this pretty one? Lack of preparation, perhaps? Or was it insolence? The youth of today –'

'Dr Hobel, *if* you please. This is not a pupil but my assistant Miss Marlova and what has brought her here is frankly none of your business.'

'Oh, but, Frau Kästner, there I am afraid you err. Following the submission the board received from the esteemed Inspector, all of your activities are my business.' It is a stand-off between two strong wills, but the continuation takes a turn that tips the balance. 'It is especially my concern to find you alone with a young lady indecorously bared, and I can only suggest that you bow out and allow me to conclude the discipline. If you will indulge me in this matter, I may be able to persuade the board to take a more tolerant view of your recent actions.'

Mrs K is silenced and I see her look as it passes from the intruder to myself and back again. My heart sinks at the thought of what this man is capable of inflicting but I know what I must do. 'First Mistress, please oblige the Doctor as he asks. If you consign me to him, I am sure he will award a just punishment.'

'Well spoken, Miss Marlova. Now, Frau Kästner, what do you say? Will you hand over the instrument and leave us to our dealings?'

'Very well, Dr Hobel. You will please report to me the details when you are done.' It is said after a pause and she goes to the door with downcast eyes. Never before have I seen the First Mistress look defeated. But now I have problems of my own as the new chastiser considers his position.

'Well, young lady, and what *was* the offence for which you have been strapped to this fine old bench?'

'Oh, it was insolence, sir. I responded without courtesy to a teacher who had made a perfectly reasonable request.' I have decided any fiction is likely to be better for Mrs K – and probably me – than the truth.

'And you repent of this behaviour?'

'Very much, sir, very much.'

'In that case, I believe two dozen strokes – in addition to the one I see on you already – should settle the matter. That is fair, is it not?'

'*Fair?* But that is far more . . .' I cannot contain my indignation at his breezy announcement of such a sentence.

'Far more than you were expecting? Miss Marlova, are you aware that the regulations permit a tally of twenty-five for each offence?'

'Yes, but –'

'Well, you have now committed a second, for which I shall award you only six more, making thirty in all. I advise you to accept this judgement while I am still in a lenient mood. Answer me, please.'

What choice do I have, immobilised on the wooden frame at the mercy of the cruel Dr Hobel? I force out a plain 'Yes' then brace myself for the onslaught.

I promised myself not to give my tormentor the satisfaction, but it is no use: by the time we have reached the original twenty-four I am howling like a baby as the cuts fall again and again on already punished flesh. Then there is a respite as he comes to the side and turns my head to him with the tip of the cane.

'I have no wish to mark you permanently, Miss Marlova, though I shall do that if I have to. However, I would much prefer to call a halt to the punishment at this stage if we can agree on one more thing.' He moves back and I flinch from his hand on my inner thigh which moves up to stroke my private parts.

'Oh no. No!' It occurs to me that the fingers are exploring the way it is intended the male organ itself should go. 'You can't, *mustn't*, I mean I have never . . .' I am aghast, the burning of welted buttocks momentarily forgotten.

'Miss Marlova, I am well aware of the importance of her virginity to a young woman in your position. However, there is another way we may proceed, if you will accept it.' The voice is patient, even insinuating. Now the agony of the last several minutes is in the past I am open to such gentle persuasion and make no objection when a fingertip is inserted between my throbbing cheeks into the ring of the anus. Greta played with me there (before I would have not thought of such a thing) and it seemed daring, though now the idea of a man's hard member invading me in that place makes me shiver. Will the thing I have never seen tear me with its thickness?

The Doctor is caressing me between the legs with gentle persistence and I am disconcerted to find that I am beginning to respond. Then I remember that I am submitting to this man for the sake of Mrs K: if I can enjoy anything about the encounter – after the horrendous beating – I should do so without hesitation.

'I'll accept whatever you want, sir, so long as . . .' It gives me quite a frisson to play the subservient Miss to the man with power.

'Don't worry yourself. There will be no – ah – consequences.' With that he puts the cane down on the desk and I see for the first time how his trousers bulge in front. Back behind me he unbuttons and there is a pressure on my tight hole. The thing that pokes me is slippery (it dawns on me that men too make juices when they are excited) and he moves it around the rim until I feel myself opening a little. Then he thrusts harder, more urgently.

'Press down, girl. Try to shit it out.' The vulgar word startles me but I do as I am told and he is right in. He reaches down to release the waist strap and lifts me enough to slide a hand under my belly. A finger hooks into my wetness, touching the secret button and he begins to pump in a steady rhythm. I am stuffed full of him in that forbidden place and the whole of my nether parts are a riot of sensation.

'Steady, girl, steady – now – now – NOW. Let it GO!' The seizure hits me all at once and I join in his shout, pushing ecstatically against his hard jerking body. Then I slump forward, all spent, and I feel him shrinking within me as he makes to pull out. Before I am released he fetches water from the washbasin behind a screen and washes carefully where he has penetrated me. Then he bathes the weals he has himself inflicted while I bask in all the remedial tending. When I dress I see he notices the lack of underwear and look down, blushing, though after what has just passed between us it is scarcely a cause for embarrassment.

'Miss Marlova, I am afraid I was rather severe with you today –' he looks for a reaction but I am suddenly tongue-tied, realising there is something I very much *want* the Doctor to say '– but I hope there are no hard feelings.' I manage to shake my head, willing him as hard as I can to continue.

'Well, if that is the case, I'll be so bold as to ask if in the future some less stringent treatment might be acceptable, might even be – ah – to your taste? Saturdays I am at my rooms in town. Would tomorrow week find you free to report to me with a suitable lapse for correction? And then perhaps afterwards – ah – as today –'

Now there are real grounds for blushes and I jump in quickly to spare his awkwardness. 'Oh yes. Yes *please*, sir.' What a perfect slut I am becoming! But I do not care and when Dr Hobel lifts my chin to kiss my mouth I kiss him back.

15

Matters of Taste

Once the Doctor's cab has taken him away I go to find Mrs K with as much haste as my stiffening bruises will allow. My mind is in a turmoil, as yet unable to register the fact that a man wants – and I can put it no other way – to have me as a mistress. His punitive demands may prove too exacting for me, but I shall try to satisfy him and who can say what I may rise to with experience. I am strangely filled with expectation rather than fear and it is in this mood that I track down the First Mistress in her own quarters. When I report Dr Hobel's parting assurance that he will speak on her behalf she looks at me with the hint of a frown.

'That is good news, Jana, but what price did you pay for his service? May I see?' The uncharacteristic deference is worrying but I have no hesitation in removing my skirt and bending over. After a brief inspection she says: 'Well, perhaps it has not turned out too badly. I have to confess I might have done quite as much to you if we had not been interrupted. It is difficult to keep a sense of proportion when one has at one's disposal such a fine pair of buttocks.'

Coming from Mrs K such talk is downright flirtatious, although she has never touched me in the way

147

I have seen her touch Sophie. The weals she is looking at are exquisitely tender and I can imagine little better than a soothing hand which went on to caress me in a more intimate place. But just as I took the initiative in the study from the unlikely position of the bench I am moved again to act. I drop to my knees and reach for the fastening on her skirt, looking up into the surprised face.

'First Mistress, do not stop me. I want so much to give you pleasure in the midst of your trouble.' Where these words come from I do not know, but they work a kind of magic. When the skirt falls I am allowed to remove the silk undergarment and press my lips to the thick pubic bush. In the bedroom she lies back and lets me spread the stockinged legs to begin my work. There is a pungency to the taste of her – befitting, indeed, a stern disciplinarian – far beyond the sweet meatiness of Greta. Dear Greta: now that I have begun to move on I can mourn her loss. Her legacy will be in the skills she taught me: skills that at this very moment are bringing Mrs K into the throes of orgasm.

'Jana, Jana!' she cries, then subsides, panting. I lie beside, close, her arm draped over my bare behind and when she is asleep I steal away. I too am ready for my bed: it has been a busy day.

My first senior class after break on Monday morning involves a written test on vacation tasks and after I have given out the sheets I sit dreaming of how to follow up my initiative with Mrs K. Mindful of my assignation at the weekend, I do not think it prudent to offer myself a second time for the castigation she was prevented from administering. Its traces would be all too visible days hence and I do not want him to think he has a competitor in my bodily correction. Then, as the period ends, Dushka the secretary appears with a message that my assistance is required in the study and I am able to put the collected papers in her hands. She tells me that the new kitchenmaid had been too busy flirting with the porter to notice the potatoes that were boiling dry on the stove. The result was a ruined pan which Cook thought merited a sharper lesson than the strap she kept was capable of delivering.

When I arrive the girl is already knickerless and benched, turning her head to me with an understandably woebegone expression. She displays the plumpest hindquarters I have ever seen presented for punishment and I see that the First Mistress has already taken down the heaviest cane from the rack. She is looking at her target with a keenness that makes me tingle: surely I shall be able to exploit the happy chance this situation represents.

'I thought to press on, Miss Marlova. I hope you don't mind.' After addressing me in this official way she turns to the miscreant herself. 'Now, Vala, you are to receive two dozen strokes and I want you to count out each one for me. It will reinforce the impression of your punishment which will, we hope, ensure your future good behaviour. Is that understood?'

'Yes, ma'am. Oh please, don't hit me too hard, ma'am, please.' If she thinks this plea will help she is sadly mistaken and when I catch the First Mistress's eye we exchange little smiles at the girl's folly. Then Mrs K rises on to her toes and delivers the hardest first stroke I believe I have ever seen. The instrument sinks right into the ample flesh and almost at once a crimson track springs up across the buttocks' whole breadth.

'Ow-ow-ow! One, ma'am. Oh, oh, it hurts, it hurts so. I can't endure it.'

'It is intended to, Vala, and endure it you shall. You can spare us the commentary: a number alone will suffice.'

'Ow-ow-owww!! Two, ma'am.'

We proceed in this manner and soon tears are flowing fast, though the maid has a resilience that keeps the numbers coming after every howl of pain. The wielder of the rattan strikes like a tiger and at the count of twenty the whole of the large posterior is barred in rich dark purples. The final four cuts are inspired: placed across the diagonal, two up and two down, they unleash a mighty screeching that rings in the ears in the uncarpeted room.

When I release the girl she bounds up and dances furiously on the spot, the hands pressed tight to hips as if that might ease the pain of the buttocks that will not bear touching. It is an exquisite moment and I see that Mrs K savours it no less than I. When Vala begins to collect herself I help her back into the discarded underwear which sets off another 'Ow-ow-ow!' but after this her recovery is rapid, aided by the washing of her face at the basin. That done, she is able to acknowledge that she has paid for her offence and promises soberly never to provide occasion for a return visit. When the girl curtsies out she is looking little the worse for her ordeal, though I know from my own experience it will be a day or two before she is back in her seat at the kitchen table.

Mrs K's colour is high and she is breathing quickly. I have seen these symptoms before but now with Sophie removed from the scene I take my chance to observe that I have a free hour. No persuasion is required, indeed words are scarcely necessary at all. In short order we are in the bedroom and this time the First Mistress is naked under her long skirt. I arrange a pillow to lift her compact behind and when she opens her legs the signs of her arousal take me by surprise. The folds of the lower lips are all bedewed and when I lay on a finger there wells up a cloudy fluid from within that trickles down through the hairs.

What an abundance of juice the making of poor Vala's stripes has created!

I am awed by such a flow and when I put my lips to hers the excretions are acrid on my tongue and my nostrils are filled with her ripe potency. Then my own desire grips me and I push hard in to suck and nibble, my chin dripping with ooze as I feel the climax rear up and break over her shuddering body.

On the Friday I receive a note from Dr Hobel that he will send a car for me at 2 o' clock and it throws me into a fever of anticipation. Eventually I decide on the uniform from my own schooldays (after all they are not two years in the past yet) for the next scene in the disciplinary drama that I am hoping he wants to enact as much as I do. And the signs are indeed good since the Doctor's gaze on me is an approving one as I am ushered discreetly into the two rooms he keeps at the back of the small hotel.

'Come in, Miss Marlova. It is good to see you.' He kisses me paternally on the forehead and looks gravely into my face. 'How are you? I hope the – ah – benchmarks laid down at our previous encounter have not proved too irksome since?'

'No, sir, but then they were intended to serve as a reminder of the occasion. Perhaps you should look for yourself and judge.' I am too keyed up for small talk but he does not seem to mind my hurry for he simply points me to a Chinese screen in the corner. When I emerge in my short cotton chemise and the old-fashioned drawers he appears delighted, taking me at once over his knee on the sofa. He finds the back tie easily and opens me up for inspection. My mirror has earlier shown me the fading tracery of blue lines that he now sees and fondles gently.

'These were well inscribed, Miss Marlova, and must still pain you a little. I have in my time, of course, seen severity taken well beyond this, but I think perhaps we should allow a further space for your recovery.' The rather ominous implication is lightened by the news that a cane is not likely to feature in today's proceedings. However, before I can begin to relax he announces that a little spanking will do my bottom no harm and decrees a dozen hard slaps. The hot sting makes me press down and when I feel his hardness against my belly a notion surfaces that I have not dared to let myself think of before. Perhaps it is madness or perhaps – and that would be ten times worse – it will make him think me too forward in these matters altogether.

Whatever the consequence, the impulse demands to be obeyed and I find myself reasoning that it will be no more than the equivalent of what I already do for Mrs K. So I slip off his lap and pull his hand, saying: 'Please, sir, will you stand up?' Dr Hobel does as he is bid though he is watching me with one eyebrow raised as I kneel in front and reach for his fly. But he does not back off. There is a flap inside and I am lucky to locate what I am looking for without too much clumsy fumbling. My heart is beating fast when I get the thing in my hand and lift it out into full view. The shaft is thick and dark with a pulsing vein and when I squeeze it a fold of skin draws back a little from the glistening head. As I watch some liquid forms at the tip and I catch it quickly with my tongue before it falls. Then my lips are round the organ and I am flicking the end of it with my tongue as I move up and down its stem. This feels to be a fine game, and the Doctor is ruffling my hair and beginning to breathe hard as matters come to a head.

'Miss Marlova – if you would rather use a hand-kerchief –' I divine his meaning but utter the best 'no' I can manage with my mouth full since I am determined for him to have his climax exactly where he is. When the jet hits the back of my throat I fear I have been too ambitious, but a hard swallow relieves the choking sensation and I am able to suck with renewed appetite. There seems a prodigious amount of it and I do not much care for the sour salty taste but it thrills me to be taking this way what was before deposited into the opposite end. I lick the rampant beast clean until it has shrunk to a curious wizened thing – altogether less impressive – that he returns rather quickly to concealment in his trousers.

Over a glass of wine I break the slightly awkward silence by asking whether men normally produce quite so much of a discharge and Dr Hobel gives a little embarrassed laugh.

'Well, you see, my dear Miss, you were in my thoughts much of the week and I did not allow myself any – ah – relief, if you take my meaning.' Indeed I do and get a little hot at the recollection of my discovery of self-stimulation and how avidly I re-sorted to it for a while. I am honoured to be the cause of such quantities of this peculiar secretion, though I keep my silence for fear of showing my naïvety. In retrospect, of course, it is clear that my virginity in relation to the territory of the male must have been part of the attraction.

'Not that I disapprove, you understand, I merely considered it wiser to conserve the supply for this afternoon. While I have a wife, as you may know, once two children had been produced she had no further taste for the – ah – sport. One which I must say you take to with real flair. But I am making you blush and there is the business of your corrective education to attend to. It was rudeness, as I recall, that you confessed to in the study, so what is the fault we have to deal with today?'

I have given this some thought, for I do not like the idea of having to invent a specific lapse to justify the disciplinary action. I can hardly cite what I have just done with the Doctor (although proper folk would think a sound whipping less than it deserved) nor what I do with Mrs K (since I do not want to make him aware of that). So I say instead: 'Dr Hobel, it will have not escaped your attention that my character has a wilfulness about it, and while that may at times lead to a positive outcome, I believe it requires curbing.'

'Oh yes, Miss Marlova, a headstrong girl needs a firm hand.' His eyes sparkle and he picks up my lead at once. 'While initiative is of course a desirable thing it should be possible for its more wayward aspects to be corrected with the judicious application of some of my instruments. I fear that is likely to require a course of treatment over some number of weeks, if you would be prepared to submit to such a thing.'

'Since it will be to my benefit, sir, I can scarcely refuse your kind offer.' In fact, it is decidedly *unkind* in what is being proposed for my body, but our game is acquiring a momentum I do not want to resist. While I have no prior experience of relations with men, I cannot believe that the rapport we have is common and I must see where it will take us.

'Excellent, my dear young lady: so let us proceed. Will you bring that upright chair with the padded back to the centre of the room and bend over it for me. That's it, right forward and hold on to the seat. Perfect.' He walks to the cupboard and returns with a bundle of thongs bound into a leather handle which he sets down on the table. It is difficult to tell from its appearance how it will feel but I shall not have to wait long to find out.

'It is known as a martinet, Miss Marlova, and since it is one of the lighter punitive devices your pretty bottom will not be harmed by a taste.' Dr Hobel has moved to the back of me and untying the drawers once more he inserts his hands and cups the cheeks. Then he reaches down into their legs to stroke the backs of my thighs, saying: 'But it is here, on the more sensitive skin, that I plan today's lesson to be written. And for that purpose this delightful garment must come right off.'

I lift my legs one by one to oblige him in its removal after which he has full access to me from waist to knees. By now the suspense is making me shivery and it is a relief when the first swishing blow lands as promised across my buttocks. It seems to take him a while to develop the right swing – I take it that a length of rattan is his forte – but once he does I am stinging as if I have sat on a hornet's nest. However, I soon realise that is nothing when the many tongues cut into the tender flesh that is to be his main concern. Soon I am yelping and jumping at every lash but I force my hands to grip tight to the wood. It would be unthinkable to leap up like a junior receiving her first reddened backside. At last he lays down the implement to run a cool hand all over my flaming parts before sliding his fingers into the wet folds between. Up and down, up and down he strokes until the tight ring that is his objective is as slippery as the rest. What I feel against it now has plainly recovered its vigour and with one slow push sinks in to the hilt.

No doubt because I have milked him once already this is a less hasty affair than his penetration of me on the bench. I can see the member now in my mind's eye as it thrusts in and pulls back like the piston of some well-oiled machine, and the steady rhythm of it has before long brought me to an imminent peak. It must show for a voice asks softly behind me if I am near and I confirm the diagnosis. The good Doctor is attentive to my state and there is no need to press the secret button today.

* * *

Afterwards he rings for food and more wine and we eat a splendid dinner. I am aglow and all awkwardness is gone: he tells stories of his medical practice while I recount some of the silly happenings one comes across in a girls' academy. When I make to leave – for it has grown late – Dr Hobel tells me he has consulted privately with members of the board and he is hopeful that Monday's meeting will put the unfortunate events in the country hotel down to a 'misunderstanding'. I thank him, though his part in the fate of the First Mistress has quite slipped my mind in spite of its being what first started me down the present path. In the car that drives me back I reflect that the next time it will be the cane, but the thought does not deter me. When it comes I shall not be tied down and it will be my chance to show that I can take my punishment as well as any.

Mrs K is waiting for me (she must have heard the engine) and I pass on the news as we walk round to her quarters. Subdued and lined with worry under the bright hallway light, she seems in the bedroom reassured when I show her that my new markings are beginning already to fade.

'Oh, Jana, I had thought to provide for you myself, though I naturally expected that you would have young friends like Greta.' She looks into my face and her whole person seems smaller, somehow diminished. 'But you are content with this liaison and intend to pursue it?' I nod vigorously, having no idea what words might serve the occasion, and it seems to be enough. And so my day reaches its final episode as the First Mistress who used to strike such terror into my heart as a pupil stands quietly for me to undress her and lead her to the bed.

16

Mo-tion Pictures

'The thing is, Marsha, that's where it stops. What you read is *it*. The lot.'

'So what does that mean: she never finished the story or the rest went missing someplace?'

'Well, I'm not certain but I have an idea of the answer.' Judith put down the folder on a table and took out a couple of sheets. She had made her way in from the back in order to catch the bar-manager before she opened up in the morning. 'There are some jottings about what happens next, for instance how Mrs K is allowed to keep her position but under closer monitoring.'

'So no replacement for the delicious little pain-toy, what was her name?'

'Sophie, though I doubt she would have recognised the description. Marsha, I swear you make these terms up.'

'Not so, honey, I just keep my ears open. And my eyes. Or better still –'

'OK, OK.' Judith laughed. 'You can stop listing organs right there and pay attention. Now these notes fizzle out into headings like "Goodbye to the Doctor" and, I quote, "The First Mistress Canes Me For The Last Time". Damn the woman, I would love to know the gory details but that's all there is. And why *last*? Is one or the other leaving, or the place closing down, or what? Anyway, the point is there aren't any notes or headings for the parts that we have in completed form so that suggests they were destroyed once she'd written the full version. No, I reckon something happened to make Great-Auntie Marlova put the project aside and she never took it up again.'

'I'm impressed, Jude. Quite the sleuth. And I would say it gives you all the more reason to go and seek out the principal prop in the whole drama – that nefarious bench. Have you got a location where it all happened?'

'Yeah, I was on the case last night. The school is – was – on the outskirts of a smallish spa town not far from the border, so we get these Czech names while German is the main language. It's called the St Thomas Academy and there's something about it that rings a bell but I can't think why.' She looked at the older woman but Marsha just shrugged.

'Don't mean a thing to me, Jude.'

'Well anyway, I've come up with a sneaky plan for my man Harry at the British Library to set his Euro-contacts digging into education records and stuff. Maybe help sweeten the pill when I tell him I'm back to hardcore dykedom. *After* the last fling this afternoon, of course. What about your girls – are they on their toes for the camera?'

'Well, honey, they're ready but I don't know about *toes* . . .' The wiry lady dodged safely out of reach of physical retribution and Judith gathered up her papers grinning.

'I'll get you one day, Marsha. But now you can let me out the front and let the diehard boozers in. I'm going to check on Grace, and then home to freshen up, as you guys say. So we're back to the parts you keep trying to bring into the conversation. And on that note . . .'

When Judith breezed into the office its occupant was busy with a nailfile. 'Hi, beautiful. How's things? You all set for later?'

'Yes, I suppose.' It was hardly a cheery response and it was matched by the secretary's petulant expression. 'It's all arranged how I'm going to redden the girls' bums and touch them up a bit before Marsha gets going with the heavy stuff.'

'Sounds good. So what's the problem?' She could guess what the answer was going to be but it was better to have it said.

'Well, Judith, if you think I'm going to get off on watching this guy ramming his prick up you till you come –'

'Look, it's a last ritual thing, right? So of course I'm going to enjoy it. But that doesn't mean I'm not –' While the trill of the phone made her jump it was a timely interruption. 'Committed' had been the word on the tip of Judith's tongue but in the aftermath of Petra that would have gone down like a lead balloon. Grace picked up the receiver.

'Nemesis Archive, how can I help you? Oh, *hi there*, Mo. Yeah, the girls are good. Spot on. Uh huh. Yes. Oh, I see. Yeah, *she's* here.' Now the face that looked up was positively sour. 'Mo wants to finalise the details of your little get-together this afternoon.'

'OK, fine. I'll take it in my office.' Judith fled and closed the door after her with a sinking heart. The road to the relationship she had invested with so much yearning was shaping up to be a rocky one. However, gloomy reflection had no chance to take hold in the teeth of the camerawoman's excitement about the imminent shoot.

'Y'see, Jude, we're gonna get some real hardcore close-ups of girls so juiced up they're fucking dripping. I mean, don't get me wrong, I got nothing against guys, specially the one who's doing you, but I get sick of the standard cumshot shit. Know what I'm saying? You got this fantastic babe, gagging for it, then either he can't make fuck all or his cock just don't match up to the size of her mouth. Fucking pathetic!'

'Too right.' Judith was finding it difficult not to smile despite her mood. 'So how's the equipment I'm getting to sample going to perform?'

'Just brill, sister, don't you worry. But I got an idea about it I wanted to check out. See, this fella has a yen for a warmed arse, it makes him get big as fuck. And laying on with a strap would get *you* nice and wet and ready, yeah? Then he'll hold back till you come – you won't be shy about letting go on camera, will you, Jude? – and when he pulls out I'll get some beauty pics of him spraying his stuff all over your fanny. Bucketloads of it, girl, I'm telling you. Bucketloads. You are gonna need hosing down after.'

The warning was followed by the dirtiest laugh Judith had ever heard and after Mo had rung off she felt cheered by the uncomplicated enthusiasm for pornography. The occasion was going to be sexy and *fun*.

When she arrived the basement was in a flurry of semi-naked figures clustered round a gesticulating Mo in a peaked cap jammed on to spiky bleached hair. Judith herself was severely attired in a high-necked white blouse befitting one who was to apply the tawse to a young man's bottom and while the plain dark skirt that went with it was similarly evocative of bygone classrooms, it had been chosen for the practicality of its pleats. These allowed it to be hoisted in a trice to allow full access to the naked (and hairless) genitals beneath at the crucial time. The effect in the mirror had been quite dramatic and on being introduced to her co-performer Judith found herself a-tingle with anticipation.

His name was Theo and he had the kind of nondescript if pleasant features that would have been no aid to a conventional film career. However, the face was not the issue and as Judith took the hand being offered with a formality that seemed slightly odd in view of what was

160

to come, her gaze flicked over the firm torso under a white singlet and the muscled thighs in their white cotton shorts. In between them was a bulge which would have made her think it had been augmented by padding had she not seen the cause of it in action on camera already. Judith became aware of his eyes on hers and flushed, caught out in the act of ogling the stud's crotch, but he flashed her a reassuring wink. Then Mo began to hustle the rest out into the observation room while a young woman in combat trousers made some adjustments to the lighting that was focused on a waist-high cubic structure. Aside from the three-tongued strap that lay on its padded surface, it was to be their sole prop, serving first for Theo to stretch over and next for Judith to lie atop, legs akimbo.

It was a simple matter to check the feasibility of the latter position for an act of copulation that would permit the tight close-ups Mo specialised in, and then they were off. The dimpled cheeks under the taut material made an inviting target and two dozen strokes were delivered with only the swish-crack of the instrument as accompaniment. Then Theo straightened up and keeping his back to camera took his shorts down and off before resuming his place, though with one startling difference. Pressed as his body was to the side of the frame there appeared pointing straight down between the parted legs a shaft like a distended dagger topped with the handle of two protuberant testicles. The sight of it pierced her with lust sharp as a pain and when Judith took up the tawse again it seemed to grow – impossibly – a little more still with each smack of leather on reddening flesh. Then, just as she thought she could wait no longer for the main event, he cried out. It was the agreed signal so she could lean thankfully forward to take the organ in her hand and feel its answering throb.

In one movement she was up on her back, spread, with the slippery head of the monster phallus nosing

161

into her liquefying vulva. Judith had been aware that some men suffered from a problem of premature ejaculation but she had never thought to find herself in an analogous position. Yet there she was, so juiced up as to be on the very point of orgasm after a single thrust. Oh God, if she couldn't slow down it was going to be all over in a flash: the shortest porn clip in the history of the universe. Even to see the lens trained on the action between her legs didn't cool her off in the slightest; instead it served to add an unwanted dash of exhibitionism to the already overspiced heat of her desire.

But then, incredibly, it happened. One moment she was teetering on the edge of explosion, the next she was gone. From somewhere high up she looked down on this curious threesome picked out by the spotlights: the pair coupled at the groin who were making noises and the third with the strange appendage that seemed held invisibly to the link connecting the other two. Time passed and the figures twitched below her with the alien motion of pre-programmed insects while she hung suspended above them. Then there was a sensation in her throat. It started as the merest tickle that grew and grew until it was a tearing rasp and she was plummeting down onto – into – the tableau below. For an instant the shriek was shockingly right in her face then she was the one who was shrieking and flailing as the climax erupted and consumed her in its molten flood.

Bit by bit Judith became aware that the last mini-scene was in progress. Theo had pulled out of her and squinting up she could see the contortions of his face as she felt the hot semen splatter over her belly and thighs. By the time he was done – and Mo was right, it took an *age* – she was more or less her old self after the extraordinary experience.

'Cool stuff, kids,' declared the camerawoman in directorial tones, although she was, Judith estimated, probably no older than herself. 'We'll take ten while I check out what I've got here.' While she bustled off towards the control room, Theo offered his hand to pull Judith to her feet.

'Were you *gone*,' he said and she realised it wasn't a question. 'The eyes, I could see they were all rolled up.'

'Yeah. I don't know where *to* exactly but it was . . . it was . . .'

'Don't try and explain.' He gave her shoulder a gentle squeeze. 'I've been to some funny places with real hot sex. Like that was. Look, Jude, er, can I help you clean up?' There was no doubt it was a proposition and she wasted no time agonising over her answer. She was in Grace's bad books anyway, so what the fuck.

'Yeah. Great. We can use the private bathroom at the front. I'll lead the way.'

Judith kept her eyes firmly ahead and they made the door without any challenge from the group filtering back into the main chamber. In the shower Theo sponged down her sticky crotch then worked his mouth over the smooth lips for a while. When he stood up there was again a full erection and they manoeuvred pressed together until he was right inside. She felt soapy fingers probing into her anus and his tongue was busy circling hers: all openings were plugged and she rocked with him back and fore, heedless of the minutes ticking by. This time there were no detonating fireworks, no bizarre out-of-body state, but a long slow voluptuous crescendo and a climax where she seemed to sense every pulse and quiver of the shaft discharging deep in her vagina.

After they had dressed she took Theo up the stairs and let him out of the main Archive door. He asked if she would care to make a date to cane him sometime but Judith declared that it was not really her thing. However, she would put it to Miss James on her return if he wanted. While she had never known her take an

163

interest in any man, when draped over her punishment
desk the display of a cock and balls might have a certain
novelty value. Privately Judith wondered if the tackle
would keep its end up under a dozen or two of the
boss's scorchers. Well, if there were to be such an
occasion she would just have to get invited to see for
herself.

Back in the basement the filming of the girls was well
underway with the punky ginger one, bare save for the
leather skirt twisted up round her waist, squirming over
Grace's knee. The expression on the secretary's face
coupled with the wince-making *crack!* of clothesbrush
on an already scarlet bottom brought Judith to a halt
and a peremptory jerk of Marsha's head was enough to
send her retreating into the control room. Her knees
went suddenly weak and she sank into the cushioned
desk chair in front of the array of screens. This time it
looked like she'd really gone and done it. Shit. It was
men who were supposed to think with their dicks. But
if she didn't have the delicious ache of a well-fucked
cunt to tell her exactly where it was, she would have to
presume the thing to be located between her ears. Where
the brain should be but patently wasn't. Shit, shit, shit.
Why couldn't she have settled for one ace fuck and left
it at that? Grace hadn't been pleased but there was a
sort of excuse and she would have come round, Judith
was sure, given time. But now . . .

The bout of self-castigation was interrupted by the
appearance of Mo making a face at her.

'Oh boy, oh boy. Have you screwed up, sister. But big
time. I had to call a break though as it is Cindy won't
be sitting comfortably all week. Can't remember when I
saw Gracie so wild.' Judith gulped.

'But, um, isn't it better like this, if she, er, gets it out
of the system?'

'Yeah, right. It's not your arse in the firing line.'

'Oh God, I didn't mean –'

'See, Judith, I know she ain't the easiest lady in the world to get on with, what with all her ups and downs. Well, sure, they can be mostly downs. But make up your fucking mind. If you want her, you gotta work at it. Instead of which you're just pissing her about. But go on, tell me to fuck off and keep my nose out.' Mo perched on the edge of the long table and made another face. 'What the fuck am I saying, anyway? It ain't very clever to mouth off at the one who decides if I get to work down here again.'

'Jesus Christ, Mo, is that what you think of me?' Judith felt sick inside and suddenly close to tears. 'That I can't take criticism without playing dirty. Look, you're absolutely right. I've been a complete shit with all this fucking about. Maybe I'm as neurotic as Grace is – or more. Can't face up to a bit of commitment or something.'

'Hey, just make up your mind what you want, Jude. That's all I'm saying, sister. Nothing wrong with casual fucking, I do it all the fucking time. Whenever I fucking can.' There was a momentary grin, as if at some tasty memory, then the earnest look was back. 'But there's no girlfriend in the picture, no one steady. It just ain't fair to Gracie. I worry about that girl. She's fucked up enough. She don't need no one making her worse. No way.'

Judith held up her hands. 'Right, Mo. You got me there. Bang to rights.' The staccato delivery was catching and she made an effort to be coherent. 'I do want her, I'm *almost* certain. I mean I've been turned on by all sorts in the past year or two but there's something else here. And it's not just how fucking beautiful she is. I could just sit and watch her face for hours when she's concentrating on something. You know the way her eyes –' Judith broke off, catching the full grin that had spread over the camerawoman's face.

'Say no more, Jude, I can see you got it bad. So what you gonna do?'

'Well, I'm working on an idea for a trip, a week or two in Europe. All I need is someone to hold the fort here and then I could take Grace along. What do you think?'

'Sounds great. But you won't get no joy asking her at the minute.'

'No. I realise that, Mo. I need to go to London for a couple of days to get some info, so suppose I went now. Like tomorrow. Give things a chance to cool down?'

'Yeah. But don't go near the girl first. Keep your distance till you get back and leave me to do the talking. Then all *you* gotta do is screw the fucking nut. Right?'

It had been easy to voice the idea of a caretaker to look after the Archive during a jaunt abroad, but the only feasible candidate for the job was Marjory Rowleigh: the woman she had not spoken to since she had bloodied her buttocks less than a week before. Yet another case of judgement being overruled by impulse and even though there had been an apology to Grace, her treatment had been out of control. And now here *she* was, having injured the secretary herself, proposing to ask a favour from the lady she had so savagely marked. It was like some ludicrous Comedy of Errors: Vice-Principal beats Secretary excessively so the Assistant Director beats *her*, only that too is disproportionate. But there was the answer! There it was staring her in the face: the one thing that could cut through this tangle of overreaction and give Marjory's usual good sense a chance to prevail.

'So can I take that as a yes?'

'Well, Judith, I would be delighted to step in and oversee your establishment for a week or two. There is very little to do at the college here so it would be no problem at all. But as to this business of reversing the roles of your last visit to my downstairs room, even if,

166

as you tell me, you have been guilty of selfishly wounding our young friend . . .'

'Marjory, please. Grace seems to have sent both of us into a spin, but I have confidence I'll get what I deserve: no more, no less. And then I can concentrate on making a fresh start with my mind at ease. If not at first the body . . .' In the pause down the line Judith heard the dry chuckle that had been missing from their recent fraught relations. Great. She received and solemnly acknowledged the instruction to appear at 8 p.m. sharp to take her place on the trestle – 'And remember, my dear, you'll need *loose* clothing for afterwards' – then rang off. It was most definitely not going to be fun, but she had the feeling it was going to do her a power of good.

Walking home, she reflected that the common idea of the masochist *enjoying* pain resulted from a confusion between corporal punishment and fetish play. Not that there was anything wrong with the kind of spanking that got you really horny, but serious discipline was quite another matter. It was a love–hate experience in which the cane left its mark in the psyche as much as on the flesh, and one that Judith had come to accept was as necessary to her as breathing. In her flat she made a plain omelette and washed it down with a glass of water, then lay quietly on her bed for an hour. Then she bathed and pulled on a sweatshirt and a baggy pair of cotton jogging pants: underclothing was superfluous to the business ahead. A comfortable pair of trainers was all that was needed to complete the outfit after which she set off to face her just desserts with a lighter heart than she had known for some time.

PART III

17

Temptations

However she tried it the result was much the same. Whether sitting forward, slouching back or leaning into the window, every jolt and lurch of the railway carriage seemed to be communicated directly to the tenderest parts of her behind. The state she was in would have made it an achievement to appear composed on a carefully placed cushion and after ten continuous minutes of unpredictable motion Judith found her self-control beginning to slip. Then came a sustained clatter across uneven points that forced out of her two audible gasps and she saw that she was being regarded from the seat opposite with a raised eyebrow.

'I don't mean to be impertinent, but you look as though you might not last the hour, and unless I'm misreading the situation there is something here that may help.' The speaker was a thirty-something woman in a business suit who proceeded to open her briefcase and pull out a white tube. 'It's a new analgesic preparation: mild but highly penetrating. Just the ticket for one suffering from a touch of – how shall I put it? – disciplinary overindulgence.'

There seemed little point in prevarication for the heat in her face would give the lie to any attempted denial. 'Last night,' said Judith, trying to appear coolly wry. 'Timing rather less than ideal.' She followed her fellow traveller's deliberate scan of the sprinkling of other passengers. All seemed busy with papers or books and the lady leaned towards her conspiratorially.

'I hope you don't think me forward, but it would be better for *me* to apply the lotion because I'll see where you need it most. If we can just find an unoccupied lavatory . . .' She stood up and led the way along the aisle with Judith following in her steps. Favourably inclined from the outset towards one of her own sexual orientation, she took little persuading to fall in with the woman's proposal. Once bolted into the small space there was really only one way the task could be managed, so while the stranger positioned herself on the toilet seat Judith eased down her trousers and briefs and dropped down over the waiting lap.

'My dear young lady,' she said, and there was a tinge of wonder in her tone, 'I guessed that you were no novice despite your lack of years. But the making of *these* marks must have stretched you.' Judith glowed inwardly at the implied praise for her powers of endurance, but tried not to show it.

'Let's just say the restraining straps got quite a workout.' Marjory had taken the job seriously, and the crescendo of anguish that had followed the final, rapid strokes was something Judith thought herself unlikely ever to forget. But the punishment had been sought and dispassionately executed and in its wake she had slept the dreamless sleep of one who has been purged of guilt. 'Ooh, ooh. That is *sore*.'

'I'm sorry. Just bear with me while the medication takes effect. There, now, just hold on for a moment . . . and a moment more . . . Now, how's that?'

'Mmm, oh yes . . . yes . . .'

It was indeed a delicious sensation of warmth and ease as the pain began to ebb from the abused flesh and Judith relaxed into the soothing rhythm of the hands. Such bliss, would it only go on for ever . . . Then she snapped back to full consciousness at the gentle but unmistakable touch of fingers between her legs.

'Oh God. No, please.' The hand withdrew at once and there was an embarrassed cough.

'Excuse me, that *was* impertinence. I'm afraid I thought that you wanted –'

'I did. I mean I would have liked nothing better, but I wasn't thinking.' Judith was on her feet, horrified at the way she had been moving her hips. Mere hours after resolving to put the lid on casual sex, there she was giving a brand-new acquaintance the come-on. 'It's my fault, not yours. You see, I've got a partner, well, she's not a partner yet and may never be in fact if I don't –' Judith broke off and took a deep breath. She could at least try to speak in proper sentences.

'Look, dear girl, we can resume our seats now that your pants are no longer swarming with angry bees. And then you can tell Auntie Bernice all about it if you want. First, though, suppose I go on ahead and leave you to some discreet hand manipulation? Has a very calming effect, I find, and will dull the prickings of desire for a while. Keep the thoughts on the lust-object and you may even reap the benefit of feeling virtuously faithful.'

It was good advice and when Judith returned to the carriage she was in a mood to plunge into conversation with her new companion. Once she had unburdened herself of her recent misjudgements to the sympathetic ear – 'I used to get into such scrapes at your age, Judith' – it was revealed that Bernice, among other things, was involved in a website devoted to depicting women chastising men.

'I'm afraid I have always been unashamedly *bi*, Judith, and your stud sounds as though he has serious potential. Do get him to email me, dear.' She sat back with a smile. 'I can remember one of our models that we played with all night without allowing him any relief, poor boy, until I softened after he'd been thoroughly tickled with the cat. By that time the thing was – and I do not lie – the size of a *truncheon*. So when I gave it just the tiniest squeeze he hit me straight in the eye before proceeding to splatter much of the camera and coat the whole of its lens. Difficult stuff to get off, dear, and I was *not* popular. But then just minutes later he gave me the most thorough rogering in the dressing room. A *real* professional.'

The lady was a fund of stories of male emissions gone awry and Judith was less than happy when the train pulled into St Pancras and it was time to say their farewells. With a head full of images of pulsing members, it was now her duty to forswear the one that had been on offer at intervals for the past year. And the keeper of the said organ – Harold Jameson, also keeper of the Catalogue of Rare Books at the British Library – was not going to be overjoyed by the news.

'I don't suppose I'm going to be given the chance to spank this nonsense out of you, am I?' The bear of a man with his grizzled beard looked up at her from his outsized swivel chair.

'Under normal circumstances, Harry, you could have *tried*, but today . . . I suppose you'd better take a look at the damage yourself.' She tried out a grin in the hope that the frown was mostly an act and rolled down her trousers. He sat up patting his lap and for the second time that morning Judith was over a pair of knees displaying her bruises.

'Hmm. I would guess that I'm not looking at the results of a little love-play here.' The touch of the big hand was surprisingly delicate when it wasn't slapping her. 'It must have been bad whatever you did to deserve this.'

'Very.'

'Then you've only got yourself to blame, eh? However, I do have something that might ease the present condition somewhat. Arnold swears by it.' Harry was referring to the young trainee often subjected to a taste of one of the canes that sprouted from a stand in the corner, so his approval presumably carried weight.

'OK.' Judith settled into position hearing the drawer being opened beside her and a lid being unscrewed. After the severities of the Vice-Principal's basement she was surely entitled to a second application of aftercare. Especially when she had kept on the string briefs to cover those places to which Harry's entry was now proscribed. The trouble was – and she really should have seen it coming – that after several minutes of careful tending, the hidden-away crotch was becoming decidedly moist. After some moments of hesitation, Judith pulled herself upright and then they were both standing, her hand on his zip. There couldn't be any harm, could there, in just taking hold of him between her thighs? No penetration, of course, just a little play between friends.

The penis was hot in her grip and she felt its end as wet as she was, aching to impale herself on it. But then she took a proper look at the thing in her hand. It was hard and quite thick, standing out from the mass of dark hairs at its base. However, set against Theo's – for which she had paid dear and would no doubt be paying yet – this one was really nothing to write home about. Or rather to have fuck you *without* the folk at home being notified. It just wasn't worth the potential angst for such an unremarkable specimen. She pulled away and released it, uncomfortably aware that being faithful had had nothing to do with her decision.

'I'm sorry, Harry.' The best she could manage was to stare fixedly at his chest. 'You'll have to get Arnold in.' Of course that should be 'get into Arnold'. Judith hoisted her trousers clumsily and fighting an impulse to giggle backed round the corner of the L-shaped room and ducked into the lavatory. Once the door was safely locked she breathed a huge sigh of relief and let her briefs join the trousers on the tiled floor. A repeat dose of the Bernice prescription was clearly called for and she sat on the toilet seat, legs spread. Now, if she could just summon up and hold that image of a bright-eyed Grace swinging the wooden paddle through the air . . .

When she emerged Harry was at his desk staring at a list of titles on his monitor screen. The office was part of an annexe to the new library complex that housed an extensive collection of pornographic materials inherited from the British Museum and its existence was barely acknowledged, let alone advertised. Permission to examine these had been – reluctantly – granted to Judith as a result of what amounted to blackmail by her boss, the redoubtable Miss James. But no licence granted access to the building occupied by the cataloguer and his boy and Judith knew she was there by his tolerance alone. It was an arrangement that she depended upon in her work and once the minor attack of hysteria had passed she decided on a peace offering. Her bag offered up a pair of hotpants she judged to be just the thing, since they would encase the loins while leaving plenty of scope for a little punitive action. So, thus equipped, she crossed to the wall-cupboard and selected a rather junior-looking tawse: the target area to be presented was, after all, very sensitive. Then she laid the article down on the desk and assumed what she hoped was an appropriately ingratiating tone.

'You know I need your help, Harry. But I'd be up for some, er, business before business, if the idea appeals.' He turned towards her and she could see him weighing up the options. 'Business' had been a code word for their brand of s/m sex and she was making a move to change its meaning. Spanking was still on the menu but there were to be no afters. Marsha had insisted that if the librarian were the decent guy Judith said he was, then he would accept their more circumscribed liaison with good grace. He would know, she'd gone on, how lucky he had been to have enjoyed the availability of a girl like herself for as long as he had. It had sounded plausible at the time but now the moment of truth had arrived she was not so sure.

'Not quite business as usual, then?' She couldn't read the expression but made an effort to hold his gaze.

'No. But still business.'

'Right. I suppose an old man has to make do with the crumbs he's thrown by the young woman of his dreams –' he put out a hand into the waistband of her shorts and pulled her towards him '– but do we have to have these things wrapped round you like a bloody chastity belt?'

'I just thought –'

'You thought you couldn't trust me, that's what. And that piece of disrespect is going to cost you.' This was more like the customary patter and Judith allowed herself a protest.

'That's not fair. It was myself I didn't trust.'

'Dear, dear. Answering back now. The extras are fair piling up.' While Judith was usually happy to play along with the role of chastising patriarch, this time she was going to have to watch her tongue or end up well sore. So she stood tight-lipped while he undid the buttons and as the pants came down was gratified to hear an intake of breath when he exposed the denuded mound and the bare lips below.

'Well, I don't know. For a girl who is no longer putting it about – or so she tells me – that is one hell of a blatant display. Nature provides a degree of modesty but the modern miss, sorry *ms*, has to strip it all away. However, it does give me an idea.' There was an unfamiliar acerbity in the fogeyish remarks that made her keep to herself the observation that *she* had opted to be covered up. The brazen visibility was all Harry's doing.

'This is going to make the boy's day. He's due for a dose of course, but first I want you on your back, legs up. That way he'll get a prime view while injecting a modicum of humiliation into the proceedings.' Harry rubbed his hands together, beaming. 'A small price, don't you agree, considering all that I'm doing for you?'

Judith grimaced. The pound of flesh she was prepared for, having offered him the strap first, but did he have to take such relish in it? And now it was coming to the point, the thought of that piece of leather biting into her flesh was anything but appealing. But she would just have to grin and bear it. And when it was over the man in Prague should have turned something up on Mrs K's Academy and its feared disciplinary apparatus. Jesus, after all this it had better be good.

'Arnold, in here, please, at once.' The librarian was at the door, holding it open and when his assistant made an entrance Judith saw him glance quickly at her naked crotch then avert his eyes. Harry gave a fruity chuckle.

'There's a sight for you, lad, that I'll wager you've not seen outside the pages of one of those magazines. Now, have you forgotten your manners?'

'Sorry, er, good afternoon, Ms Wilson.' Lean and dark, he looked more appealing than she had remembered. Judith perked up a little. There was surely no need to fret about displaying her sexual parts to this young man.

'Hi, Arnold. How are you?'

'Oh, fine, thank you.'

'We'll see how fine you are after a dozen of the best, my boy. But first it's the lady's turn. If you please, Judith . . .' He indicated the table against the wall. She climbed obediently onto its surface, sticking her legs in the air, and Arnold was instructed to pull them back towards her head. It was a peculiarly defenceless position and Judith bit her lip and waited. The first six smacks of the leather she suffered in silence even though the sting was worse than she had feared. But then the interrogation began and it seemed that once opened for answers the mouth was obliged also to register her pain.

'So who is she?'

'Who? Ow.'

'The one you've fallen for?'

'Ow. Oww.'

'I'm waiting . . .'

'Ow.'

'I want to know who's pushed me out."

'Oww. The name's Grace. Ow.'

'Sounds rather old-fashioned.'

'Ow. Well, *she*'s not. Ow, ow.'

'And *who* is she, pray?'

'Ow. Our secretary. Ow, ow, ow!'

Three sharp strokes had her writhing. Oh God, was he drawing this out.

'The Assistant Director –'

'Oww.'

'– of the Nemesis Archive –'

'Oww.'

'– going with a *secretary*?'

'Oww! Yes, why not? Oww!'

'She must have a really hot arse.'

'Oww! None of your fucking business. Oww, oww, ow-ow-owww!'

'Those were for the language. Six more then we're done, right? Hold her still now, lad.'

'Go on.' It came out through clenched teeth, as Judith felt the grip tighten round her calves. Harry hit hard and fast, and when released she was left rolling about clutching at the blazing sting of her ill-treated thighs.

'Come along, girl, you can spare us the theatricals.' He took a cane from the stand and stood looking at them both with something approaching a smirk on his face. Judith was rapidly deciding that when he didn't get his way with her, Harry was not quite the paragon she had once fondly imagined.

'Let's be having you then. Judith, as you were before; Arnold drop those trousers and pants and get in position between. That's it, boy. You've got the idea. Splendid.' All at once the plan became horribly clear. Arnold was in front of her holding her legs to his chest and between them his erection extended along her pubic mound. She could even feel the balls against the lips of her vulva.

'Damn you, Harry,' she muttered with a surge of irritation.

'All part of the payment plan to give the boy a little pleasure in the midst of his pain. Don't worry, Judith, he's well trained. *He* isn't going to make a move.' The implication was as subtle as a slap in the face: while Arnold was capable of restraint, *she* was not. Maybe it was true, maybe not. But how *dare* he? Anger welled up and Judith knew what she was going to do. In this situation considerations about Grace would have to take a back seat.

'Bend over more, lad. Let's see that backside properly presented.' As Arnold leaned towards her Judith put her hands on his and freed her legs. His half-closed eyes popped open and she grinned at him, then eased back a little before thrusting her pelvis up. Primed as she was from the strap, he was inside in a trice and she flung her legs round him in a scissor grip, pulling him hard down.

'There you are, Harry, how about that? I've got him nice and tight for you. *And* I've made sure he'll get that pleasure you were talking about.'

'Hmm, I suppose. But they'll be twelve good ones, lad, and you can count them out for me.' He sounded decidedly miffed and Judith guessed that Arnold's behind was going to suffer as a result of her impulsive action. Well, she would just have to keep his cock well stimulated meantime.

'Yes, Mr Jameson.' The face above hers was tense and she blew it a little kiss as the length of rattan sliced down with a zip-crack!

'Uh. One, Mr Jameson.'

Zip-crack!

'Uh. Two, Mr Jameson.' It was a well-practised ritual between them that Judith had witnessed before, though this time her presence had thrown it somewhat out of kilter. But Arnold would survive: as the punishment proceeded it became evident he was tough enough to keep his erection despite the efforts of his displeased boss. And its rigidity provided the means whereby every jerk of the boy's hips was conveyed into her throbbing centre. It was a novel way of participating in a caning that she must recommend to others.

When the last stripe had been inflicted things moved – as Judith was hoping – swiftly to a conclusion. With an obvious intention Harry came up close at the boy's back and she felt him stiffen. Then the older man was in him thrusting hard and it was as though two bodies speared her as one. All the pent-up frustration and tension seemed to gather itself up and then her voice was sounding among the others as the moment of shuddering sweetness coursed through her.

18

Sex-ercises

'If she's the real thing, isn't it worth sacrificing some of your freedom? Look at me – I played about one time too many and lost mine. And not a day goes by I don't regret it.'

'Charlie, for fuck's sake spare us the sob story. If you'd copped off with the wee blonde sensation last night it would be a different story. So stop talking shite, will ya?'

'That's simply not true, Izzy, and you know it. You're just in a mood because she wouldn't even give *you* a dance.'

'Bollocks! She was no' my fucking type anyway.'

'Children, children. Save the slanging match for the street, or you'll have us all out there.' Scowling, the spiky carrot-top with the prominent lip-ring did as she was told and the Saturday lunchtime drinkers at the neighbouring tables turned back to their desultory conversations. Released for a few hours from managing The Phoenix, Marsha was holding court nearby in a basement bar with the recent stars of Mo's mini-movie. It was not uncommon in term for there to be rowdy interchanges with university feminists who disapproved of what they saw as her perverse influence on the impressionable young women of the town. But in the holidays, the mainly tourist clientele was less inured than the students to raised voices and strong language.

Knowing that Charlotte was still fixated on her split with Cassandra and oblivious to Isobel's patent doting on *her*, Judith was hardly surprised to find that her own inept courtship of Grace was a source of disagreement. 'Haven't you two ever wondered what you'd do without the other to quarrel with?'

'Och, she's such a pain in the jacksie with that poncy accent and those prissy ideas –'

'And *she*'s just so rude and vulgar –'

'Enough, girls, enough. Judith's quite right. Whaddya say I book us all in to the gym so you guys can get into the boxing ring. And afterwards you can kiss and make up, and kiss some more, and then get down to what you both really want to do. If you would only admit it.' Ignoring the bemused looks that greeted her proposal, the grey-cropped American surveyed her young protégées with a speculative eye. 'The point *is*, honeys, our friend here from the Archive is having trouble making up her mind: casual encounters at will, or denying them in the interests of a deep and meaningful relationship? A topic that touches all of us, so let's have some thoughts on the matter. The English rose plumps for true love but the tough Scot prefers to play the field. What I wanna know is how we tell when we've got something that's worth pursuing?' The question was bizarrely like something out of a seminar back in Judith's first – and last – year at the university, but it had the effect of producing at least a temporary cease-fire.

'Well, the way she lammed into my arse when she kent Jude had been for seconds – fucking murder it was. OK, I'm no beefing about it now, I got some great stills to tout round the mags. What I'm getting at is there's strong feelings there, no question.'

'Izzy's right – for once in her life – so if Judith feels the same, what's the problem? She should go for it.'

'Aye, Charlie, but we're no' just talking about being stuck on a bird. Like the way you're sitting there right now and it's twisting my guts. Um, well, I mean . . .' The sentence died and the speaker glugged at her bottle of lager with frowning concentration.

'Izzy, I didn't know. You never let on . . .' It was hard to say whether the apple-cheeks under the pretty ringlets or the freckled face topped with ginger hair were the redder. Marsha chuckled and Judith dropped her own particular concern into the embarrassed silence.

'But I've got another question. Let's say our heroine is keen to give commitment a try but she's run out of grovelling apologies for her promiscuous behaviour? How does she get another chance?' Charlie sat up, suddenly focused.

'Well, I remember something Mrs Rowleigh arranged when I'd done that with Cassie, I mean before I did it again –'

'And again, and again, and –'

'Shut *up*, Izzy. Basically it was an erotic massage: we had to do her without touching each other and she would do each of us. But singly with the other one watching, and there was a total ban on talking. It just made us both so randy that after a couple of sessions we just screwed like crazy and all was forgiven.'

'Hey, girl, that's not bad. I don't suppose Marjory would turn down the idea either. Do you reckon, Jude?'

'So we could get together without me getting slagged off.' Judith laughed. 'Now *that* sounds promising.'

'Yeah.' Charlie smiled at the reception of her idea then turned quickly and hissed at her companion. 'Izzy, did you really just say what I thought you said?'

'You heard.'

'But why didn't you tell me? I thought –'

'You thought I can't stand you. Well, there's times I could kick your arse, but that's only because –'

'Right, girls, allow me my two bits' worth,' Marsha interrupted firmly. 'You have things to talk about and Judith and I could well be left to discuss how we might

184

follow through your suggestion.' She reached down and came up with a large brown envelope. 'Here's a whole bunch more pics of Wednesday's session that came today. Why don't you take them and have a look? If you let yourselves into the room at the back of The Phoenix, no one will bother you for a few hours and you can have a heart-to-heart. Or whatever. OK?'

'I just love nudging the kids along the course of true lust. Though with those two I guess we can expect a few bumps. But you haven't told me yet, honey. How did the news go down with our national keeper of porn?'

'Rare Books, *if* you please. And not exactly as hoped.' Judith made a face. 'He played dirty but I managed to trump him, though at the cost of taking the boy instead.'

'You mean –'

'Yeah, into that place supposedly now dedicated to Grace. Do you think if I got a chastity belt made and gave her the only key –'

'Jude, this does not bode well for your monogamous future. I could kinda see a *last* last fling with the man himself who is doing you a service, but his assistant . . .'

'Well, that's the worst of it, Marsha. He hasn't come through with the goods yet. All I've got is that the school closed its doors in nineteen-twenty-eight, but where exactly it was and whether the buildings are still in use his source couldn't tell him. For all we know it's an ancient heap of rubble with the bench buried underneath.'

'You think he's lost enthusiasm for the post of Assistant Director's dogsbody now her fanny's not in the deal?'

Judith stuck out her tongue. 'To be fair, it is only a couple of days. I should give the man a chance. Thing is, I – or *we*, if Grace ever speaks to me again – can't go haring off without confirmation that the one-time object

185

of Bohemian schoolgirl nightmares is still around. To say nothing of being up for offers.'

'Well, so long as the bench is stashed somewhere there, it's unlikely to be in use. Come to the push, you could always go on spec. The new lovebirds can take a holiday wandering through the picturesque scenery of Middle Europe.'

'Marsha, I've heard of jumping the gun, but this one isn't even loaded yet.'

'OK, OK. First things first.' The bartender swallowed the rest of her beer and leaned forward. 'Let's resist the temptation to have another. You can go check your emails for news of foreign parts, while I have a cosy little chat with a certain Vice Principal to see if she will once again live up to her designation. I'll speak to you later and meanwhile, girl, keep a grip.' Marsha wagged an admonitory finger. *'Don't* approach Grace – she won't be in today, will she? – and when you do see her don't even *think* about owning up to your doings in the capital city.'

By Monday morning there was still no news from Harry but a message had come through from Marjory's home computer. Not only was the lady amenable to the idea, she had gone one better than Charlotte's homegrown affair to make an arrangement with a new local establishment that specialised in the combination of sexual stimulation with physical workout. Since the prices charged put the place beyond the reach of a sleazy 'massage parlour' trade, local opposition to its opening had been less than expected and Judith was aware that Marjory had helped by throwing her weight behind the planning application. The Business College was in the process of becoming a rather select conference venue for which such a discreet upmarket facility (she had claimed) could be an added attraction for the stressed-out executive. The note said that a session had been offered to her (no doubt in return for the support) that would run from noon that day until noon the next during which certain conditions were to obtain. Physical communication was to be minimised between the two young women: talking, touching and even eye-contact were forbidden. Vigorous exercise interspersed with bodily manipulation of each while the other watched would be repeated to raise erotic tension to a high level and maintain it there. The final condition was that the whole operation would require herself and Grace to remain overnight in restraints that would rule out the possibility of self-induced release.

Judith smiled a little grimly to herself. While the prospect of a free visit to the expensive salon was enticing, it all seemed a little intimidating set out cut and dried on the screen. Knowing only too well her proclivity to be led by the state of her cunt it was going to be a testing twenty-four hours. And then what if it didn't work? Supposing that after all the rigours of prolonged frustration Grace still presented the cold shoulder? But what option was there other than to give it a try: none that she could see. Anything that might kickstart the relationship again – and preferably boot it up to a new level – had to be given a chance. Peering at the clock Judith realised with a start it was nearly eleven. No sooner than she had reached home, showered and changed she would have to come straight back. It was time to get moving.

When she arrived a little flushed at the shopfront tucked away down a short cobbled close it was five minutes before twelve and she found a figure already in occupation of a small ante-room. Clad in a sweatshirt and jogging trousers similar to her own, Grace sat with her head turned studiously away from the newcomer. Judith supposed it was a good sign that the girl was actually there, but her feelings about the whole thing fell rather short of what could truthfully be called optimistic. There was no sign of the organiser of the event so she squatted awkwardly on the remaining chair until the inner door was opened by a dark-haired woman with high cheekbones wearing a white leotard and white leather ankle-boots.

'You are Judith and Grace, yes? Then please come through. My name is Kim and this is my sister and associate Nancy.' The companion was of almost identical appearance though dressed in a contrasting black. 'We shall be in charge of you both for the next twenty-four hours. Now, I understand that you have been acquainted with the rules –' Kim looked at each in turn to receive assent '– so I'll just say that Nancy and I will keep our speech to the minimum necessary. So no chat and no questions, OK?'

There was a brief smile and Judith nodded, taking care *not* to look over for Grace's reaction. Suddenly she was impatient to get started.

'Right. First we prepare the ground with a few simple exercises for which you will be separated. What comes next you will find out when it comes. That is enough talk: let's go do it!'

In a room off the main pine-panelled area Judith removed her clothes, willing herself to appear nonchalant about her nakedness. There was no special equipment in it and none had been necessary to bring her panting and sweating to the massage table. For one whose days were spent mostly at a desk, a concentrated burst of press-ups, squat bends and running on the spot, in tandem with her shamingly unruffled instructor, was enough to have little-used muscles screaming for respite. She leaned obediently forward over the padded edge and felt a finger trace one of the fading lines left by Marjory's cane.

'I see you are into discipline, Judith.' Nancy kept her voice low. It seemed she intended it to be unheard beyond their small space. 'With buttocks like these you must be much in demand. It is plain they would permit the most rigorous treatment.' Hands lifted and separated the cheeks, squeezing hard, and Judith's loins responded at once. The speaker sighed and released her grip. 'If I had my way with you for just one evening you would be left unable ever to forget. But I should not be saying this. We have a job to do. Come, up on the table.'

The fingers on her neck and shoulders were far from gentle and their manipulations were followed by chopping and pummelling that took her breath away. But she was glad to be distracted from contemplating the degree and duration of corporal correction that would be to Nancy's taste. Without doubt it would take her to the limits of endurance and well beyond. The idea was to the mind unthinkable but the body's fierce excitement at the mention of it told a different story. Judith suspected – indeed feared – that one day the recurring thought would get made into reality. And then perhaps the obsession would lose its grip. She had been ritually thrashed once with a penal cane and after two years the memory still caused her on occasion to wake in a sweat. But that had been an impromptu affair. God help her if she ever entered by design into a black hole of expert and systematic flagellation.

It was a gruelling afternoon of hard exercise and harder massage that left Judith sagging against the wall of the shower until the reviving heat of the water did its work. A brisk towelling completed the restoration and she followed her trainer into the main area where Grace lay over the apex of a triangular punishment horse with her wrists and ankles secured to its legs. Her position provided a stimulating exhibition of private parts but Judith saw with a sinking heart that *they* showed no sign of stimulation themselves. In contrast to the copious flow of her own juices under Nancy's hands, Grace's distinctive vulva was set in a dry disapproving line that gave no hint of the engorged glories Judith had once explored.

There was a murmured conference in the corner of the room after which Kim released the occupant of the horse and signalled Judith to take her place. The fastening of the ties that held her so lewdly open was enough to make her lubricate afresh and her heart sank. She was already uncomfortably aroused and the direct genital stimulation was yet to start. And Grace – damn her! – was refusing to play ball with a level of restraint that was making Judith feel ashamed. But then it occurred to her that perhaps it was not so much a refusal as an inability to let go. It was the other side of her craving for punishment once started to continue: in both cases an issue of control. Hmm. She would have to hold on to a thought which located the problem in the secretary's pathology rather than her own inveterate sluttiness. It might see her through what promised to be a long night.

In the event, it was not enough. At three o'clock in the morning, a decidedly overwrought Judith twisted in her bonds and hissed at the figure fastened to the opposite side of the huge divan.

'I have to tell you. I didn't fuck him in London, I fucked his boy, the assistant.' There was a silence the length of which almost gave her hope that Grace was asleep and the utterance would become something she had never actually said. But then there came an angry snarl.

'I hate you Judith. I *hate* you.' And after that the silence lasted until her hypertension succumbed eventually to sleep.

Returning consciousness brought the realisation of what she had done and Judith tried to sink back into the confused remnants of a dream. But the sound of a voice pulled her eyes open and she saw the two sisters at the foot of the bed.

'You were monitored during the night according to our instructions. I had expected the tape to confirm your compliance to the rules but instead I find a serious breach.' Kim's tone was stiff with displeasure and Nancy was flexing a slender black wand with a gleam in her eye. 'I will free you both when you have consented to correction at our hands. Otherwise I must fetch Mrs Rowleigh to take charge.'

'No, no,' said Judith quickly, 'I agree.' It was unthinkable that Marjory should be brought in to deal with her lapse.

'Good. And Grace?'

'I suppose. Well, yes. Yes.'

After they had been untied, Kim ordered Grace to take up position over her knee. Since she had not instigated the forbidden interchange a spanking would be sufficient redress. Judith made a face. It didn't take a brilliant mind to work out who was going to get the benefit of Nancy's evil-looking instrument. She looked on as the arm rose and fell, bringing the taut hand again and again into vigorous contact with the bare hindquarters.

'Ow. Ow. Ow-ow-ow!'

It should have been a joy to watch the bouncing arse of her heart's desire but the experience was marred by anxiety. The girl was being unexpectedly vocal in response to every slap and as the head jerked tears were clearly visible. Suppose instead of letting the punishment come straightforwardly to a close she broke down and demanded more. However, the worry was groundless. Released from the chastiser's grip Grace shot up and rubbed furiously at the red-blotched cheeks for several seconds. Then she stood quietly and waited. Judith shivered: now it was her turn and she guessed that her pain was not going to be so easily allayed.

Nancy pointed to the massage table with a smirk of anticipation.

'Judith, across that, please, face down, keeping your feet on the ground. Kim will hold your legs in place. Grace, climb up and sit astride your friend's back. That's right, facing me.' She beamed and whipped the elastic rod twice through the air with unconcealed relish. 'It is only a light thing but a dozen cuts across the thighs should produce a reaction.'

Ashamed as she was of her outburst in the night, the idea of atoning for it was in itself almost welcome. However, the actuality was something else for, as was already plain, Nancy possessed a talent for nicely judged cruelty. It took a mere three strokes to make her writhe and shriek with the intolerable smart of the tender flesh just below the crease of the buttocks. But then, pushing up under the straddling weight that pinned her down Judith became aware of something that gave her the determination to endure the rest of her punishment with a little more dignity. Between the pressing heat of the twin spanked globes was the unmistakable imprint of a very wet cunt.

19

Flesh

The first spray of cool water falling on the thin lines of fire took Judith's breath away and she froze in a moment of exquisite collision between pleasure and pain. Then she turned up the temperature and washed between her legs with scrupulous avoidance of anything resembling masturbation. In her head there was only one thought: Grace had been turned on! Whether by her own hot bottom or Judith's stripes or even the physical contact from riding her back didn't matter.

When she emerged from the shower naked – a condition that was getting to seem quite natural – she found the similarly unclothed secretary already installed at breakfast in a small alcove. Judith squeezed in next to her and lowered herself with care on to the wooden bench. There was no reason to give a hovering Nancy the satisfaction of a display of wincing. She poured out a large cup of coffee from the steaming jug then helped herself to muesli and strawberries which she doused in cream. A quick peek at her partner showed the girl eating with apparent concentration but there was the hint of a smile and a flicker of the eyes as if she might like to return the glance. And then she felt the definite if transient pressure of a bare thigh against hers. So far so good. Judith took a spoonful from her bowl and chewed on the nutty mixture. It tasted delicious and made her suddenly aware how hungry she actually was. There was an expanse of literally insatiable desire to negotiate before noon arrived and its level was in danger of a premature boost from the pinkly erect nipples on the edge of her vision. She put down her head and focused on the food. It was time to stoke up before things got tough.

For a while after Grace had been 'horsed' and two pairs of hands commenced to pet and caress the oiled flesh Judith thought she had perhaps been over-apprehensive. Though required to watch, she was not restrained in any way and when the genitals began visibly to respond she rather enjoyed the frisson. It was akin to the vicarious pleasure of skilful pornography, and since not involved in stimulating the body herself she was able to attend to every detail of the vulva that was flowering into the dramatic crimson of its glistening whorls and crevices. And, unlike the voyeur condemned to be merely such, there seemed a good chance she could land in the thick of it for *real*. In the fullness of time, of course. But it was when the moaning started up that the folly of facile optimism became clear. It was a low, throaty sound and already there was an edge of desperation in it that hit her straight between the legs. She could have Grace all right – they could have each other – in the end. Later. *Hours* later.

The realisation was bad enough but when Judith's time came it brought a change for the worse. While its prior occupant was put through a brief and vigorous workout she was secured to the horse and found her belly pressing into the moist heat that had been left behind. She rubbed against the sweaty traces as lasciviously as the bonds allowed and was rewarded by a finger that jabbed straight into her engorged clitoris.

'Oh no. No! Please, I can't bear it.'

'Then behave yourself. The only stimulation will be

what we provide –' Nancy gave a malicious chuckle '– and *that* isn't going to let you come.'

Judith clamped shut her mouth and bowed her head. Damn the woman. It was indecent to take such pleasure in her agonies of frustration. She was just going to have to deny her tormentor further opportunities to gloat. It was called self-control and now was her chance to show what she was made of. OK, it wasn't exactly what she was noted for, but with a bit of *real* effort, surely . . .

Heroically, she managed to remain tight-lipped through what seemed an eternity of bottom stroking and squeezing that communicated directly to her deliquescent centre. When at last it stopped, the substitution of the muscle-wrenching exertion of press-ups as Grace took her place was almost a relief. She even lasted through a second bout of guttural moans by giving rein to her irritation in an internal rant that helped block the sympathetic response of her vagina. Fuck it girl, have you no shame? What an exhibition! If you could see yourself now . . .

Too soon, however, it was her turn again and after wrists and ankles had been tied she braced herself for the touch to her brimming cunt. But instead she felt a pull on the left buttock followed by a flurry of smacks into the exposed cleft. Then the right was moved and there was the same repeated impact of something like a soft leather paddle. *And it was suddenly quite intolerable.* When Harry spanked her he finished with a harder version of what was happening now, with the aim of bringing her to a climax. But this, *this* . . . This was intended purely to tease, to increase lust to a pitch that simply could not be borne. And it broke her. The first sob tore out of her throat with the force of a disgorged object and then she was bawling with all the angry petulance of a frustrated infant. Her whole being screamed with longing. There was nothing in the world save this one unbearable, incessant aching ITCH. And it had to stop or, or –

Then a voice said: 'That's it. We're done. You will be cuffed in the shower while I wash you. Just to make sure, you understand.' Judith leaned weakly against her while Nancy soaped her behind. 'I put a card in your pocket. Mail me if you ever decide to submit to some serious discipline.' She curled a hand round the side of Judith's neck and looked her full in the face. 'I think deep down you know it's what you need.'

Outside Grace was waiting and Kim handed them the clothes they had arrived in. 'One last thing. You are to jog round to Marjory's house, but separately. You go by Market Street, Judith, and Grace by the Close. There you will find instructions.'

The note was short and to the point: *The guestroom at the end of the landing is yours. I'll return tonight. M.* Judith's had been the longer route and she climbed the stairs, heart thumping as much from nervous anticipation as from the run. Grace was standing framed in the window and the bright sunlight made it impossible to discern her expression. It was no time to be faint-hearted and Judith forced herself to step forward until she was standing face to face with the cause of so much turbulent longing. Now she could see there were beads of sweat on the forehead, and a drop that hung from the left nostril. With the tip of her tongue she licked it up, tasting its salt, and kissed the eyes one by one, feeling the tickle of the lashes on her lower lip. They flicked back open at once and Judith stared into their depths as the unblinking gaze stared back. Then slowly, very slowly, she tilted her head and pushed it forward until the two pairs of lips met. It started as a small tingle at the back of her neck that travelled, growing, down the spine until it was an electric current in her loins that made her gasp with the shock of it.

'Oh God, Jude, I'm going to – oh – oh –'

'So am I. Gracie, stay, just stay – oh – oh –'

Her fingers dug into the shoulders and hands clawed at

her back. Then they were locked in an impossible intensification of feeling until at last the storm broke and honey raged up inside.

It became an afternoon like no other she had ever spent. Once the sluice-gate had been opened the pressure of pent-up desire demanded full release. Driven into ever more intricate and intimate entanglements, the bodies' tangy sweat was soon spiked with orgasmic secretions and lust begot more lust. A still point at the centre of it all found the lovers on the bed, eyes locked, mutually impaled on the opposing heads of a double dildo. Every nerve ending was as raw as if it had been flayed of its protective skin and Judith lay not daring to move across from the trembling frame of her partner. Then with a wild howl Grace drove her hips forward along the shaft that connected them and they were off again, bucking and thrusting with furious hunger. In the end, she fell back panting and arms folded her head into the softness of breasts while the pumping heartbeat slowly subsided. Reserves of energy commandeered by passion were used up and try as she might to hold them off, encroaching clouds of black weariness rolled in and enveloped her.

She came to herself out of a fog that contained a distant voice. As her surroundings clicked back into focus she saw Grace propped on an elbow looking down at her. Except that she wasn't. In an image that was the stuff of nightmare the luminous blue eyes oddly tinged with amber were open but blank and the face was a flawless empty mask. Judith struggled up with a lurch of panic then the voice called again from outside the bedroom door.

'Did you hear me? I said I've run a bath, then it will be time for supper. Keep your strength up, you know. Come down when you're ready.'

'Yeah. Thanks, Marjory, will do.' Now the features were formed into a broad grin and the spell was broken.

Grace leaped out of bed with a giggle and made for the door. 'Last one in gets a smacked bum. OK?'

Once they had patted each other dry Judith dropped her towel and began to plant kisses from the cleft of the perfect arse all the way up the wriggling spine. When she reached the back of the neck she cupped her hands round taut-nippled breasts and pulled the body in to her own.

'I was going to mention this a while back, but then we weren't speaking. You know that manuscript I've been editing – Jana's story?' She spoke into the pink-lobed ear and the head half-turned so that she could see close up the curl of the lashes.

'You want to track down the bench, is that it? Ugh. Sounds a horrible thing.' From what Judith could see of the one eye it was fixed on the space ahead.

'I wanted *us* to go and find it, yeah? And maybe there would be some old records or something. Take time out and drive down there.' Now the head swivelled and Judith was being regarded from the corner of the eye. Soft buttock flesh rubbed into her crotch.

'Sounds good. And who's going to do my job while we're gone?'

'I thought Marjory – and mine too. There's not much on for a week or two.'

'OK. So where is this place exactly?'

'Well, I'm waiting to hear.' Judith returned the pressure with her thighs and ran a hand over the firm round of the belly. 'I could go and check my emails on the PC downstairs.'

'So you could.' Grace freed herself from the grip and reached curling fingers down into Judith's wet cunt. '*And* we've got to eat. But first things first, lover . . .'

From B L Rare Books Department
To Assistant Director, Nemesis Archive
Subject St Thomas Academy

Jude:

(a) At last here's the gen. What you're after is now part of a complex located outside the old spa town (see map attached). The closest I've come to what happens there is the phrase 'corrective experiment' but I get the idea your building is used only as a kind of adjunct. So perhaps there is a chance of finding the original furnishings stored within. Contact details to follow shortly – then it's in your hands. (By the way, I'm told the locals call it the Thomas-Halle after the school.)

(b) Getting the above was like extracting teeth. There's something hush-hush/disreputable going on here. If you go watch your back(s).

(c) The boy has what he calls a *gaypal* (you tell *me*) in the area and he's due time off. So if he could be useful, e.g. as with advice in (b), let me know. I *don't* mean as (regrettably) before since I assume his equipment has become surplus to requirements.

Affectionately, HC

Judith sat frowning at the screen on Marjory's basement desk. It would have been wiser to do what she was doing *before* loading up with lasagne and chilled white wine, but after the urgent fuck on the bathroom floor there was another appetite that would not be denied. Now, however, she had the sense of failing to grasp the full import of Harry's rather strange message and the fuzz in her brain wasn't helping at all.

OK, try and think it through. The basic point was that the contents of Mrs K's office and the old headmaster's study that Jana had described might still be there, lying unremarked in a corner under decades of dust. Was that really feasible? Difficult to say until she could quiz an occupant of the new set-up. It wouldn't do, of course, to mention the bench as such at the outset. The first approach could be in terms of background research to a memoir she had acquired on Academy life in the 1920s. When there was someone *to* approach. Get a move on, Harry. This place without name or admitted function was beginning to intrigue her. 'Thomas-Halle' rang a bell although her less than crystal-clear mind refused to come up with even a hint of where she could have heard it before. And what about Arnold? He was a cute boy all right, but unless he was a black belt or the like on the quiet not exactly bodyguard material. Was the man up to mischief again? On balance she thought not since the tone of the mail seemed conciliatory. Though she couldn't quite work out whether having Arnold's cock inside her called 'regrettable' meant that Harry was shouldering at least some of the blame for that outcome. Well, she would give him the benefit of the doubt. For the moment.

After closing the file she put the computer on stand-by. It was time to go upstairs. While Marjory would be taking her place to do some work, Judith fancied a little more wine before the night in the big sumptuous bed. And a chance to broach the idea of an expedition properly with Grace and maybe even to sound her out cautiously on a certain young man's – what was the word? – equipment. Suppose, just suppose he did go with them and then they both took him on together. One could even use a cane while the other . . .

'Down, girl!' Judith admonished herself out loud and stood up. Alcohol-fuelled fantasies. The male organ was no longer on the agenda and that was that. Tut, tut; she should be ashamed. With a female form as ravishing as the one waiting for her tonight, who could possibly want more?

Marjory was at the top about to descend. 'I don't suppose I'll see you again tonight, Judith. There's a contract to finish that will – if it comes off – tie the college in with a European outfit. This could be an important new direction, so it's the midnight oil for me.' She nodded in the direction of the sitting room. 'I'm sure you two can look after yourselves.'

'I never said thanks, Marjory.'

'Think nothing of it, dear. I'm pleased the sisters seem to have done the trick, for now at least. Let's hope it lasts.' The older woman disappeared, closing the door behind her. Now what was *that* comment all about? As often with Marjory where Grace was concerned, Judith had the feeling there were things she was not being told. Then again, such suspicions could be seen as unworthy, even a touch neurotic. If anyone was in a position to understand what went on in that pretty head it was surely herself. So she had better stop mystery-mongering and proceed on that basis.

The object of her concerns was curled up clutching a cushion in the cormer of an outsize chesterfield. The vulnerable beauty of the girl made Judith ache inside and the dazzling smile she flashed was greatly reassuring. Once glasses had been recharged they clinked them together.

'Here's to you, Jude.'

'Here's to *us*, Gracie.'

After they drank the toast she sat on the sofa and Grace snuggled up laying her head on Judith's lap.

'So did you get your info, boss lady?'

Judith wrinkled her nose. 'Hey, I'm not really that and certainly won't be once she who must be obeyed arrives back. *Then* you'd better watch points, girl.'

'OK, I get the message – *lover*. Is that better?'

'Much.'

'Right then. If we've got that settled, spill the beans. What did you find out?'

'Well, it seems we may be in luck since the old building is amongst new ones and not used for much. Maybe the goods are stashed there yet. So what do you reckon to a trip, Gracie? And does any place grab you for a stopover on the way?'

'Hmm. I kinda like the sound of Berlin and all those sleazy clubs. You know, Jude, lots of strict doms to whip that luscious arse of yours into shape while I watch.' She gave a little giggle and flashed Judith an upside-down glance. '*Only* joking. But not about the city. Are we going to be anywhere near?'

'Not really, but I need to check a proper map. We can always do a detour.'

'It's in Germany, though, yeah? I mean the names . . .' Suddenly there was a hollow in the pit of Judith's stomach and a strong sense of foreboding.

'No. I thought you knew. It's over the border in the Czech Republic.'

The head jerked up from her lap. 'And what's the place called these days when it's not a school?'

Judith's mouth was dry and she felt her heart thudding. The memory that escaped her downstairs had returned unbidden. And she wished it hadn't, but there was no going back now. She tried to moisten her lips. 'I don't know its proper name but it's apparently known as the Thomas-Halle.' She longed to be mistaken, but the recollection was far too vivid. Where she had planned – with Grace in tow – to bag the trophy of a veteran punishment bench was the very place from which the girl had been rescued by Marjory. Oh shit. Shit, shit, shit!

At once Grace was on her feet, clenching and unclenching her fists. The beautiful features were contorted and there was an ugly truculence in the set of her mouth. For a wild moment Judith flinched in fear of a physical assault.

'Oh God, Gracie. I didn't realise. I should have done because I did hear that name before but I just didn't connect. You've got to believe me.' She held out her arms but the cold silence of the stare stopped her dead. 'Gracie, *please*. I would never have set something like that up knowingly. Surely I'm due that much credit?'

'You'll have to go by yourself. I can't – won't –'

At least she was speaking and Judith grabbed at a hand. 'Of course you can't. Oh, I'm such a fool. If only I'd thought.' She dropped to her knees and put her hands on the hips of the rigid body. Then in a do-or-die gesture Judith pulled down the waistband of the cotton shorts until the pubic mound came into view and took a tuft of its hair firmly in her teeth.

'Ow. Ow! Stop it, Jude, will you?' There was less of anger than exasperation in the response and Judith was encouraged to persist. Slackening her bite a little she reached round and massaged the ripe globes until the tension in them begin to ease.

'That's better.' She turned her eyes up to the face that looked down impassively at hers. 'Listen, Gracie. No way am I going on my own. Not to that place where you were, were –' She broke off, recognising that she didn't know what exactly *had* been done to Grace there. It was another missing piece of the puzzle. But this was scarcely the time to pursue the matter so she changed tack. 'I mean the place you got away from. It just wouldn't be right and anyway, it would churn *me* up too much. So just forget the whole thing, right?' She gave the bush in front of her nose another tug and then there were hands each side of her head bringing her to her feet.

'OK. Let's drop the subject like you say. For now.' Grace kissed Judith once on the lips. The expression was solemn but the hard edge had softened. Phew. It looked like there was still desire on the other side to meet hers. Then a corner of the mouth twitched and the lips formed into a sexy pout. 'So, *lover*, are you going to take *me* to bed, or am I going to have to take *you*?'

20

Rapport

It was ten o'clock on Wednesday morning before Judith was inserting her key into the heavy outer door of the Nemesis Archive. Alone in her own flat after two days of intense erotic activity she had slept the sleep of the dead and its foggy remnants still clung to her as she punched the code into the wall-panel by the lift. And when she reached the office the sight she saw did nothing to dispel the air of unreality. The figure that rose to greet her glowed in a sheen of white latex that coated jutting breasts and nipples, the scraped-back hair fastened with ornate white clips on the two sides. As Judith's jaw dropped, Grace blew a kiss from blood-red lips then put a finger to them in a gesture of silence. Turning slightly away she bent as if hinged at the waist and clasped her ankles above the gleaming white stilettos.

The sheath of the micro-dress had ridden up and the unspoken intention seemed plain. Judith swallowed. Despite the girl's problematic history this had to be an invitation, and when the buttocks gave what looked like an impatient twitch inside the sheer silk pants she brought the flat of her hand down on the left one with an almighty SMACK! There was a yelp but at once the back arched and she used her stinging palm with as much force as she could muster on the right target. Then she drew down the white wisp and removed it carefully over each shoe in turn. There were two perfect imprints of five fingers and a thumb on the fair-skinned globes and Judith pressed her hot hand to the liquefying lips between them.

'Oh yes. Yes. But I've got to say this first.' The head twisted and the slate-blue eyes looked up from under unfeasibly long lashes. 'I'm coming with you to the Hall. No ifs or buts and no arguments. We're *both* going to go. And now, lover, you can get those digits working.'

With the barriers down Grace was nothing if not sexually enthusiastic and in the end Judith frogmarched her to the desk that contained the neat pile of mail left by Marjory's caretaking.

'*You* are our secretary: so do secretary-type things with this little lot. And that's an order.' Grace stuck out her tongue but sat obediently down and Judith continued. 'I'm off to my hideaway in the stacks. If you behave, girl, your big, bad – and strictly temporary – boss might come and take you for some lunch.'

Since the mail she had received on Monday, Harry had been incommunicado and Judith realised she could hardly plan a trip without access to someone on the inside of the penal outfit. It was certainly such from Marjory's account of the place, and a pretty shady one, which made it rather difficult to accept Grace's sudden change of heart. Could she really be set to confront what had happened or would she revert to the previous state of denial? And what on earth would happen when – if – they actually got there? The questions circled in her mind and her attempts to draw up a summary of what she knew of Jana's life ground to a halt. So it was with relief rather than irritation that she heard the tentative steps on the iron stair that brought Grace standing meekly before her. If, that is, meekness could ever be ascribed to one clothed so provocatively in skin-tight rubber.

'I dealt with the correspondence and I've put two things you need to see on your desk. And I know it's only twelve, but I, er, thought you needed a break before we go out.' She shifted awkwardly from one foot to the other and Judith grinned.

'OK, let me guess. Would this break you have in mind involve any of the activities we've been doing rather a lot of lately?'

'Got it in one, boss lady.' Grace clapped delightedly. 'But with a difference. Y'see, a catalogue came from AAA and it got me thinking.'

'AAA?'

'All Anal Appliances Limited. Things that you would *never* guess . . .'

Judith followed her visitor down the two flights of stairs and across the aisle through the array of shelves that brought them out in the secretary's office. All the while the prattle continued and Judith was unsure whether to be charmed or disconcerted by the ingenuous enthusiasm for a novel sexual practice. At the bathroom entrance the flow of talk dried up and Grace blushed.

'I *have* been going on, haven't I? Oh dear.' The woebegone expression made Judith take her arm.

'Don't worry, girl. I get carried away now and then too.'

'It's just I feel so ignorant.' She flung open the door and there on the narrow side-table lay the orange bulb and pink tube of an enema kit. It was not so long since her own encounter with a similar device at Dykes 'n' Sluts and the queasy memory of a bloated colon was all too clear. Judith looked doubtfully at Grace.

'Are you sure, now?'

'Of course I'm not sure, Jude. But how will I find out if I don't try?' She picked up a black cylinder with almost the girth of a cucumber. 'So, after, if you would –'

'I get the picture, Gracie, but let's be realistic here.' Judith took the dildo from her and found in the wall-cabinet a flesh-coloured tube the size of a largish carrot. She put on the worldly-wise air of a parent who knows things her offspring doesn't. 'In time, who can say? But for now ... Though you're right, of course. There is only one way to learn.'

It took a minute or two before she was happy with the temperature of the water, then another to fix the greased nozzle in place. The recipient was silent while the transfer of liquid into her body took place, and when it was done she looked decidedly pink.

'Right,' said Judith. 'Now I'm told some good hard slaps help churn it all up and get you nice and clean inside.' She looked at Grace who leaned forward obligingly over the bath and stuck out an enticing rump.

'OK, Jude, you're in charge. Spank away. We want to do the job properly.'

It took three administrations of the contents of the bulb before they agreed to be satisfied with the state of the fluid noisily expelled into the lavatory bowl, and it was thus a very red pair of cheeks that Judith separated to expose the sanitised anus. She took a bead of jelly from the jar and pressed it into the brown pucker, then scooped out another.

'Ooh, lover. Ooh, that feels funny and it's *cold*.'

'Stop wriggling. Until I can get my whole finger up this tight little hole there is no chance of Bertie here getting a look-in.' Grace giggled but held still until the lubricating had been done. Then Judith pulled the cork-topped clothes bin out from under the wash basin, arranged the secretary face-down over it and straddled her. Dildo in hand, she examined the cleft below her with its vulval pink peeping through damp curls underneath the glistening orifice that was the present object of concern. 'OK, girl, hold tight. Here we go.'

'If you don't mind, folks, I'll pass on the stool.'

Marsha flipped the top off a bottle of Pils and looked up. 'Am I to infer that the young beauty is suffering the after-effects of the Director's strap? Or worse, even?' She fixed Judith with narrowed eyes. 'You should be ashamed.'

'Oh, no. It's not *that*. There was just a few smacks before I got, er –'

A red-faced Grace broke off and Judith looked at her American pal. She had helped set up the 'exercises' and would of course have heard how successful they had been. It was fine that she knew in a general way that they'd been fucking like crazy, but Judith shrank from spilling the beans about a bruised sphincter acquired from vigorous buggering on the floor of the Archive's office bathroom. Somehow things with Grace were too raw to be the subject of even friendly banter, so she tried to switch topics. 'In any case, I reckon a girl in *that* dress should think twice about perching at the bar unless she's prepared to fend off unwanted proposals.'

'OK, OK.' Grace made a moue and tugged fruitlessly at the latex hem which reverted to crotch level as soon as she let go. Marsha caught Judith's eye and she was pleased to see a just perceptible wink.

'Too right. I gotta watch the reputation of my bar. Already those guys by the door look like they're gonna come over for the tariff. And they won't be asking about drinks. So why don't you two grab your sandwiches and go hide round the corner. I'll come over when I can.'

It was sooner rather than later for they had barely finished eating when Marsha appeared with more beers and plonked herself down opposite. 'So the trip's on, eh? That's good. Now tell all.' She looked expectantly from one to the other but Grace waved Judith on.

'Well, I finally got the contact I was after: one Sibyl Metzger. Comes across as a sort of PR person for what she refers to as "The Program". We haven't been given an official name and I'm communicating through what looks like a personal email address.'

She glanced at Grace who chipped in: 'We just called it the Hall. I don't remember seeing anything else. And

I don't remember *her*.' The girl seemed fine with the topic being broached and Judith relaxed slightly.

'I gave her the pitch about our interest in the St Thomas Academy eighty years back and it went down no problem. Our Ms Metzger said that as far as she knew a lot of the original furniture and records were packed away untouched. It was pretty obvious she had no interest in the place except as additional storage space for their operation. So it looks like we can go and poke about. Naturally, I didn't mention anything about Grace's past association with this so-called Program, just that I'd be hoping to bring along a colleague.'

'Dig the promotion,' said the secretary with a little smirk, but Marsha looked less happy.

'I don't want to put a damper on things, guys, but have you thought this through? I mean the bench stuff is cool, but are you then going to say: "Thanks for your help, Sibyl, and by the way, this is former inmate No. 57322"?'

Judith hesitated. 'Well, it's up to Gracie what she wants to do. I mean, she doesn't *have* to do anything. This Sibyl couldn't have been around when she was there, and, after all, it's not as if she absconded or anything.'

'Sure. But this outfit is too secretive for my taste. If you just had a fail-safe plan to fall back on –' Marsha stopped short, eyes on the scowling beauty biting her lip and picking at a beer mat. 'OK, sister, none of my business. I'll keep my nose out. Now, what was that about a stop-over on the way?'

'Yeah, we were, er, thinking about Berlin,' Judith put in awkwardly, but then Grace looked up with a bright smile that made her sigh. Would she ever get used to the abrupt changes of mood?

'Jude said you might know about BDSM joints – it's supposed to be big for that kind of thing, right?' The bar manager raised an eyebrow.

'Honey, I do have a couple of addresses you could get in touch with. Skilled, hard bondage is their bag.'

'Yes, yes. That's exactly it. Not so much the SM end, I simply want to watch her trussed up completely naked, and then –' The eyes were bright and Judith cut in quickly to stop the flow, feeling her colour rise. Damn the girl, did she have no sense of discretion?

'Hold it there, Gracie. I think our imaginations can take over for now.'

'I'll dig out the details and pass them on. You girls are going to have fun.' Marsha was chuckling, but Judith was a bit unnerved by the childlike pursuit of new games. In one way it was quite a turn-on, but it left her with the breathless feeling of running to catch up. 'So have you decided when you're going?'

'We thought early next week –' Judith looked at Grace who nodded happily '– once we get the travel arrangements sorted out. And Marjory's going to babysit the Archive till we get back.'

'Tell her if she needs a break to give me a call.' Marsha stood up briskly. 'But now I had better let Monica go for some lunch. If I don't see you guys, take care. And Grace, if you could bring me back a couple of stills of the Assistant Director all tied up and going nowhere . . .' She headed back towards the bar leaving Judith once again with her colour rising. But it was good to hear Grace joining in the older woman's laughter.

After work they took a cab to Grace's bedsit where she bundled some clothes into a backpack and changed into jeans and trainers for the walk over to Judith's flat. Halfway across the park, within sight of their destination, Grace made for a bench beside the pond and pulled Judith down beside her. They sat for a few minutes in silence in the warmth of the late afternoon sun then Grace said: 'This Jana, at the old school. What do you make of her?'

'How do you mean?'

'She's kind of on her own, isn't she?'

'Yeah. There's background stuff about her mother dying young and the old father being in an institution. So she went to the Academy as a boarder then gets taken on. It's where she lives, holidays as well as term.'

'That's what I thought. So the woman in charge, this Mrs – what is it?'

'Mrs K. The First Mistress.'

'Right. Well, d'you think she's a kind of stand-in for the family the girl doesn't have?'

'Uh huh. Could be.' There was a pause while Grace picked at a piece of mud sticking to her shoe and Judith wondered where these questions were heading.

'I was just wondering. Does Jana maybe want – or need – Mrs K to beat her right from the start? Though she doesn't know it.'

'You mean like a strict parent or something?'

'Yeah. Y'see, Jude, I can get the stuff with the guy, when he fucks her and all. Like it hurts but it's dead sexy. But when it comes to going over that bench thing by *choice* . . .' Grace had hold of a stick and was jabbing at the ground, brow furrowed.

'Well, it's no fun at the time, that's for certain. But it would turn *me* on and that's without there being any *sex* sex along with it, if you see what I mean. I thought you were the same, Gracie. At least you used to be with the boss and her strap, yeah?' They hadn't really talked since getting physically to grips. It was a new terrain and it was going to take a careful tread to avoid finding one of its undoubted mines.

'Yes, I suppose. But she was sweet on me really, until you guys brought that Penny back.' Uh oh. Wrong step number one. But she just had to probe a bit more.

'Thing is, Gracie, you say you don't understand Jana going for the bench off her own bat, but isn't that what you did at the Hall? I thought you didn't get walloped without asking for it – literally.'

'There was pressure. You couldn't get through – and *out* – by just keeping mum. If you did that you'd be in the place for fucking ever.'

'OK, I get the point –'

'I'm not sure you do. It wasn't you locked up there expecting to be shipped back any time to a rat-infested hole.' She was flushed, mouth working at the corners, gazing down, and Judith put a hand on her arm. 'I couldn't deal with it – couldn't cope – couldn't –' The speech cut off and the secretary jerked to her feet, facing away. Damn. Why had she not let it go? With a bit more patience maybe the girl would have volunteered things of her own accord.

Judith sat watching the figure who had moved the few yards to the water's edge and now stood hands in pockets and shoulders hunched. Grace shivered as a cool breeze spattered a few drops of light rain on her head but all of a sudden the clouds parted and they were both caught in a shaft of sunlight. Then Grace swung round and the expression was miraculously as clear as the weather.

'Whatever. Who cares anyway?' She swung her arms back and forth and gave a little jump. 'Come on, Jude. Race you to the gate.'

'No way, girl. I am far too wrecked.' To say nothing of emotional stress. 'But you go on. See the Chinese at the end of the street? Why don't you get the menu and pick what we're going to take home?'

Out of deep sleep Judith became aware that another body was sliding into the narrow bed at her back. They had agreed earlier that Grace would occupy the small spare room with similarly cramped sleeping quarters, so after a long and languorous entanglement Judith had pushed her new lover out to her own quarters and shut the door. And here she was again.

Sliding a hand over the warm body she rounded a buttock and fingered the anus in its damp cleft.

'Oo-ooh.' The soft complaint came in a waft of breath on her ear, then teeth nibbled gently on the lobe.

'Still sore?'

'Mmm. Bit.'

'But it was good, yeah?'

'Mmm.'

All at once the thought of Arnold on their trip popped into Judith's head. No, she couldn't, could she? Oh, why the fuck not? Her sleep-addled brain tried to find the right words. 'What would you say to the real thing? Like attached to a male of the species. We've had the offer of a young guy to come with us. I mean, he's gay but he'd be amenable . . .'

'You know this 'cos he's the one you fucked, right?' Oh shit. Of course, Grace *knew*. How could she have forgotten the anguished confession? Wide awake Judith tried to turn but a hand held her shoulder. 'So he gets to fuck *me* now, eh? OK, let's give it a whirl. A live cock up the bum: sounds cool. Or do I mean hot?' There was a small but distinct giggle and Judith lay scarcely able to believe what she had just heard.

'You mean it, Gracie? That's OK?' She felt a touch between her legs that extended into her moistening vulva.

'Yeah. But not in *here*, right? This –' she pressed the swelling clitoris in a way that made its owner gasp '– this is mine. Male – or other female – entry prohibited. Is that clear, lover?'

'Aah. Crystal.'

'Are you quite sure you've got it?'

'A-a-aah. Ooh. Got it, got it, got it . . .'

213

21

The Thomas-Halle

As the lull continued Judith guessed the latterly wakeful librarian's 'boy' had crashed out with the rest in the capacious cross between a limo and a people carrier they had hired for the journey. At getting on for three in the morning it was about time. The map showed a straight run down the autobahn to the Czech border and as she settled at the wheel behind the powerful headlights she was glad of the chance to put her thoughts into some kind of order.

It had been a hectic couple of days that began well at Marsha's designated parlour in Berlin. Slowly and methodically, the eager Grace was taught a sequence of knots, loops and crossings that had left a denuded Judith trussed in jack-knife position around a long-legged stool. While breathing was unimpeded, other muscular activity was curtailed to the point of immobility and once they were alone the student of bondage lost no time in attending to the exposed genital area. It was not so much the fingers that did it, for efficient as they were in making the juices run their technique was becoming familiar. No, it was when the mouth came in close, mixing warm wafts of breath with strong cool puffs of air deep into the parted lips. Blowing hot and cold, quite literally, and it brought her in a trice to the point of orgasm, where she hung constricted and panting. Until the tip of the tongue connected with the swollen bud and set off contractions that, despite the bonds, threatened to topple her and her wooden perch to the floor.

The recollection of it made Judith shift in the driver's seat with a sharp stab of desire. It had been quite an experience, even if things had gone rather downhill since. Arnold had duly collected his similarly bisexual web contact Luka, but instead of the foursome she had rather vaguely envisaged, Grace had taken sole charge of the newly available organs, demanding anal penetration by one while putting the other under close examination. Quite a leap for a lesbian with a single initiation under her belt, though one that had the unfortunate effect of relegating Judith to the role of non-participant adviser. However, the ensuing exchange was not one she was likely to forget in a hurry.

'Girl, that beast you're playing with is about to go off.' Hunkered down over Arnold with Luka's cock planted in her bum, the figure looked up from her manipulations of the boy's foreskin.

'Go off? You mean –'

'Shoot. E-jac-ul-ate. You've done this close-up before, on camera, remember?'

The upturned face coloured. 'Um, that bit wasn't actually *me*. Cunt and arse were yours truly's all right, but then I didn't get a proper look at what was going on.'

'Jesus, girl, and I thought you were the real deal. Well, anyway, this gizmo is going to squirt. And unless you want it in the eye you'd better get your gob round it pronto.'

'You're the boss.' Grace set to work obediently but when a trickle of semen appeared running down the chin the performance tailed off into what sounded like expressions of distaste.

'Ugh. U-u-ugh.'

'Hey, gorgeous, are you trying to tell me you're not so keen on a nice mouthful of sperm?'

'Too fucking salty.' She made a face, but then resumed the task so that subsequent comments were interspersed by the far-from-decorous noises that came from spirited sucking. 'But now it's stopped doing that it's a good thick thing –' slurp, slurp '– yummy –' slurp, slurp '– and well hard. I could get into this. But if I keep on will it go off again?'

'Yeah, I expect so. Though I'm no expert on the subject.' The women continued the discussion as if the organ had a life independent of the boy who lay back moaning with eyes screwed tight. 'But I do know the second helping should be way smaller than the first.'

'That's good news, lover –' slurp, slu-u-urp '– though it'd be better still if you could lace their beer with something that would tone down the fucking taste.'

The episode concluded in grand style with Arnold's promised second ejaculation being matched by a discharge from Luka pumping at the other end. In so far as she could with her mouth occupied, the prime mover of the exercise joined in with the orgasmic noises and the memory of it made Judith smile as she drove. Later in the day, however, Grace had become taciturn, even morose. While she would not confirm or deny it, Judith had no doubt the mood was related to the approach of their journey's end at the Hall where the girl had once been incarcerated. Better face up to it: the enterprise was going to be a tricky one to pull off. Perhaps the best she could expect was to be able to locate the relics of the old Academy she was looking for and do a deal as quickly as possible. If only Grace would stay in the background, her former identity might not come to light, but her volatility made events dangerously unpredictable. Withdrawn and tight-lipped for the past several hours, she could easily lurch into upfront mode once they reached the establishment itself. And Judith had a nasty feeling that was just what might happen.

They made the border crossing at dawn without incident and after the hunt for documents the yawning trio made no objection to Judith's proposal to drive the last hundred kilometres or so that would take them to their destination. They were scheduled to meet Chief Officer Metzger at ten and she wanted to keep awake until their first encounter had taken place. Over breakfast at a roadside café, washed down with plenty of strong coffee, the final plans were made. Since there was no way two young men – whether ostensibly gay or not – would be welcomed into a secretive all-female institution, Arnold and his friend would keep their distance in the vehicle while she and Grace were admitted. Thanks to Luka they were equipped with functioning mobiles, so the boys could stay in the vicinity until they received an OK. Beyond that, they would remain prepared to return at short notice if called in case of an emergency.

When it came into view on the edge of a run-down industrial estate, the long high wall looked a good bet. Over the top of it could be glimpsed an old stone gable at the end of a steeply pitched roof, but that was dwarfed by a concrete façade scored with vertical strips of dark tinted glass. While there was the sound of machinery from the half-raised door of a large garage, most of the buildings were boarded up. No one was in sight and there was a general air of dereliction. Judith edged the traveller forward down the dead-end street until she saw as expected a recess in the expanse of concrete at the back of which stood the solid metal surface of a door. She drove past and turned at the end of the cul-de-sac, then stopped the vehicle and glanced across at Grace who was chewing on a lower lip.

'OK, girl. Seems like the time has come. But you don't *have* to do this, you know.'

'Yeah, I know.' She scowled into the middle distance. 'How about I keep a low profile – just to start with, like? Let you sweet-talk the lady first.'

'If that's what you want, sure.' Even with the surly expression Judith was struck afresh by her looks with a shock that was almost physical. There was something about it that distinguished the girl from others of similarly flawless complexion and model features. She was vulnerable, certainly, but that wasn't the whole of it. No, there was an otherness that felt like it came from an alien core: she could play a part all right, even a few parts, but when she wasn't acting it was as if she was somewhere of which Judith had no inkling. She tried to remind herself that the bench was the main object of the trip: if anything useful came out about what had happened to Grace three years earlier that would be a bonus. Judith cleared her throat and put on a grin. Enough wool-gathering: there was a job to do.

'Right, beautiful, let's go.' When they got out Judith went to the tailgate and removed a large black attaché case. While it held little more than clean underwear it looked the part of the business-like researcher and would with luck be holding some useful papers on the way out.

'All set, guys? Once we're in, wait till you're texted an all-clear, then you can head off. One of us will call you later when we're on our own.' Arnold nodded assent though he looked rather apprehensive. Judith grinned. 'Hey, don't look so worried: you're not going to have to send in a rescue mission. It's just comforting to know we've got transport at the ready just in case we need to make a fast getaway.'

However, it soon became apparent that if the exit procedure was anything like what it took to get *in*, there wasn't going to be anything quick about it. After Judith had identified herself at the mesh grille beside the entrance, a panel slid back to allow the memorised code

218

to be punched into a set of numeric keys. Then, with the clunk of a solenoid-operated bolt, the heavy door swung open to give the visitors access to a vestibule where they were faced by another door exactly like the one they had come through. Before Judith realised what was happening, that had clanged shut at their backs and a harsh and heavily accented voice from above their heads made them both jump.

'You will be scanned. Remain still and wait, please.' In the confined space Judith took a deep breath and cast a worried eye over the pale tense face of her companion. Then the security camera in the top left corner of the cubicle winked its red light at them and with a grating rasp of metal on metal they were released into a neon-lit tunnel by a young blonde in a dark serge bodysuit.

'*Kommen Sie, bitte*. Offizier Metzger will see you now.'

She strode away and they followed her obediently down the passage. Judith's gaze homed in on the plump little buttocks which gave a bounce with each clunk of the heeled boots, until there came a sharp dig in her ribs and a terse mutter of prohibition in her ear: 'Uh, *uh*.'

Fuck it, here she was being reined in for eyeing up a nice pair of cheeks when the girl had been cheerfully hogging two cocks for most of the ride. But then they belonged to males and so didn't count. To Judith's mind sex was sex whatever gender combinations you went for, but she wasn't going to quibble. With Grace about to re-enter the scene of past angst, maybe a bit of common or garden jealousy would help keep things normal.

After more locks had been negotiated, they found themselves in an entrance hall from which ran bare corridors to left and right. Ahead was a lift which took the party in silence to the carpeted fourth floor where their guide tapped on the door opposite and without waiting for a reply ushered them in. In contrast to the closed spaces they had traversed the office was all light and air from the sheet of glass that commanded a view of the whole complex contained within the perimeter wall. But more striking than the vista that opened out was the 'Offizier' who rose to greet them. Tall and lean in a uniform of tailored grey silk, she shook out her auburn bob and peered at the arrivals over the top of steel-rimmed spectacles.

'Sibyl Metzger. Welcome to the Program.' There was a perceptible transatlantic burr, but the clipped English was otherwise perfect. Judith swallowed and shook the offered hand firmly.

'Judith Wilson. Thank you for agreeing to see us. However, I'm afraid that my colleague, er, Carol isn't feeling very well.' She avoided Grace's eye praying that she would go along with the spur-of-the-moment double subterfuge. 'A lot of travelling in a short time . . .'

'Of course. My assistant will show her the accommodation where she can recuperate from your journey while we talk. *Bitte*, Helga . . .' With relief Judith saw the door close behind the pair and lowered herself gratefully into the indicated armchair across from the desk.

'Very good, Ms Wilson –'

'Judith, please.'

'So, Judith, shall we get down to business? You have expressed an interest in the former Academy, which is of course now part of our facilities, and I believe you are particularly concerned with its methods of corporal correction.' The carefully modulated speech allowed a hint of relish to colour the final phrase, and it made Judith decide to tell the whole story. It was perhaps excusable to try to protect Grace from recognition, but that was no reason to conceal anything of her mission from a fellow enthusiast for the disciplinary arts. So she spoke of the MS that had come her way, with its interlocking themes of passion and punishment played out so close at hand in the second quarter of the previous century. The Chief Officer listened, head cocked attentively, interrupting only once to ask an astute question about authenticity. When Judith had finished she added a couple of notes to the deskpad in front of her, then swivelled her chair and gestured towards the tiled roofs of the old buildings below.

'It is good that you have an account of what happened in the school. I am as you know rather occupied with the training of some of today's young women, so I have not spared much thought for past methods of discipline on our own doorstep. As a result I shall be interested to read your publication when it appears and am, of course, happy for you to look into what things may be left over from that time. Ah, Helga.' The door had opened quietly to admit the said member of staff, following which several sentences were exchanged in German that were quite beyond Judith's perfunctory grasp of the language.

'You will excuse us, I hope. Helga's English progresses only slowly, despite my best efforts to motivate her. If there is still no improvement, I may have to fall back on the *bare* recitation of numbers at the lesson tonight.' The merest hint of a wink might have passed Judith by were it not for Helga's blush and wiggle. There was no doubt that *she* had got the message.

'You will go and help our guest locate what she wants, and practise your English at the same time. If she gives me a good account of you, perhaps there will be no need for the counting of strokes later. Is that understood?'

'*Ja – ach nein.* Yes, Offizier Metzger.' The pretty blonde's renewed flush as she caught Judith's eye made her loins prickle at once. And the thought that she could decide the fate of the girl's bottom was too arousing altogether. Now if she were to give Helga's performance one of those school reports that said could try harder, then there would be another 'motivation' session to which she might even be invited . . . Judith pulled her attention back to the present as Officer Sibyl cleared her throat.

'You have been open, Judith, about your wish to acquire the bench and any relevant papers, and I appreciate your frankness. There is no reason I can see why we should not dispose of assets for which the Program has no use, and I shall put my mind to drafting a protocol. So, as I believe the expression goes, happy hunting!'

'What we search for is named a flogging rack?'

'Er, caning. And they called it a bench. It would be about so high.'

They were standing in the old headmaster's study, though its state would hardly have met with his or Mrs K's approval. Fully half of the space was filled with a jumble of boxes, filing cabinets, tables and chairs, stacked one upon the other almost to the ceiling. But what Judith homed in on first was the grand, dark-wood desk that had been pushed back against a wall and she set about exploring its contents.

'I'm looking for papers, too, Helga. Anything official.'

'*Richtig*. I start to move things, yes?'

'Yeah.' While the assistant set to work Judith closed the last drawer and scratched her head. All empty, and yet there was something . . . Then it hit her: the majestic piece of furniture was very like the one her own boss posed behind, right down to the intricate inlaid border round its heavy top. And that one had a special feature Miss James had shown her on the day it was installed. Concealed in the shallow tray that opened above your lap was a lever which, if pulled, released a panel on the inside of the leg space. Bingo! There it was, and with bated breath Judith bent down and felt inside the narrow opening. Her hand closed at once on a small bundle that she drew out with care. Letters. They were letters, maybe a dozen of them in their original envelopes and addressed by hand to Frau Kästner at the St Thomas Akademie. Was it possible – could she be so lucky – that they were from Jana? And of course if they were she was not going to be able to read them.

Judith sat on the edge of the desk and berated herself for lack of application on the language front. She pulled out the folded sheets of the first, inscribed in faded ink that was the colour of slate, and saw the date at the top was written as VI:5:27. Nineteen-twenty-seven – that was the year before the school had been closed down. With trembling fingers Judith turned the page to the final paragraph to find the initials J.M. Jana Marlova. She had in her hands new material from the author of the memoir that was to form the opening case study of the NemArch imprint.

Then a word of the text above caught her eye: 'trying'. Trying? *I was trying to set down an account of my time at the Academy and it made me realise that leaving was a mistake.* Bewildered, Judith turned to the first page and there at the beginning was the explanation. *First Mistress:* it read, *Will you hear me please? I shall use for this my poor English – which I know you understand well – to make difficulty for a spy to learn what I write to you.* Saved. That was brilliant. She didn't deserve it, but she was going to be able to find out what business Jana had had with Mrs K at the end of it all.

'Yoodit. Yoodit!' The tug at her sleeve came with the realisation that the strange-sounding word was the German rendering of her name. In front of her the excited assistant was pointing at a wooden frame she had extricated from the assorted debris.

'This is it, yes? The cane bench? And the bad girls go over like so.' She flopped down across the slatted top and Judith saw the stout straps that were perfectly positioned to encircle thighs and forearms. Helga giggled.

'*Geht in Ordnung*, Judith. Tie me tight for spanking.' She stuck out her bum and between the parted legs was the clear outline of the split vulva. Judith felt her own moisten.

'Helga, get up, please.' The young blonde turned her head and displayed a pout.

'You don't want to play with me? OK. I am good.' She got to her feet. 'I understand. The fraulein I take to her room is your girlfriend. You are – *was ist's?* – a couple.' Judith winced at the term, but it was after all what she was aiming to make into the truth.

'But you will say I put the effort into the English? I got training the last day –'

'*Yester*-day,' Judith suggested gently.

'Yesterday, *gut*. And this day – *to*day, yes? – is too soon again. I show you.' Before Judith could stop her the zip of the one-piece garment was open and turning her back she had shucked it off the shoulders right down round the knees. Judith stared at the purple-black lines that formed a horizontal grid on the pert buttocks. Twelve were easily countable and there were three further marks below the overhang that must have stung like hell. The neat accuracy of it all could scarcely have been equalled by Miss James and the colouring betokened a thinnish instrument forcefully applied. She imagined for a moment being on the receiving end of that punishment then pulled the girl to her and laid a hand carefully on the pubic fuzz.

'I'll say you were trying really hard, Helga. So it should be all right.'

'If I must take *der Stock* again then I must. It is not so bad really.' It was plainly an act, but the bravado was very sexy. Far too sexy. Judith allowed herself to dip one finger carefully between the cunt lips she knew would be as wet as her own then gave the punished bottom a slap.

'Ow – ow! I am sore.'

'Come on, Helga, zip up now and get back to your duties. You have work to do, yes?' The interrogative style of conversation was catching. This time, though, the answer was a simple 'Right', and the assistant did as she was told. Once she was alone Judith felt drained and pulled over a chair to sit at the desk and spread out her discovery. The bench was a terrific find and she must examine it carefully. But first she was bursting to know why Jana had been writing a series of letters to Mrs K.

22

Example

Judith woke with a crick in her neck and half of her face numb from pressing down on the pages covered with carefully formed script. Shit, what time was it? Just then there was a sharp knock and the door opened. She shook her muzzy head and blinked at the pony-tailed young woman who stood there in a light cotton boilersuit.

'Ms Wilson, I have come to ask you to attend my passing-out event this afternoon. But first, you go to lunch, please?' Lunch. That was all right; she couldn't have slept for very long. She got stiffly to her feet.

'Call me Judith, yeah? I'm sorry, I must have fallen asleep. Er, what is a "passing out"?'

'OK. My name is Käthe. I have a job if I pass one more test. The employer will be there. Do you understand?'

'You mean an ordeal. With the cane – *der Stock*?'

'*Ja. Und anderen* – um – other implements also.' She made a grimace. 'It will not be easy. *Der Hauptoffizier* thought you would wish to see.'

'But what about you? I don't want to –'

'There is already *eine Audienz*.'

'Right. Fine.' This must be the kind of thing Marjorie had talked about: setting the limits of pain as high as one dared. And then suffering it. At which Grace had failed so utterly. Oh God, Grace. Or rather, 'Carol'. The alias now seemed a piece of silliness, but she must check on her lover.

'An associate came with me but she went to lie down. Can we fetch her to eat with us?' Käthe shook her head.

'I do not eat for I must prepare. And your friend is gone with the young men. But please search in the room if you like. I take you there now.'

The accommodation was cell-like with its small square window set high in the wall. On the lower of its two bunks lay a sheet of paper with the scrawled words: *Back soon. BEHAVE! G xxx*. Irritated, Judith screwed the note up into a ball and tossed it in the bin. Then she stripped and padded through to the compact shower cubicle. It was bad enough that Grace had taken off to God knows where, but in the process to broadcast the fact that they had two guys in tow was inexcusable. What kind of impression was that going to make on the formidable – and indubitably lesbian – Sibyl Metzger?

Over lunch in the gleaming stainless steel of the staff canteen Judith had a chance to quiz Helga about the 'event' she had been invited to witness.

'It is good for Käthe, you know? She was nothing – a juvenile criminal and a junkie and now – now she will be in the care of a mistress.'

'A *strict* mistress.' Judith looked sideways at the earnest face of the young staff member.

'She is *Direktor* of the large company with much money to spend. It is true she will be strict, but Käthe has the taste for it. And –' Helga caught Judith's eye and snorted. 'Ha. You make fun of me, yes? You – and I also – we both submit to the stern lady. Your Miss James has a – *was ist das Wort*? – a reputation.' One that had found its way into the walls of the Thomas-Halle, apparently.

'OK, Helga. The girl will be looked after in *all* ways. But what is actually going to happen this afternoon?'

'I tell you. First the new mistress will take an hour alone to prepare her. She will be well warmed out.'

'Up. I think you mean warmed *up*. If we're talking about spanked bottoms.'

'*Very* spanked.' Helga giggled. 'Hot and red like the coals in the fire. Then she is before the arbiters and must give a number for the cane. The chief will apply the strokes with her own hand. But for Käthe it is not a trial really because she has been already accepted. She will not fail. It is – what do you say? – *eine Vorstellung*.'

'A demonstration? Where she will show she can take her punishment.'

'*Ja*. Is so. You will enjoy it, Judith.'

'You're not going to be there?'

'*Nein*. I am only the junior assistant who bends over while the others watch.' She made a sour face but then it rapidly cleared. 'I told Offizier Metzger you might give me a good report – that is right, yes? – and then I might get a prize. To watch someone else, if they . . . Oh, but I must not say more.' She put an embarrassed hand to her mouth but it failed to hide a sly smile. Watch someone else? Surely she couldn't mean –

'Helga! *Komm hier. Auf der Stelle!*' At the barked command from the doorway, the young blonde sprang to her feet, toppling the metal stool with a clang on to the parquet flooring. Leaning over to set it right she mouthed the words 'good report' then scurried off, leaving Judith to mull over her enigmatic remarks.

An hour later she was installed in a large room on the top floor opposite the Chief Officer's base. While it was similarly laid out, a curtain had been drawn along the length of the glazed wall. Judith guessed that closing off the outside was intended to preclude distraction from the proceedings within, though it would have taken a spectacular view to compete for her attention. She was seated discreetly at the back of three uniformed guards with notepads who were joking amongst themselves. No doubt they regarded their job of appraising the candidate as a kind of technical exercise of no great moment, whereas coming fresh to the ritual that was about to take place she was a-tingle with anticipation. To sit in on a young woman's formal punishment – one that would mark the beginning of a chosen masochistic career – was a rare enough prospect to make Judith impatient with their banter.

But she did not have to wait long for the main event. Before half a minute had passed the door opened to admit Sibyl Metzger and following her a thick-set woman of around forty or fifty whose finely tailored exterior seemed only to accentuate the powerful frame beneath. That its musculature had enjoyed recent exercise soon became clear for between them stood a dimunitive figure clothed only in a croptop and boots who was at once turned to display a rear view. Judith had heard of a punished bottom described as having the colours of 'Hawaiian sunset' but had been able to bring to mind only an imprecise picture. Now there, in front of her, was without question the thing itself in archetypal form. The meaty rounds glowed a deep ruby, laced with dark streaks and framed by the salmon-pink of strap-weals layered round hips and thighs. It was, Judith thought, a sight that took the notion of a good spanking about as far as you could go (Helga's 'warmed *out*', indeed!) and when the Chief Officer picked up the long cane and swished it through the air she winced inwardly.

'Director Kohlstadt, please take a seat. Käthe Weigl, I ask you now. Are you ready to allocate yourself a number of strokes? Please consider your answer with care.' There was no more chatter; instead the room was tense with expectantly held breath. How many *could* the girl take on flesh so marked already? Three? Six? Surely nothing like as many. Heart in mouth Judith waited, convinced that were *she* in such a state a single cut would send her howling out of the door. The girl still faced away, arms straight down her sides. After a slight pause she held up her head and made the announcement in a clear voice.

'*Zwölf, bitte, Hauptoffizier.* I am sorry, I forget myself. I mean to say a dozen strokes, please, ma'am.' Then she bent forward at the waist and gripped her ankles in a movement that parted the swollen cheeks to show genital lips nestling into a dark tuft at the apex of the legs.

Judith sat hardly daring to look as the Officer took up position to the right and stroked the end section of the rod over the posterior contours on display. Sibyl Metzger's face was impassive as she raised the weapon above her head where it quivered for a full second before lashing down across its target. Judith flinched at the impact which drove the slight figure forward though the 'examinee' held her balance without a sound. The buttocks bounced back into shape imprinted instantly with a fresh line and Judith gripped the edges of her chair, mouth dry.

Six more followed in like manner, though the next – number eight – brought a first cry of pain. Then nine jerked Käthe upright with a screech to clutch at her purple-barred rump, and it was a long moment before she dropped back in to place with a moan.

'*Es tut mir leid.* I am sorry. I –' The words were spoken at the floor in a low voice and it seemed she was weeping. Anyone could see that a code of conduct had been breached and the Director looked across to the Chief Officer. Receiving a slight nod of the head she rose from her seat to stand by the stricken girl who turned up an anguished face. Allowing her hand to graze the wet cheek for a moment the woman pushed down the head and leaned the young woman's body into her own. Then she encircled the bare waist with powerful arms, faced the audience and presented the blistered behind for the rest of its allotted count. Käthe would not fall supported thus by the strength of her new mistress and Judith watched the three remaining strokes inflicted with a lump in her throat to add to the juices flowing between her legs.

However, the occasion was not quite at an end. Tight-lipped at the further irregularity the assessors conferred and made a request, of which Judith understood only the word *drei*. Oh God, she was to get more. There was only the tiniest of hesitations before the chastiser uttered the word '*Natürlich*' with a small inclination of the head. After bending to inspect the ravaged buttocks of the tightly held girl she drew back and in short order painted three lines of pain across the less-marked thighs.

Somehow the recipient of the beating now stood unaided, face contorted while the hands opened and closed at her sides. The Chief Officer placed the cane carefully on the table.

'*Es ist vollbracht*. You are free to go.' The Director shook her hand and made a bow in the direction of the panel: 'Ladies.' Then she stretched an arm round the shivering Käthe and steered her out of the door into her new life.

Whatever else, the situation called for a change of knickers and in the still-empty cell Judith sat on the bunk to unlace her boots. Socks off, she thumbed down her black trousers and stripped the briefs from her seeping crotch with a sigh. The affecting combination of cruelty and solicitude just witnessed had put an ache in her loins that would not be denied. Judith swung her legs up and lay back, the rough weave of the blanket prickling against her bare skin. There was still a frisson in finding the vulva hairless and one finger then two slipped easily into the slick opening. It may have been Käthe's trial that had brought her to this state, but as she caressed herself different images appeared to her.

Images of Helga, her bottom jiggling down the corridor and stuck out later in play over the bench: now if she could give *that* body a closer inspection. There had been no doubt of the invitation or the sexual tone of those last strange remarks. Judith saw in her mind's eye the assistant peeling her body suit provocatively off the nakedness beneath and gasped at the stab of sensation in her clitoris. Then she gasped again at the sound of a lock turning and shot up, grabbing for her clothing, as the door was flung wide.

'Hey, lover. Guess who's back!' For a moment the two young women faced each other across the room then Grace gave a dirty cackle. 'Timing, Jude, timing. Have I got it or what? I swear to you – no lies – I was dreaming of a nice wet cunt all the way back. And what do I smell as soon as I open the door? So let's not waste any time, boss. You just lie back down and let me in there . . .'

It was a tremendous orgasm. Orgasm*s*, more like. Single or multiple, whatever, Judith only hoped the accommodation had good sound insulation. Grace's tongue had launched her into the stratosphere and every time she sought to cry enough it had executed a funny kind of clit-flick that sent her higher still. At last, limp and sweaty, she made to pull the girl down beside her, but Grace had other ideas. She wanted to talk. It began as a laugh-a-minute tale of new acquaintances and escapades of the hours she had been gone, but shifted quickly up a gear and then another into a full-blown rant on the theme of how she had never been given a proper chance. With sinking heart Judith heard it through to the conclusion: first thing in the morning she was going to present herself to that principal woman (whatever she was called) and demand to prove herself. She was going to show them all and after that everything would be OK.

It was the worst that Judith had feared and protesting was useless. The speech was as manic as the oral sex that had preceded it and there was no halting its flow until it had run its course. And then the secretary was gone again as abruptly as she had arrived. What was she to do? Grace had to be stopped: if the experienced Käthe could misjudge a 'passing-out' in the way she had witnessed, what chance was there for the erratic secretary? Somehow Judith would have to intervene to avert disaster but her mind was refusing to come up with any kind of plan. So she had returned to the old headmaster's study to the diversion of the letters: Jana's letters to Mrs K. The slim packet lay where she had left it and she took out once again the single sheet that was contained in the first envelope. That morning she had only skimmed it yawning; now she read carefully the message from the summer of 1927 headed by an address in Prague.

First Mistress:
Will you hear me please? I shall use for this my poor English – which I know you understand better – to make difficulty for a spy to learn what I write to you. I do not know how is your situation or if you will wish at all to communicate. I was silent for many months. I try not to annoy you with a long explanation: only make this letter short and hope you will stay to the end.

I was trying to set down an account of my time at the Academy and it made me realise that leaving was a mistake. I expect you to know that the Doctor started me with pupils and he told me to keep away from the scandal. Though now he is gone I see I was wrong. If you will have me, I come back – on any terms. One time I asked for the bench but we were interrupted. I think now my errors deserve the full correction you did not give then.

Please answer.

I am your repentant Jana.

* * *

So the young lady who had been 'taking charge' of the relationship at the ending of her memoir wanted once more to give herself up to her old mentor and strict mistress. However, perhaps Mrs K had been less than enthusiastic about the proposal for the next sheet bore a date more than a month later than the first. But it soon became clear that that was not the case.

Dear Frau Kästner,

I am very pleased to receive your reply, but I cannot address you as you ask. I am less formal with the name above which is as far as I can go for now. It is more likely that after I have been well benched – oh how the thought of it makes me tremble although it is so MUCH what I need – I am going to do as you wish.

It is wonderful that I may work again as your assistant for the ending year of St Thomas. My few girls are finished their year's work so I am free to come when you tell me. One of them is 'promising' (you understand me?) and if my little plan would work out we could see her in the future. I must not say more until we meet, only that I have the means to carry it out, if you would approve.

Waiting for you to answer me, I shall be impatient. But I am still your repentant

Jana

The remaining three letters were given over to practical details such as when the re-appointed Assistant to the First Mistress would leave her rooms in the city and take up residence. Any addition to the text of the memoir – which seemed indeed to have been abandoned rather than interrupted – was naturally welcome, but the few short paragraphs left Judith with more questions than they answered. Jana's 'little plan', for instance: could it involve more private tutoring, and what were the 'means' referred to? And what had happened to the affair with Dr Hobel that had burst into such lusty life? She longed to know what was to become of the two women and the promise of an act of total submission she could not be privy to was plain tantalising. But then ... but then ...

Judith stowed the envelopes with their contents in her attaché case and got to her feet, her mind suddenly clear. She couldn't share in Jana's voluntary subjugation, but what she could do – *must* do – was follow the girl's example. Grace had vowed to call on the Chief Officer in the morning so Judith had to pre-empt her visit. It was only just after 9 p.m.: she was going to find Sibyl Metzger and make a proposal of her own. And if she judged right it would be one that the dominant lady would find difficult to refuse.

23

In Her Hands

'I shall speak plainly, Judith. I do not strike bargains.'
The pale grey eyes were cool, appraising. 'However,
once a young woman has submitted to my pleasure she
is likely to find me favourably disposed to a request.
And in your particular case there may be an extra
dividend once I am ready to elucidate a certain lack of
candour at our earlier meeting.'

'Oh.' The precisely phrased admission seemed to rule
out any direct question so Judith held herself in wait for
the verdict that was still to be delivered. She was
perched somewhat awkwardly on the edge of a seat
fashioned out of transparent formica facing the speaker
who lounged back in the elegant informality of a fine
silk shirt, open at the collar and with sleeves rolled.
Beyond the undrawn blinds of the Chief Officer's private
rooms lighted windows were visible through the gathering dark of the old schoolyard.

'But that will come later; for now I am content to
accept the offer I hoped you would make. There is (I
believe the expression goes) no time like the present, so
if you consent to it I should like to enlist the aid of my
assistant. Helga is, as you may have recognised, quite
enamoured of your person and will, I know, be thrilled
to be invited.' Judith bowed her head, swallowing down
a flutter of panic at the speed with which events were

moving. They were of course events which she had herself not sanctioned until that moment, but the fact of their anticipation gave her the feeling of being caught up in something preordained.

Sibyl Metzger reached for a small handset on the low table between them and spoke a few indecipherable words into it. Then she stood up and Judith followed suit. 'I shall show you to the next room, if I may, Judith, and leave you there. Helga will arrive directly to prepare you for our little scene.'

A short step across the hallway took them from clean lines of metal and plastic into a riot of decoration from the embossed wallpaper to the ornately canopied and carved four-poster bed. Its atmosphere was heavy and Judith lowered herself onto the brocade of an upright chair and tried to steady her breathing. In the space before an ornate dressing-table there was a small punishment horse that resembled nothing so much as a tooled leather pouffe on splayed legs. Compared with some brutal apparatuses she had seen it was an inno-cent-looking thing without visible restraining straps of any kind. However, picked out as it was by a ceiling spotlight, Judith guessed she was due to make a closer acquaintance with the device in the course of which it was likely to lose some of its present charm.

A tap on the door signalled the arrival of the young assistant and Judith's pulse quickened at the sight of the croptop and brief cotton shorts Helga was wearing. She placed a few items on the bed then turned to Judith. '*Komm*. I am to take your clothes.' Obediently she raised her arms and allowed the T-shirt to be pulled over her head. It was laid carefully over the chair she had just vacated before Helga touched the exposed breasts.

'What a pathetic pair. Now yours –' She was cut short by Helga's finger on her lips.

'*Nichts sage*. And anyway, they are beautiful.' She bent down and took each nipple in turn into her mouth, licking and sucking until they stood out hard and wet. Then she pushed Judith down and unlaced her boots, removing them with the socks. After the trousers had come off too, she was made to lean over the chair while the string briefs were peeled away from the cleft in her buttocks. Helga then parted the cheeks and a nose pressed into the anus while lips kissed their nether counterparts. Judith felt a shiver run down her from head to toe: this was what she called love-making. Then Helga turned her round and fixed her eyes on the bare pubic mound.

'Oh. It is so . . . I did not think . . . Please, may I make a proper taste?' While she knelt, busying herself in the liquefying cunt Judith basked in the girl's eager guileless eroticism, trying not to dwell on its contrast with the contrived tours de force that Grace executed when the urge took her. Then Helga pulled back and stood up looking worried.

'I have to ready you now – for her. She will hurt you, Yoodit, but I am going to help you to bear it.' Judith saw with a pang that tears had welled up in the girl's eyes, but she wiped them away with a small determined smile. 'How I am silly. You will love the pain, yes?' Judith kissed her solemnly on the mouth, tasting salt tears among the residue of her own secretions.

'Yes, Helga, and when I can't bear it I'll love it the most. Do you understand?' Brave words, but they didn't stop her stomach churning as the assistant guided Judith into position over the warm stuffed leather of the horse. Its size was such that her feet were planted firmly on the floor while her hands reached to the very point where the legs disappeared into the thick pile of the carpet. Twisting her head she saw Helga take up a flat piece of wood with a handle at each end unlike anything she had seen before. The girl came up at her back and she felt a rough surface pressed against the top of her jutting rump.

238

'You must stay here – you do not get up when Offizier Metzger comes. Now keep still while I use the *Sandpapier*. It will not hurt but it is to make you more sensitive.' She drew the board down with a firm movement and Judith flinched at the abrasive pull. Vertical scrapes alternated with horizontals and Judith gritted her teeth to bite back a protest. It *didn't* exactly hurt but the raw scouring made her bottom-flesh feel like so much meat – meat that was being systematically tenderised. It was all rather fiendish and Judith tried not to think about the kind of instrument that would have its effect especially enhanced by the treatment. Then an astringent perfume in the air and the faint swish of expensive fabric brought the lurid imaginings to a stop. Sibyl Metzger stood beside her dangling a bundle of knotted thongs. Her nostrils caught the reek of freshly tanned leather and Judith turned her head but mindful of the instruction she had been given remained obediently in place.

'*Das ist gut*, Helga.' There was the touch of fingers on her sore skin then the Officer squatted down with the whip spread across her trousered knees. 'It was once favoured for military punishments, I believe. In the old days it was pickled until hard enough to draw blood with a single good stroke.' She looked into Judith's face for a moment, then gave out the small bark of a laugh. 'Do not worry, *meines Kind*, the leather is new and will not easily cut you. However, the preparation you have undergone will ensure that you feel every knot. One thing more and we are ready. Helga, *bitte*, the pessary.'

Judith squirmed as a smooth slippery object entered her anus and was pushed home at the end of a finger. Then she felt the Officer's hand stroking the small of her back.

'You will have noticed that there are no fastenings to hold you down, Judith. It is our way here. So there is nothing to prevent you terminating at any time the discipline I am going to administer. However, you are where you are by your own will, so I take it that you intend to present yourself to me until I judge you to have been adequately whipped. But we are private and the occasion is unofficial so I have asked Helga to provide physical contact to support your resolve. So I ask you again, Judith, before we start: do you place yourself freely in my hands?' *Adequately whipped.* She had a feeling the phrase would turn out to be a gem of understatement, but she was too far in to back out now.

'Yes, I do. Aah!' Throughout the little speech she had been aware of a growing sensation inside, but just as Judith uttered the final words of submission a burning spasm passed from the colon to her anal ring. It made her want to wrench the cheeks apart with her hands but she tightened her grip on the horse's legs and instead strained to push out and separate the buttocks as much as she could.

'Ha! I see the ginger suppository is beginning to take effect. An old trick, but one that is not as well known as it should be. In my experience it acts as a deterrent to clenching and thus allows the tails to do their best work inside the bottom parting. Very good. So let us begin.'

At first Helga stood at the head, leaning to hold Judith's waist and imparting a reassuring pressure of thighs against her upper arms. Six quick cuts made her catch her breath though the sting was not quite as sharp as she had feared. But then she guessed that the chastiser was getting her eye in – taking the measure of the new contours at her disposal in order to combine force with accuracy. And indeed, as stroke followed stroke she was soon writhing in the assistant's grip, yelping each time the knots found their way into the most intimate parts.

Judith had been punished splayed before, but each time under restraint. Never had she been so obscenely open, straining to spread and cool the fire in her arsehole. She must be providing the Chief Officer with quite a sight, one no doubt enhanced by the copious lubrication she could feel spilling from her genitals. It seemed to be the way of it that a leathered arse made a leaking cunt, however much it hurt her. And she *hurt*. The whipping had taken on a steady rhythm with each swish-crack punctuated by her grunts and cries. As she strove to endure, the young assistant's body pressed hard on her and the waist-hold tightened, so she was able to push against it while she struggled to keep the hands locked in place. Suddenly, miraculously, there was a pause while she tensed for the next cut but instead a hand squeezed and lifted each throbbing globe in turn, forcing a prolonged yell of pain from her throat. Helga stepped back and Judith felt something hard enter between her seeping labia. Oh God, please not. But there was no mistaking it: she was being probed with the tip of a cane and when it touched the engorged clitoris the intensity of the sensation sent her rigid with shock. When her vision cleared Sibyl Metzger was at her side and in her hand was a slim length of brown wood with pronounced bamboo-like joints.

'Malacca.' She spoke the word that had been forming on Judith's lips, a word she knew to have a special connotation if only her fogged brain would identify it. 'I think to start with we shall try six. You will take six, Judith, won't you? There is after all a lead to follow here.' Moving back out of view, the Officer tapped the instrument across the buttocks just above the crease. The flesh was so indescribably tender that the light touch was enough to take her breath away and in an instant the connection came to her. Jana's journal, it was in *there*: where the already-beaten Sophie is finished off with a malacca cane. The Chief Officer takes on the part of the First Mistress – how appropriate – but how did she *know*? Judith's mind made a brief stab at

241

comprehension but a second tap of the implement brought her back to earth.

'Helga, *bitte*. Take the water. You will tend her while I finish the work.' Sibyl Metzger was going to thrash her with the cane and understanding would have to wait. For now her role was to suffer . . .

It may have been a role, assigned and unequivocally assumed, but it was no *act*. Although the material of the weapon lacked the resonant bite of top-grade rattan, the target it was to be applied to had been exceptionally primed. So Judith babbled and shrieked and howled her way through six full doses of six before Officer Metzger pronounced enough to be enough and cast her instrument aside. While Helga valiantly bathed and stroked and caressed it, sweat poured from the upper body that contorted in parallel to the torments of its lower half.

Eased off the horse at the end, Judith sank to her knees and allowed herself to be half-dragged, half-carried through to the adjoining cloakroom. Once there she resisted the move to lay her out face-down on a cloth-covered table for there was one paramount need that impressed itself on Judith's semi-consciousness. While the excoriated flesh could be tended, it would in time heal itself, but there was one source of pain that she could – *must* – remove at once. So with Helga's assistance she squatted above the seat in the corner (any contact being out of the question) and expelled what was left of the ginger suppository, together with regrettably much else, into the lavatory bowl beneath. Once the patient hands had washed away the last irritating traces, Judith lay as bid for them to minister to her welts and bruises. And, of course, above all to the needs of the other places between her legs that were beginning urgently to re-assert themselves.

The best part of an hour later she was standing in T-shirt and thong before the Chief Officer of the

Thomas-Halle who was seated at the desk of a compact den tucked away in the back of the house. The offer of an armchair had been wryly made and as wryly declined: since Judith had been unable to contemplate restoring the tight trousers she habitually wore, the presence of a cushion, however soft, was not going to make sitting down any more feasible. But the sore and weary body was swept up in an overriding elation that seemed in direct proportion to the rigours undergone: it was the feeling of being bathed in the first full light of morning to follow the dark night. So when Sibyl Metzger asked to inspect 'the damage' she presented her rear view without hesitation, albeit acutely aware of the swollen weight of wealed buttocks spilling out around the narrow band of material. Cool fingers brushed lightly against the hot skin and the Officer spoke quietly.

'It is good. You have done well, Judith, matching the best I have encountered in my corrective career. As a mere recruit of sixteen I was treated on one occasion to a generous dose of the barrack-room ashplant, and when my commanding officer heard the fuss she insisted on rounding off the impromptu affair by putting me across her knee. Only a bare-bottomed hand-spanking but you can understand that in my condition it was something that has remained in the memory.'

The very idea made Judith shudder but she pulled herself up and reached for the waist band of her pants. At once there was a tell-tale contraction in her loins. 'Ma'am, if it would please you to follow her example . . .' She faltered, blushing at a term of address she had never thought to hear herself use, but the lady was regarding her gravely over the top of her steel rims.

'Judith, I am tempted. Perhaps in the future, if you were to be once again willing . . .' She inclined her head and the auburn sheen of hair swung in the desklight as she bent to open a drawer. 'Now, however, we have business. First, you may be surprised to learn of the existence of this.' The thick A4 sheaf landed with a smack on the table and Judith peered at its title page, puzzled. A few long German words did little to enlighten her until she read with a start the name that was printed underneath: Mathilde Kästner.

'Yes, it is indeed your Mrs K, the First Mistress. I had known nothing of those old days so when your enquiry came in I conducted a search. It fell to you to locate the hidden letters, but these pages – or rather the handwritten originals – were found abandoned in an old box. They are less than polished which inclines me to the thought they were a rough draft of something more finished and therefore intended simply to be destroyed.'

Judith turned a few pages and lit upon the name Sophie in the foreign text. 'So she wrote about those times – the times that I know about through Jana –'

'Indeed so. You will of course need to have a translation made, but it is yours for the taking. I hope it will be of use.'

Of use? It was brilliant, utterly brilliant. Jana's memoir was, it had to be owned, on the thin side, even when fleshed out with background material and wrapped up in her own editorial contribution. But now the title that would launch their NemArch imprint had suddenly acquired the potential to be a significant piece of work.

'This is wonderful, Officer Metzger. I don't know how to thank you.'

'Our encounter has not been without reward for me, Judith.' There was the glimmer of a smile then the grey eyes were again serious. 'There is something else I have decided you should see. It may come as rather a shock.' She held out a single sheet of bold handwriting that was disconcertingly familiar. Under the masthead of 'The British Library' it read:

Dear S –

A brief supplement to e-communications that is for your eyes only.

Suggest you make her pay in kind (so to speak). J will be none the worse for a really good hiding and I trust you will capture the proceedings on disc.

The neurotic bitch was one of yours (before your time) and you would do me a service to break her. I gather that would not be difficult.

Books you requested are enclosed. They will not be missed. I approve your taste in the engravings which show a rare sadistic imagination.

Yours, H

The bastard. The utter scheming *bastard*! Her own treatment didn't matter. Now that it was over, she was quite gratified to have had 'a good hiding' (for which she had in any case volunteered) and thereby passed through to a relationship with her chastiser that promised much. But Grace, poor Grace. Far from getting the chance to redeem herself – however unrealistic that might have been – she was to be 'broken', if Harry Jameson had his way. Though since she had been shown this letter . . .

'Yes, it is disgraceful. Quite breathtaking in its arrogance and egoism. No doubt you will want to revise the terms of your association with the Keeper of the Rare Books.'

'Well, I –' Judith looked down, reddening. What exactly did Sibyl Metzger know about her and Harry?

'Don't let me embarrass you, Judith. I was thinking merely that its content made me decide to reduce my own future dealings with the man to a minimum. However, it serves to bring us, I think, to the matter of your associate. Carol: was that her name?' Judith felt the flush hot on her neck as she tried to stammer out an explanation. But the Officer stopped her with an unexpected chuckle.

'I am afraid she was detected almost at once. One so beautiful does not easily escape recognition by those who have seen her before. I am not annoyed at your attempted deception for I know it was done to protect a difficult and vulnerable young woman. The question we face is what to do about the need she has to settle with her past. You told me that you expect her to ask, even insist, on a formal disciplinary trial which – I have to say – I should feel obliged to grant. And you fear the worst, even without any of the deliberate malevolence sought by the librarian?'

Judith grimaced, trying to find a phrase for Grace's alarming unpredictability that would not make her sound a complete nutter. Though if Sibyl Metzger had been inspecting her old records, she no doubt already knew the worst.

'It's the mood swings that are the worst. If she could hold on to her resolve I think she could get through almost anything. But how that can be brought about I have no idea.' Weariness washed over her at the attempt to confront the intractable problem and Judith yawned a mighty yawn. The Chief Officer gave her a little smile and waved away the apology.

'It is close on midnight and I recommend that you should, as the expression goes, sleep on it. I have the impression that your Grace is a jealous person, so perhaps with my young assistant's counsel you could accomplish something. Now go to your bed, please: I shall have Helga call on you early in the morning.' Sibyl Metzger took her hand, pressed it briefly, and with that Judith found herself dismissed. What did the lady mean about Helga helping? The effort of thought was too much and she concentrated on finding her way back to the corridor where her quarters was located. At present they would be empty: but before the other occupant returned she had to find a solution.

24

Passing Out

If only she could make it to the end of the passage she could reach her, stop her . . . But her legs felt like they were stuck in treacle and she held out her arms, despairing, calling her name. There was a hand on her shoulder and her heart leapt. The girl wasn't ahead at all; she was just behind her and she was going to be safe. She tried to turn but there was a weight stopping her and that voice, the voice that kept hissing something at her –

'Yoodit. Yoodit! Wake up, Yoodit.'

'Oh, Gr–' Judith snapped awake and bit back the name just in time. 'Helga. Oh, Helga. I was in this strange dream. I had to move fast and I couldn't. And the time was running out. Ugh.' She squinted at the figure framed in the dawn light of the high window and pulled her close enough to slip a hand between her legs. The young blonde kissed her on the mouth and unzipped the snug body suit, giggling, but Judith drew back.

'Ha! You dream of your girlfriend and think of her still. All right. I don't care.' Helga pouted, letting the garment slip to uncover breasts and a pubic bush trimmed into the shape of a heart. With the intimacies of the evening yet vivid in her mind Judith's loins responded at once, and it was only with an effort that she held off.

'Look, Helga –'

'I only inspect your rear end, OK? To make sure you start to recover from what was done by *meiner Befehlshaber*. She is cruel – I know it well myself.' Judith turned over and allowed the bedcovers to be removed, wincing when fingers explored the still sensitive flesh. 'As I expected. Many colours and some are dark. You are injured and must let me massage the bruises.'

'Helga, I thought you were going to help me come up with a plan. You know – before Grace gets here.' She said the words but the girl was already busy petting and stroking and she forbore to stop her.

'We have the time. I am to tell to you that the door outside is closed, with a bolt – yes? – before the clock reaches eight. So no person can enter.' Since it was barely a quarter to seven, that was the clincher. Judith gave up the unequal struggle against renewed desire and lifted her behind up into the air. After a while she pushed the assistant on to her back, spread her legs wide and inserted two fingers into the slippery vagina.

'My turn, right? Before I come I want a proper taste of you.' It was the work of a moment to slip a pillow under the firm buttocks and bring into clear view the labia that glistened under the matted hairs. Helga whimpered softly as Judith licked and nibbled at the tangy folds with increasing absorption. Lost as she was in the total intimacy of the act, it was with something of a shock that she became aware that the vocal noises had transformed themselves into a series of full-blooded groans. She glanced up with the sudden thought that, even given the early hour, the door would be better tight shut. What she saw froze her exactly as she was: crouched over the naked body with its secretions running down her chin. In the now open doorway stood Grace, and Judith shrank back as the eyes blazed.

'That's it! I'm finished. I want outta here. Today. Fucking now!' Quavering with emotion, the voice was rising to a yell. 'But first I'm gonna show you. You think I'm rubbish and I just don't matter. Well, you bastards, I'll fucking show you!' In her hand was a small carrier which she threw down on the bunk. 'Here, you better have this anyway – at least it'll give you a cheap laugh.' She swung out of the door and crashed it shut at her back. Helga, already dressed, pulled on her trainers and pushed the open-mouthed Judith back.

'You keep away. Stay here, yes? I deal with the situation.' She was off down the corridor at a run before Judith could argue and she sank stunned down on the bed. Mechanically she reached inside the bag, took out the package and fumbled with the wrapping. Inside was a fuschia thong that sported at the crotch a dayglo-green heart. And in the middle of that was embroidered the letter G.

At another time the sentimentality of the gift would have made Judith squirm but in her overwrought state it brought a lump to the throat. She ached with the pathos – *bathos* – of it all and eyes brimming she railed against her penchant for heedless dalliance. It had been the intention to dissuade Grace from making any rash move to rehabilitate herself at the Hall and she had in fact made things worse. What the girl would do now was anybody's guess, but it was likely to be extreme and Judith felt sick with apprehension. For all her disgust at Harry's cold-blooded malignity, her own actions may have achieved the result his could not. The irony was too, too much and Judith rocked helplessly backwards and forwards, squeezing her eyelids shut on the tears. Time passed until at last, as the flow began to abate, she curled up in a ball. To intervene now was likely only to compound the folly. Maybe – just maybe – Helga could retrieve something from the wreckage: she herself had done quite enough damage for one day. Worn out, Judith buried her face in the pillows and abandoned herself to sleep.

* * *

She woke to find the assistant standing at her side and struggled into a sitting position. 'Shit, what's happened? What time is it?' She croaked out of a dry throat and her head ached.

Helga thrust a tall glass into her hand saying, 'Drink.' It had the tang of citrus fruits about it and Judith sipped gratefully. 'It is ten. In thirty minutes you must go where you went before to watch Käthe.'

'Käthe? You mean that Grace *is* going to – just like she threatened. Oh God, no! She can't.'

'The passing-out will be done. She is being spanked now with a paddle, but she will keep on her pants for the cane. It is maybe not as bad as you think. The *Hauptoffizier* says it. The girl will come from it better than she has been and you will love her, yes?' Touched, Judith took hold of the blonde's arm, but a suspicion was forming in her mind.

'Helga – earlier, when you came and we got caught – that wasn't just an accident, was it?' The blonde looked at her for a second then dropped her gaze.

'You have to get ready. I will not see you again, so I give you the buzz-tube on the table. Use it in the shower and relax. And – and perhaps you use again sometimes and think of me, yes?'

There was a catch in the voice that made Judith want to fold her up and – and what? But in the moment of hesitation the girl had turned and was gone. Judith hauled herself out of bed and stomped into the tiny bathroom. She made a face into the mirror, inspecting the smudges round the eyes under the short dark hair. What was she doing leaving the adorable – and ador*ing* – young German for a dodgy neurotic whose head might be even more seriously fucked up before the morning was out?

Judith looked over at the electric-blue vibrator on the bedside shelf then thought better of it. She showered quickly and towelled herself dry in a burst of energy. At the end of the bunk the vulgar briefs lay where she had discarded them and in a moment of decision Judith pulled them on and snapped the elastic in place. She would wear them not so much as a charm – someone about to undergo ritual thrashing needed rather more than good luck – but as a gesture of solidarity. Grace was going to get through this and she, Judith, was going to stop pissing about with other women and make it up to her. A white shirt, black trousers and the customary black boots completed the dress and it took only a moment to throw her few things into the attaché case with its haul of papers before heading out to make her way to the top-floor room. At the door Judith paused and after brief deliberation turned back to tuck the shiny phallic object into a button-down side pocket. After all, there was nothing wrong with *thinking* about Helga now and then, was there?

The lift-doors opened as Sibyl Metzger was leaving her office and she handed over an envelope with the request that it remained sealed until Judith had returned to the Archive's computer. Ushered into the fateful chamber, she opted for a position behind the single uniformed figure at the front and lowered herself into the seat with due attention to her own bruised condition. There was an audience already assembled of half a dozen from which came a small buzz of anticipation. While the previous event had occasioned in Judith a similar curiosity and excitement, the prospect of this one filled her with fear and it was almost a relief when the door opened and Grace was led in. The sooner it began, the sooner it would all be over.

'*Damen*, I believe you all know why we are gathered. A former resident has petitioned to enhance her somewhat less than impressive record. I have agreed to the request and in view of the circumstances have allowed the changes you will note in our customary practice.'

251

There were some blank looks that Judith guessed were the result of the Chief Officer's elaborate English and the speaker waited until some murmurs of explanation had passed round the room. 'Grace Marshall, I ask you: how many strokes?'

For the first time Judith dared to look at her lover who was turned to face the questioner. She was wearing a bra-top in gunmetal grey and hipster pants with the currently obligatory thong visible above their narrow waistband. Below it, small pleats fitted the satin sheen of the material close to the curve of the dimpled behind and the trouser legs flared out over boots with thick high heels.

'Twelve strokes, Officer. Please.' The words came staccato out of the red mouth in a deathly pale face and Judith felt her stomach knot.

'Very well. *Zwölf Schlagen.* Confirm to us that you have been suitably prepared.' Without the slightest hesitation Grace peeled down the trousers and showed herself. The deep cherry-red of the bared buttocks betokened a prolonged and systematic application of leather and a ripple ran through the small audience. Judith fancied she could almost feel the heat of them from where she sat and she looked grimly at the cane in the Officer's hand. It was at least a four-footer that would be hard to take at the best of times and the restoration of the trousers did little to reduce her sense of foreboding. Their snug seat would provide precious little protection to the drastically inflamed flesh that swelled beneath.

'Offizier Gartner! Will you please show the candidate to her place.' The second deviation from normal procedure took the form of a plain wooden workbench with the addition of a handrail at one end and a pair of brackets secured to the legs at the other. Under direction, Grace bent and grasped the rail while the duty officer took a bar and slotted it in behind the knees. It was not exactly a restraint of the kind frowned upon at the Thomas-Halle for the secretary's behind was positioned for the chastiser's attentions only for as long as she held on. At any time she would be free to straighten, remove the knee-bar with her own hands and walk away.

'Is the candidate ready for the passing-out to begin?'

Grace lifted her head and twisted it back, scanning the assembled viewers. 'She is ready. *I* am ready.' She spat the words out and as her eyes fell on Judith they flashed with a pure venom that made her shrink down behind the broad uniformed shoulders in the front row. Oh fuck. If she did – just conceivably – come out of this in one piece, the girl was never going to speak to her again.

The cane tapped imperiously on the presented backside and the head went down again. Before Judith could blink there was a sound like tearing silk and the body drove forward against the wood with a gasp of expelled air. The figure clung white-knuckled to her support and when the buttocks bounced back a line appeared across the whole breadth of the stretched cloth. Sibyl Metzger stood motionless, head bowed, while it seemed the whole room held its breath, then she rose on to the balls of her feet and lammed the pitiless ash a second time into the waiting rump. As the trial proceeded it was like a repeating nightmare from which there was no escape, except that each time it became marginally worse. The figure jerked more wildly, the grunts became cries and the horizontal grid etched on the seat of the pants acquired one remorseless line after another. To have the state of the punished flesh concealed in that way allowed the imagination to run wild and Judith wished fervently for the spectacle to end. Let Grace's control break, anything – who cared any longer? – if only it would stop!

But stop it did not, not until the ultimate stroke had whipped into the abused mounds and added its mark to the rest. The perpetrator of the damage pronounced the trial finished and Judith slumped in her chair suddenly aware of the sweat-stains spreading from her armpits and the seeping wetness between her legs. There was the lover – would-be lover – about whom she was guilty and upset, and here she was *turned on* by her ordeal. Shit. How sick was that? Thank God it was done. There was a slight hiccup when it was found that the victim's hands had locked on to the rail in a muscular spasm, but the guard came to the rescue with some timely massage. The affair was indeed at an end and Sibyl Metzger set the seal on it.

'The record of previous failure will be expunged. Offizier Gartner will take the candidate for interim first-aid then make sure she is escorted safely from the building. Our business is concluded.' She swept from the room and the Officer helped Grace in the same direction, after which the remaining watchers made their way out one by one. When the door had closed on the last of them Judith sat staring at the white wall until she felt as blank and still as its empty surface, then she went slowly down the stairs to face the reception committee that would be waiting at their vehicle outside.

At first Judith was glad to drive. Partitioned off and cocooned in the dance beat she kept pulsing out of the dashboard speakers it was possible to ignore what might – or might not – be happening in the back. Even after a stop at a sandwich bar just across the border, where she remained determinedly in her seat, she was happy enough to continue at the wheel. However, when it came to late afternoon Judith had had enough of dodging the issue. Sooner or later she was going to have to look Grace in the eye and beg forgiveness. It would not be granted, of course, and she was likely to be the cause of tears and recriminations, but it had to be tried. So she pulled off for fuel, paid with her card and parked near the exit. Then she got out and tapped on the glass of a side window. Inside she could see lips set tight in a line of disapproval but the boy unlocked and slid open the door.

'Your go,' she said in an attempt to sound merely practical. 'I need a break.' He made no move to let her in but she persevered. 'Arnold, I've got to do this. I can't avoid Grace for ever.' Grudgingly he got up and stepped down, his companion following, and there was a brief interchange in German.

'OK, we'll go in front. She's asleep – or *was*. It'd be better if you don't wake her, right?' The lad once shy and blushing in Judith's presence had plainly become struck on Grace during the intimacies of their trip and the deference to 'Ms Wilson' was a thing of the past.

'Whatever you say. Now just go and drive. And keep your eyes on the road, OK?' She shooed the boys round the front of the people carrier and climbed in, swivelling one of the seats to face the figure that lay prone under a sheet at the back. There was no sign that her arrival had been registered and after a while Judith began to relax. After the turmoil of the past twenty-four hours she felt suddenly weary and the steady drone of the engine as they sped along the autobahn was soothing, hypnotic. Now if she were to close her eyes for just a minute . . .

It was an odd, throaty sort of noise, a kind of sputtering or spluttering and it insinuated itself disruptively into the images of smooth soaring flight. Then as the reality of wheels on tarmac returned to consciousness the new noise was still there. Judith blinked and sat up with a blank stare of incomprehension at what she saw. The corner seat across from her had been turned away and above the back of it was a mask fixed in a rictus more ghastly than any gargoyle. For a split second she was rigid with shock, then the features dissolved and reformed themselves into those of Grace: a Grace who was being overtaken by an uncontrollable bout of giggling.

'It worked. It fucking worked! I was so mad I got through. You're a genius. It – fucking – worked!' The words came out amid hoots and shrieks as the hysterical episode passed and Judith struggled to get a handle on the situation. The girl thought it was all a plan to get her angry enough to 'pass out' successfully. Well, if it was something cooked up by the Chief Officer and her Assistant – and that had to be on the cards – they hadn't bothered to put *her* in the picture. *She* had just been doing the usual: going in cunt-first without a thought for the consequences. But she was not going to explain all that. At least not yet.

'Look, Grace, I don't know what to say. Are you OK?'

'I'm all right now the penny's dropped. But I'm going to tell you something, Jude. When I heard that bitch moaning halfway down the fucking corridor, I thought there's only one girl I know who gives head like that.' It was a backhanded compliment and she eyed Grace uncertainly. The secretary pursed her lips and poked Judith in the chest, emphasising each word.

'And if I *ever* catch her tongue in a strange fanny again, that is it. End of story. *Kaput. Finito.* Get the picture?' Judith gulped and raised a hand to fend off the stabbing finger, but to no avail. 'And there's one more thing, boss. If I see you so much as fucking look at another arse, then I'm going to wrap *this* round yours. Got it?' With a flourish she lifted up from the floor a long yellowish rod that Judith stared at stupidly.

'Is that, er, the one, I mean *the* one –'

'The very same. A trophy from the Duty Officer 'cos I did well.' She grinned and Judith grinned back in relief. It was not long since she had seen the cane used on Grace's bottom and there was no doubt that it hurt like hell. But the thought of bending over for Grace to apply it to the seat of *her* trousers gave her an instant tingle between the legs. So maybe a little planned flirting could become all part of the game. She could hardly believe it, but some kind of future for the two of them was looking almost feasible. In the present, though, there was a very sore behind to tend and Judith moved round to the back of the kneeling figure.

'Let's have a look, Gracie. I got some special stuff from a woman on the train – that's one I *didn't* fuck, OK – and it's just what you need.' She lifted up the long T-shirt that was all the girl wore and winced at the mass of purple contusions. 'Now then, you had better hold on tight until the effect starts to kick in . . .'

Two days later the Assistant Director and Secretary were back at work, and in another three a bulky crate arrived at the Nemesis Archive by special delivery. Hardly had they removed the packing and dragged the contents to a prominent position in the basement than the Director herself returned from her month-long sojourn at the Rigorist Order in Brittany. Judith's report on the augmented MS was well received and Samantha James enthused over the solid construction and unique design of their recent acquisition. However, as she suspected, there was a catch. As she had learned from painful experience, with Miss James there was nearly always a catch.

'It is good work, Judith, both theoretical and practical in its results. But not achieved, I'm afraid, without a certain presumption on your part. You took our secretary away from her work and left the Archive in the hands of Mrs Rowleigh for a whole week. Hers are of course very capable hands, but, as I think you are well aware, I should have first been consulted on the matter. Would you accept that as a fair statement?' The raven-haired woman in her late forties looked up from her desk and Judith made herself return the penetrating gaze.

'Yes, Miss James. I acted too hastily where there was no real need to do so. I apologise.' She lowered her eyes

257

and stood still. There was always a frisson of masochistic pleasure in owning up to a fault and awaiting the Director's judgement.

'Your apology is accepted, naturally. That leaves the small matter of due reparation, and there I have a suggestion to make. Since I need to see the splendid caning bench in action, so to speak, you could serve both these ends by providing the subject for a demonstration. Is that agreed? Good. Then have Grace secure you in place downstairs while I consult your excellent work on its former mode of use. I shall be with you shortly.'

'Ow. These bloody straps are too tight.'

'Stop complaining. You want to show her nibs how well it holds the victim down, don't you? Even when her arse is on fire.'

'You'd better be ready with the cream, OK?'

'Sure, lover.' Through the satin thong that separated her rear cheeks Judith felt fingers caress her vulva then the secretary kissed her on the lips. 'I'll be waiting.' No sooner was she gone than Judith became aware of the presence of the Director at her back, though there was a pause before she spoke.

'Hmm. I see we have some quite interesting marks here. They lead me to suspect that the area will be rather sensitive and I'm told that my new rattan has an exceptional zip to it.' The dispassionate assessment of her impending pain made Judith quail but she steeled herself to hear the sentence. 'So I am inclined to think that we could settle on the thirteen strokes that seems on my cursory reading to have been associated with the device. The phrase used was, I believe, "a butcher's dozen".' There was a cool line of pressure across the centre of her bottom and Judith tensed herself.

'Ah, my dear, it is so good to be back. And now, if you are quite braced and ready . . .'

Nexus

NEXUS NEW BOOKS

To be published in June

THE ENGLISH VICE
Yolanda Celbridge

Nineteen-year-old Beryl Beaton takes up a place at Trismegist Towers Finishing School. She is soon mixed up haplessly in a bizarre, longstanding boundary dispute with the neighbouring Parvex Hall. The discipline at Trismegist runs a gamut from traditional corporal punishment to inhumation in mud, and worse. But Beryl soon finds it is as nothing compared to the flagellant excesses of the sybarites of Parvex.

£6.99   ISBN 0 352 33805 9

THE DEBUTANTE
Jacqueline Masterson

In 1950s Britain, a group of decadent aristocrats operate their own 'secret season', an alternative to the tedious official round of balls and court presentations. Instead of being groomed for marriage, pretty young 'debutantes' are trained, tormented and finally auctioned off in a bizarre parody of the real debutantes' presentation at court. Angela Carstairs is inducted into this secret world and soon consumed by curiosity – which of these cruel men and women will acquire her?

£6.99   ISBN 0 352 33802 4

THE SCHOOLING OF STELLA
Yolanda Celbridge

When English rose Stella Shawn wins a coveted scholarship to Castle Kernece, Scotland's sternest training college, she plans to fulfil her ambition of becoming a schoolmistress. More than just a college, Kernece is a way of life: a fierce and perverse arena of dominant and submissive females where punishments are frequent and taken 'on the bare'. She meets the enigmatic headmistress, Miss Dancer, the insatiable Morag, and feared Bull, and the beautiful Italian, Alberta; all adepts of discipline. Only by her own total submission to the rules can Stella learn to dominate.

£6.99   ISBN 0 352 33803 2

If you would like more information about Nexus titles, please visit our website at www.nexus-books.co.uk, or send a stamped addressed envelope to:

Nexus, Thames Wharf Studios,
Rainville Road, London W6 9HA

NEXUS BACKLIST

This information is correct at time of printing. For up-to-date information, please visit our website at www.nexus-books.co.uk

All books are priced at £5.99 unless another price is given.

Samplers and collections

NEW EROTICA 5	Various	☐
	ISBN 0 352 33540 8	
EROTICON 1	Various	☐
	ISBN 0 352 33593 9	
EROTICON 2	Various	☐
	ISBN 0 352 33594 7	
EROTICON 3	Various	☐
	ISBN 0 352 33597 1	
EROTICON 4	Various	☐
	ISBN 0 352 33602 1	
THE NEXUS LETTERS	Various	☐
	ISBN 0 352 33621 8	
SATURNALIA	ed. Paul Scott	☐
£7.99	ISBN 0 352 33717 6	
MY SECRET GARDEN SHED	ed. Paul Scott	☐
£7.99	ISBN 0 352 33725 7	

Nexus Classics

A new imprint dedicated to putting the finest works of erotic fiction back in print.

AMANDA IN THE PRIVATE HOUSE	Esme Ombreux	☐
£6.99	ISBN 0 352 33705 2	
BAD PENNY	Penny Birch	☐
	ISBN 0 352 33661 7	
BRAT	Penny Birch	☐
£6.99	ISBN 0 352 33674 9	
DARK DELIGHTS	Maria del Rey	☐
£6.99	ISBN 0 352 33667 6	
DARK DESIRES	Maria del Rey	☐
	ISBN 0 352 33648 X	
DISPLAYS OF INNOCENTS	Lucy Golden	☐
£6.99	ISBN 0 352 33679 X	
DISCIPLINE OF THE PRIVATE HOUSE	Esme Ombreux	☐
£6.99	ISBN 0 352 33459 2	
EDEN UNVEILED	Maria del Rey	☐
	ISBN 0 352 33542 4	

Please send me the books I have ticked above.

Name ....

Address ....

....

....

.... Post code....................

Send to: **Cash Sales, Nexus Books, Thames Wharf Studios, Rainville Road, London W6 9HA**

US customers: for prices and details of how to order books for delivery by mail, call 1-800-343-4499.

Please enclose a cheque or postal order, made payable to **Nexus Books Ltd**, to the value of the books you have ordered plus postage and packing costs as follows:

UK and BFPO – £1.00 for the first book, 50p for each subsequent book.

Overseas (including Republic of Ireland) – £2.00 for the first book, £1.00 for each subsequent book.

If you would prefer to pay by VISA, ACCESS/MASTERCARD, AMEX, DINERS CLUB or SWITCH, please write your card number and expiry date here:

....

Please allow up to 28 days for delivery.

Signature ....

Our privacy policy.

We will not disclose information you supply us to any other parties. We will not disclose any information which identifies you personally to any person without your express consent.

From time to time we may send out information about Nexus books and special offers. Please tick here if you do *not* wish to receive Nexus information.   ☐